# How the Planet Lost Its Tail

♦

## J.D. McMorine

One Mouse Press
PORTLAND · OREGON · USA

ISBN: 978-0-692-85071-8
Library of Congress Control Number: 2017904347

Available in e-book format:
ISBN : 978-0-692-85072-5

**One Mouse Press**
Portland, Oregon, USA
onemousepress.com

*Dedicated to KC, Tyrone, and Slim,*
*a/k/a "El Guapo"*

# HOW THE PLANET LOST ITS TAIL

## Part I    The Beast

## Part II    Loose Pawns

## Part III    The Mission

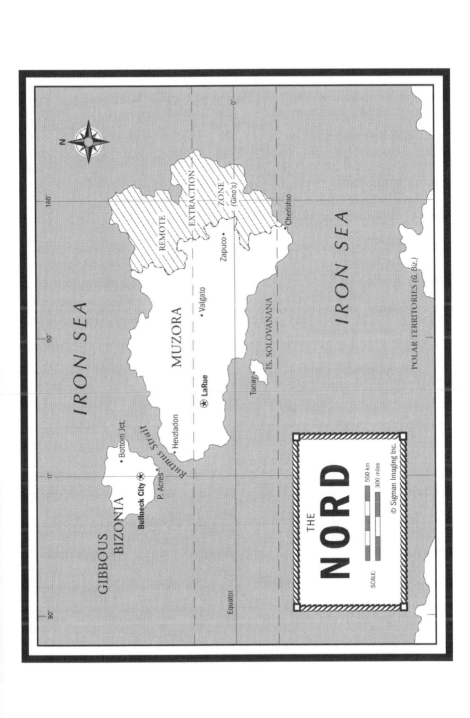

"The quality of the light was such that it could forever
increase in intensity yet never become painful to the eyes.
The warmth such that it could forever rise in temperature
yet never become painful to the body."

*~Abacus*

# Prologue

On a moonless night on planet Earth, a young man sat gazing at stars through the bare, motionless branches outside his bedroom window. "If only the Earth were half as large," he whispered as he gnawed on his pencil, "we would solve the world's most puzzling and urgent problems twice as fast, or even faster…"

At that precise moment, in the young man's line of sight, a speck of stardust sliced burning through Earth's atmosphere—a shooting star born of a distant, ancient, massive stellar explosion. The shooting star was a burning message of love etched forever in the young man's mind.

It was a hope.

Also at that precise moment, two specks of stardust from the very same exploding star found tiny, precious planet Nord, half a galaxy away. Nord, a planet far less than half the size of Earth, is where our tale begins.

# PART I

# The Beast

CHAPTER ONE

# Incorporated

*While the nation waged war in a distant land, Rod Bankman sighed to the whisper of seven chrome pistons. Rod's goose down mattress tilted sideways with the lengthening pistons, rolling Rod half-asleep from between his sheets into a trough of warm cologne. The snaking trough flowed by candlelight from room to room beneath vaulted ceilings as white-robed servants polished Rod's body with sea sponges. A sharp, shaved, and confident Rod emerged smelling sweet and woody to waltz through his granite kitchen, pressed into glowing business attire. A jointed aluminum arm lowered a small, oval sandwich into Rod's alligator briefcase alongside the completed text for the Buckingham Project. The briefcase snapped shut. As the planet died, Helicopter Three trumpeted its horn from the driveway, impatient to carry Rod away.*

Rolling over on his lumpy, sweat-stained mattress, Rod Bankman crossed the trumpeting of Helicopter Three in his dream with the boisterous honking of his alarm clock. His recurring dream of clean sheets, whispering pistons, and helicopter rides was blown away in an instant. Rod's slender fingers pounced to stop the honking alarm.

It was that time.

Lost in a stew of ratty blankets, grumbling to himself about this and that, Rod twisted away from the clock. Another day at Magic Wands lay ahead.

Belinda, the troll upstairs, was up and pounding on Rod's ceiling with a broom handle. "You'll hear from me, Bankman!" she croaked at the honking of Rod's alarm, "The racket!" Rod snatched a wand off of his nightstand, tempted with curses to cast on Belinda. He slammed the wand back down without a word—foggy morning curses were, at best, unpredictable.

Little did Rod know, but in two weeks' time, neither Belinda nor his lumpy mattress would matter in the least. After unravelling the deepest secrets of magic wands and of his own true identity, Rod would be dead.

Pushing himself up out of bed, Rod stepped on half a sandwich—bologna and cheese hidden for days under yellowing utility bills. Rod kicked aside a moldy loaf of bread only to find that the loaf was Slim, Rod's black and white tuxedo cat. His best little buddy.

Unapologetic at this early hour, Rod staggered into the bathroom and landed almost completely naked in the shower, drooling under its icy spray. The landlord, always slow with a fix, was still two weeks out with a solution to Rod's hot water. Looking down at his now drenched night socks, Rod wondered if he hadn't stumbled upon a way to clean both his socks and his mottled shower floor at the same time. He smeared his feet back and forth.

Still outraged at the honking of Rod's alarm, upstairs Belinda flushed her empty toilet, knowing well that it would turn Rod's shower searing hot. The water steamed from the nozzle onto Rod's squirming, scorching body. When the water cooled to soothe and then ice Rod over once again, that was enough. Rod cranked off the cracked chrome handle at the spigot and raked a brittle towel over his fair skin, still covered in a froth of soap bubbles. He then peeled off his socks, wringing their cloudy water into the rust-stained sink.

# INCORPORATED

It bears mentioning that Rod Bankman was not of this Earth. He was not a human being. Rod Bankman was a baybeetle. Like Earth's humans, baybeetles were ape-like, bipedal, ten-fingered, ten-toed, and hairy in all of the right and all of the wrong places. If Rod was to have landed, properly clothed, in the center of New York City, passersby would not have looked twice at the smallish, wide-eyed baybeetle.

It never came to bother Rod that he was not of this Earth. In fact, Rod had never even heard of planet Earth. Rod was a resident of planet Nord—an astoundingly Earth-like world spinning away on the far side of the Milky Way galaxy. Nord, however, was tiny. On such a tiny planet as Nord, the consequences of even the smallest, most personal actions were far more obvious than on massive planet Earth.

Rod slopped a handful of Gino's Grooming Compound onto his head and sculpted the same ruthlessly parted hairstyle he had worn since early childhood. Shaking the breadcrumbs from a collared shirt that smelled decent enough, Rod buttoned up, wiped off his necktie, and clicked on the television.

"Our fair city of Bottom Junction will be cold and drizzly again today," read sleek meteorologist Tawny Witherspoon, "and perhaps through Sunday when we will begin to see increasing precipitation throughout the nation."

Rod pulled a mug out of the sink from beneath a pile of pots and pans. A rugged aroma drifted across the room. "Thank you, Tawny," said the anchorman, "We'll be right back for more of Gino's News Morning after this word from our sponsors." Rod's ears perked as he filled his mug with yesterday's coffee and plunged some sourdough into his new seven-slice toaster.

"Hey hey!" charmed the frenetic sponsor jumping from side to side in a tucked-in polo, "Gino here, and we here at Gino's Emporium would like to take a moment right *now* to take advantage of this opportune moment to give *you* the opportunity to take advantage of this chance to give *us* a chance to save *you* some money on these incredible buys!" Rod's inked quill raced across a piece of scrap paper, noting deals on disposable can openers and kitty litter. "That's right, only seventy-nine ninety-five, that's seventy-nine *ninety*-five *today* at a Gino's Emporium near you."

Rod glanced at his list of bargains and then to the cuckoo clock. "Oh dear." Riddled and perspiring, Rod made a grab for his overcoat and the torn paper bag that held the still incomplete text for the Buckingham Project. He bounded out of his standard residential unit under the watchful eye of Chet, tirelessly leering out at Rod from the window of his large, luxury unit. Rod jumped into Babe, shoved his key into her ignition, and disappeared into a glistening cloud of smoke.

Babe was Rod's weathered but cozy Tugliner Plus. A hand-me-down from his folks, Babe was once the pinnacle of economy station wagons, but her exhaust filter was now beyond repair. Her once shiny, olive coat had gone flat and pimpled like Rod's arms. Smarmy Chet continued to watch, arms crossed, as Babe emerged from her cloud of smoke and disappeared again into a left-hand turn.

The city of Bottom Junction—an industrial center in the nation of Gibbous Bizonia—growled as vehicles oozed over highways and turnpikes, spreading themselves throughout the maze of monuments to war. Though buried in six lanes of traffic, Rod was tempted to sneak Babe into the vacant diamond lane, the express lane reserved for larger, pricier vehicles such as the new Freedomcraft models. Law enforcement could be wicked and Babe was already conspicuous—dwarfed within the parade of MacroCruisers, Gargatons, and other heaving automobiles—so Rod pooh-poohed himself and let his coffee and the gray drizzle fertilize his thoughts. He and Babe wended their way over mounds of fertile soil compressed under layer upon layer of asphalt.

With morning coffee stretching thin the walls of Rod's bladder, the halo of MWI, Magic Wands Incorporated, came into view. MWI, a proud member of the Gino's Family of Industries, had been Rod's home away from home for the past sixteen years. Babe vaulted out of the slug of traffic to ascend the challenging spiral of the company garage. The garage was full, again, and Rod was relegated, again, to the muddied pasture across the river from MWI. Rod mucked himself up in the now stiff rain, and to a chorus of car alarms, he made his way to the Magic Wand compound.

Wet and winded, Rod cradled his soggy paper bag next to the MWI front desk as security guard Carl scanned his left eyeball with a green laser. "Good morning Mister Flounders, sir," grinned Rod, bladder pounding, at the approach of his half-troll boss.

"You're LATE, Bankman."

Rod looked to his wristwatch and then to the company clock. "Thank you, sir, but I believe I'm seven minutes early, sir."

"That's SIX minutes early, and did you not receive the Spirit Department MEMO?"

"Which one, sir?" Rod had received so many crass memos from the Spirit Department—short for Employee Spirit Evaluation Department—that they all blended into one prolonged beating.

"Which ONE? How about the ONE that asks all of our employees to please stop STEALING company TIME by showing up LATE!"

"But I'm...six minutes early, sir."

"Looks more like FIVE minutes, Bankman, and STILL NOT WORKING!"

"But—"

"But THIS, Bankman!" steamed Flounders from beneath his black caterpillar moustache as he shoved a stack of papers into Rod's chest. Flounders turned on his heels and bullied his way down the cramped hallway, spouting tiny droplets of saliva onto his pinstriped suit and onto Rod's coworkers. Rod made a dash for the lift.

On the seventh floor, Rod settled into his cubicle to resume the task of climbing the invisible company ladder. The ladder led from one job to the next, each job more lucrative and powerful than the last. As a copywriter assigned to the Buckingham Project, Rod's current task was to compose the literature—terms of use, warning labels, user's guide—that would accompany the new Buckingham line of wands, the next generation of MWI magic wands. The Buckingham Project would be Rod's springboard to the next invisible rung of the ladder.

They were conjuring magnificent results with the Buckingham prototypes in Product Testing. The high alchemists were certainly impressed with the wand's effect on potions of varying colors and consistencies. The future of the Buckingham Project was so promising that Rod was already shopping caviar and itching his nose from the imaginary tingle of ancient sparkling wine.

Like the rain pouring outside, Rod passed the hours raining crumpled papers covered with rejected drafts into his waste basket.

Despite the intensity of his efforts, Rod kept his senses tuned at all times to the possibility of catching gorgeous Dorothy Tarnuckle walking the corridor to the ladies' room. Rod skipped lunch to labor over words and phrases, banking on coffee refills and the chance of seeing Tarnuckle for inspiration. As the coffee delivered its diminishing returns, Rod began to get distracted.

A circling office fly landed on Rod's computer monitor and took a few hurried steps. The fly zipped from the monitor to the rim of Rod's coffee cup and from there into the coffee itself where the fly struggled for its very survival. With agile typing fingers, Rod scooped the fly up from its tragic circumstances and onto a stack of paper napkins that came every morning tucked under his chocolate doughnut hole. Rod continued to work, head nodding and snapping with exhaustion.

Reaching for another sip of Gino's Dark Roast, Rod's hand stopped at the sight of the fly returned to the coffee. This time the fly crouched cautiously at the coffee's shore, taking light sips. With drooping eyelids, Rod imagined how pretty the fly would have looked curled up in a blanket under a shade tree next to the ocean of coffee. Rod pictured himself curled up next to the fly, spooning on a sunny afternoon. He then pictured himself easing away from the fly, slipping on his shorts, and burying his toes in the sands of Isle Solovanana, a tropical paradise in the nation of Muzora.

"Are you HAPPY, Bankman?"

Rod's eyes snapped open to the sight of Flounders' cratered bulb of a nose hovering inches in front his own. "Yes, sir. Very happy, sir."

"Well GREAT then. Hate to interrupt your cozy little NAP, but THAT means you must be DONE with the TEXT for the BUCKINGHAM Project."

"Almost done, sir."

"*Almost done, sir*," mocked Flounders in a lispy tongue. He left Rod with a knowing sneer and a foul scent. Rod flew to the restroom where he could finish his nap and his dreams of Isle Solovanana.

Six thirty, quitting time, arrived with the chiming of fairy bells and a collective sigh. Rod wrapped up his product description and packed his still damp paper bag. He was mere days away from completing the Buckingham's final drafts. As team leader, Rod had completed Gary, Lance, and Dorene's projects for them while they rehashed daring twists in television's daytime drama "The Onion Cleavers".

With raindrops sliding down office windows like tears in "The Onion Cleavers", Rod threw on his overcoat, grabbed his bag, and set to thinking about being home with Slim the cat and an evening of bird watching. With the first step outside of his cubicle, Rod heard that voice from behind.

"Where do you think YOU'RE going?"

It was Flounders, of course.

"I'm going home to my kitty ca—"

"Do you think you're BETTER than everyone else, BANKMAN?"

Rod looked around the office, noting bitter expressions on the faces of his coworkers—Gary, Lance, and Dorene included. "No, sir, I was just—"

"Just WHAT?"

"Just—"

"You...make...me...SICK!" Mister Flounders turned completely red, shot out his arm, and pointed Rod towards the lift with a flaming index finger.

Rod descended alone to the lobby.

Not a bad day.

Rod dug Babe out of overflow parking with little more than his bare hands. Caked with mud, the two endured the Sigman Expressway standstill and eventually sliced onto the off-ramp for Roadview Drive.

Humming a nifty tune as he scanned the radio for the latest hit from pop sensation Ace Redworm, Rod's hand froze on the dial. There was a baybeetle ahead—a short, chocolate brown baybeetle out for a stroll. And it wasn't even Sunday.

Not only was this short, dark baybeetle out for a stroll on a Thursday, but he was also completely *off* the sidewalk, on the ribbon of grass next to the road. He appeared to be lollygagging. "How odd," whispered Rod as Babe swerved to avoid running straight into War Monument Six.

Three other cars swerved as well, distracted by the gray-bearded pedestrian in a caramel three-piece suit and matching fedora. The next vehicle, a MacroCruiser, ran straight into War Monument Six, knocked it to the ground, and kept on rolling without a scratch.

Babe backfired.

In unison, Ace Redworm's "Show Me the Money" popped onto the radio. *"Show me the mon-ey. Gotta get me some lovin' hon-ey..."* Rod slid down in his seat and grooved, forgetting all about the awkward pedestrian and the loss of Monument Six.

Once safe behind the walls of Grace Peck Apartments, Rod stripped off everything but his boxers and bifocals. He sweet talked

Slim, dished him up some vittles, unfurled a tin of Iron Sea sardines, and threw on his knee-length birdwatching jacket covered with pockets of various sizes.

Donning headphones and bulky aluminum goggles, Rod eased back in his recliner and began to toggle a peculiar apparatus. Piped into the goggles via a tangle of outdated cables was a virtual jungle, and by toggling his apparatus, Rod was able to maneuver like a spirit through these tropical wilds in search of exotic feathered critters. With stereophonic sound as his guide, Rod had sighted many rare species such as the Pebbled Rimmett, the Dank Foosler, and Rafael's Wax Trumpet—all of which now had bright red check marks next to them on the wall chart. Next to the Foiled Hoverbean, a hummingbird so elusive in the virtual jungle that its very existence was the subject of debate, a red smudge was visible where Rod had once made a check...and then rubbed it out.

After logging a Spindle Grouse and two Rourke's Chiblers, it was bedtime. "Well I guess it's just you and me, Slim," sighed Rod, "Let's turn in and call it a day." Rod rubbed the cat's nose and the bridge of his own nose, sore from the dilapidated goggles.

Rod rectified the morning's bologna sandwich mess. Once the mess of bedding was rectified, Rod tucked Slim in and together they enjoyed the final minutes of a pro roundball game on the Roundball Channel. As the two faded off to the pounding of night rains, Clint Mosaby, the king of roundball, rammed it home at the final buzzer. In his victory celebration, Mosaby broke his clavicle and punched two opposing players in the face, sparking drunken riots throughout most of greater Bluntville.

# CHAPTER TWO

# One Bad Bounce

*Lounging in the cockpit of Helicopter Five, Rod surveyed a Gino's battery plant in the nation of Muzora. Using binoculars on a swivel, Rod spotted six of Gino's employees taking rest from shouldering their loads of rare metals. All six were natives of Muzora and all six were terminated on the spot, by Rod, a Gino's executive. The net below Helicopter Five drug the sweaty workers into the air, tan arms and legs poking through the twisted net. The Muzorans were dropped into a sluice pond in the outskirts.*

*"Work, work, work," Rod smirked to helmeted Pilot Seven. When Helicopter Five banked into a turn, sending butterflies to Rod's tummy, the Muzoran landscape gave way to a dark body of water dancing with the sun—the Rutmus Strait. The skyscrapers of Gibbous Bizonia bejeweled the coastline afar. As the helicopter approached Rod's penthouse landing, the scene at street level forty floors below was manic.*

*A green creeper had escaped the Age of Nature diorama in the lobby. The National Guard was called in and they were pounding away at the creeper's network of crawling vines. With a shrill cry, the Guard's Sergeant Crowley rushed the creeper and seemingly saved the day, sinking his bayonet deep into the creeper's main stalk. Cozying up to a dirty martini, Rod turned on the news.*

*Staring back at Rod via a live feed was the horrified mug of Sergeant Crowley. A second creeper had escaped and it was spreading, heading Rod's way. Rod curled up into a ball and watched from the corner as the hard edges of his windows began to darken with savage greenery. When Rod was surrounded by the creeper's web, his ceiling faded to black and filled with stars. Moonlight touched Rod's face and hands as a shooting star parted the night sky. Rod's bare toes shifted in the dirt and a dusty moth brushed Rod's eyelashes and tickled his nose.*

Rod awoke in a giggle. He couldn't remember ever waking up in a giggle before. It was still twelve minutes before his alarm, so Rod hit the off button and eased out from beneath the covers so as not to wake Slim or upstairs Belinda. Rod made it into the shower completely naked and it was the best shower of the week until Belinda caught on.

With no intent to bathe, for she seldom did, Belinda got up, cranked on her shower's hot and cold, and began to laugh as Rod's shower was reduced to a useless trickle. "Take that, craphead!" she howled.

Pleased with the shower that God gave him, Rod got out and put himself together.

With three slices toasting in his seven-slicer, Rod whistled his way back to the bedroom and Slim. Slim's catatonia was betrayed only by a twitch of the whiskers. "What are you dreaming about, my good Slim?" Rod wondered. Catnip? She-kittens? Chasing moths in the moonlight? A shooting star? At the thought of a shooting star, Rod recalled a foggy trace of the dream that had left him in this chipper mood. He stopped fluffing his pillows. His chipper mood had come from the plants, the dirt, the moon, and the shooting star in his dream.

This was not good.

# ONE BAD BOUNCE

The Age of Nature was long, *long* gone and baybeetles had eliminated nature for good reason.

"Any Foiled Hoverbeans lately, Bankman?" jeered Gary, one of Rod's underlings at MWI. Gary, a fellow virtual birder, never let an opportunity slip by to make fun of Rod and his claim to have spied the rare virtual hummingbird.

"Stick it where the sun don't shine, Gary," replied Rod, typing away. After a Spirit Department review of Rod's crude reply, Rod was sent to detention where he spent the rest of the day under the abrasive supervision of fellow go-getters.

Meanwhile, rumors continued to leak out of Product Testing. "The new Buckingham wand passed durability with a nine-point-four, no reports of splinters." "Clint Mosaby, *the* Clint Mosaby, king of roundball, tested one and *liked* it." Could all of this really be true? The dollar signs that flashed with each murmur about the Buckingham wands helped Rod survive another bumpy workday.

After work, as Babe relaxed into evening rush hour, Rod flipped open his phone to give Jake a ring, only to find that his phone battery had gone dead. Jake was Rod's baby brother who was in the throes of an unacceptable lifestyle. Jake was not only irresponsible, but dirty and unrealistic, at times unshaven and even a little strange. Completely unprofessional. The solution to Jake, however, was not lost onto Rod, who at thirty-two was almost seven years Jake's senior.

Rod had been composing a list. In the list's left-hand column was a succession of Jake's most compromising faults, such as,

"Needs a better paying job". In the right-hand column would be corrective actions, such as, "Apply for sales job at MWI". Jake's List had been fermenting to perfection for months. Tomorrow night, at family dinner, Rod would finally present Jake with the list in crystalized form.

With his phone sitting useless and still in his pocket, Rod was left to face the remaining miles to the gray speck of Grace Peck Apartments with only his thoughts of Slim.

Rod made it home to see fading dusk outline the blooming bingalee tree just outside his tiny window. It was one of only two trees left in the county. This bingalee had been slated for removal, as it attracted troublesome squirrels who loved to scamper about its branches. Rod and Slim were both exhausted, Rod from detention and Slim from sleeping all day, so after dinner they decided to skip the evening's birding and call it an early night.

As Rod and his pillow became one, he began to dream. In his dream, Rod was blazing around a blind corner in his new convertible when he ran over something with a quick double thump. In the rear-view mirror, Rod saw a squirrel tumbling off the side of the road. Nice.

The looks on the faces of Rod's workers would be tinted green with envy when he walked into Gino's, *his* Gino's, after a fresh kill. They would see his wind-tossed hair and the fluorescent lights beaming off his sunburn, leaving no doubt that it was *he* who had pulled into the first spot on parking level A1 with the top all of the way down, braving the smog of the day.

# ONE BAD BOUNCE

"Stinking insects!" Rod cried to the cloudless sky, squirting wiper fluid onto a smashed bug that had ruined his otherwise spotless windshield. The next bug hit and this time, it left one of its black and orange wings clinging to the windshield. "Disgusting." A mist of wiper fluid broke over the windshield and settled into the combed furrows of Rod's lacquered hair. The windshield was hit by another butterfly, then another. Rod could not keep up. He could hardly see through the mash of wings, wiper fluid, and bug guts collecting on his windshield.

Stopping next to a bank of flashing parking meters, Rod got out to summon a car wash with a wave of his wand. Even this was impossible for the growing swarm of sunset orange butterflies. The butterflies whispered past Rod's reddened ears and clung unnoticeably to his back and shoulders.

While Rod was fussing with his wand, a short, dark baybeetle wrapped in a clean, white cloth emerged from within the gentle chaos of flying insects. The baybeetle's stare was warm and frightening. A strange elation sprang from Rod's heart when the baybeetle lifted his cupped hands in front of his long, peppered beard. Leaning in towards Rod, the baybeetle opened his hands to free a single Foiled Hoverbean. The presumably extinct hummingbird darted to and fro, right before Rod's very eyes.

Grinning but distressed, Rod turned over and over in bed. Losing patience with his bedmate's antics, Slim stretched, bounded, and fell asleep on the bookshelf next to Rod's most recent copy of "Virtual Birding Quarterly".

Rod's eyes popped open.

They were happening again.

These strange dreams, dreams in which he was being overcome by a fearsome happiness when faced with unrealistic visions of the natural world. And this latest dream even included the strange, dark baybeetle he caught lollygagging on the Thursday drive home. Video games were one thing, but dreams were real to the touch. "These dreams are ridiculous," Rod laughed nervously to a dozing Slim, "Utterly ludicrous. Foiled Hoverbean, indeed."

Once fooled into believing otherwise, Rod was now convinced that these hoverbeans were good and gone. Extinct, even in the virtual world. And nature? Wilderness? The unspoiled wilderness? Beyond sporadic tales told by returning REZ workers, there was absolutely no evidence of such a thing. Besides, fringe baybeetles who worked in the REZ, the Remote Extraction Zone, were loud and unsavory, not to be trusted.

Though it was the middle of the night, Rod dared not risk any more dreams, so he pushed aside the covers and headed into his slippers. Three cups of coffee later, Rod found his favorite game show, "Celebrity Spank and Rumble", on the television, so with this and a bowl of popcorn, Rod was able to sit up in bed and flush out the madness of his dreams. When starlet Sally Brighton laid a two-handed spanking on an unknown contestant in the bonus round, Rod nearly fell off the bed. "She's too much," the game show host said with an electric smile.

"She's too much," Rod repeated to himself, slouching a little lower against his headboard, "too much."

Rod was still wondering about a good spanking on national television from the likes of Sally Brighton when the first Common Nuthatch began chirping in the bingalee at the break of dawn. Closing his eyes, Rod could imagine the "Spank and Rumble" studio audience roaring and the exhilaration of moving into the final round. Rod's eyes remained closed as the sky brightened with the rising sun and his thoughts of Sally Brighton turned to dreams.

Rod dreamed that he was floating through outer space next to Brighton. They were two among many, floating in a cluster. Neither Rod nor his companions had developed much beyond the fetal stage, and each was anchored by an umbilical tether to a common central yolk sack. The pod was protected by a translucent membrane that obscured their view of the heavens.

Nobody saw it coming.

Nobody sounded the alarm before the pod collided with a massive object. Rod, Brighton, and a handful of their underdeveloped companions survived the collision.

Strange species observed through the settling haze as Rod and the others clumsily examined their ruptured yolk sack and their new environment. The object they had run into was so large that it appeared to stretch forever in every direction. Yolkless, the castaways cast away their umbilicals and intuitively commenced a honey hunt. The dirt between his tender toes and the sunshine on his shoulders made Rod happy and everyone shared all of the honey and all of the pain inflicted by angry bees.

Someone discovered that a stick could be used for poking and hitting things. The stick could be tossed to dislodge fruit from the trees. It could dig into the ground to dislodge tasty tubers. Rod could bend the stick and put leaves over it for shelter. So beautiful their new planet and so curious their minds that Rod and his companions wandered freely and slept untroubled, submerged in fireflies.

Rod and Brighton learned to reproduce via the genital mingling technique, but did so only to the point that their numbers did not plunder the beauty of their new home nor deplete the jungle of food. Rod and his kin splintered off and wandered to a place where there were fewer fruits for the nibbling. Everyone remained curious and appreciative as they searched more thoroughly for their meals, finding hardly any honey at all.

One day while high in a tree, Rod saw an unfamiliar baybeetle approaching—though they may have once shared the same yolk sack, the newcomer was now strange in his hairdo and the cut of his loin cloth. He was singing songs in a language that Rod did not comprehend. Out of fear, Rod remained hidden and observed.

Days passed, and a growing number of these strange baybeetles were arriving. These outsiders were tolerated, if not welcomed, until Rod became famished and these stupid jerks were digging up his very favorite tubers. "That's it," Rod said under his breath, "This has gone on long enough."

Emerging from a thicket, Rod screamed incantations and hurled his good stick at the outsiders just to get a rise out of them. The good stick took a bad bounce, one really bad bounce, and hit the largest weirdo square in the nose. The burly weirdo got immensely pissed off and out of spite, he urinated on the last edible tuber in sight.

Things simply went downhill from there.

Rod's party began to hoard all of the food they could in order to fortify themselves against outsiders. Rod spent more and more time hiding in the dark behind thicker and thicker walls. Without the sun, Rod's body, once a rich brown, faded to pale pink.

Rod began to hunt the enemy with increasing sophistication. Rod's once loving, wandering, celestial mind became occupied with ways to hunker down, build, fight, and work. Rod's magical sensibilities got tangled up as they took to technologies ever more distant from the natural logic of pure Nord. Having lost sight of the natural world on the other side of their walls, Rod's group grew in number and in their numbers, they began to unwittingly plunder the beauty of their new planet.

When walls had grown up to the sky and waste dumps could not be contained, a two-headed beast reeking of stale urine arose from the sewers. With calculated blows from its many arms, the beast began leveling walls and buildings, one after the other. All Rod could see was shaking, crumbling walls and suffering, dying baybeetles. After the civilization that Rod and his kind had built was reduced to piles of smoking rubble, Rod spied the beast as it turned and walked away, heads hung low.

As he dreamed this dream, cold sweat rubbed off of Rod's churning body onto his sheets and pillows. His last fading memory of the dream was the sight of a lone magic wand, gyrating to a stop on a slab of mangled concrete in a mist of settling dust. Next to the wand crouched one sunset orange butterfly, barely breathing, wings grounded.

Rod's instinctual, half-asleep reach for the security of Slim's soft pelt was in vain. The alert feline was perched atop Rod's dresser, watching, quiet as a vulture.

CHAPTER THREE

# Bullneck City

Pulling himself together and getting out of bed was simply not going to happen, not this morning. Not any morning. Ever. Rod's dreams were killing him. He called Magic Wands.

"Good morning! Magic Wands Incorporated. How may I direct your call?"

"Mister Archibald Flound—"

"Please choose from the following options. For a staff directory, press 'one'. For Product Testing, press 'two'. For Marketing, press 'three'. For—" Rod pressed the zero button.

"What."

"Mister Archibald Flounders, please."

"Bankman?"

"Yes—cough—good    morning,    Mister—cough    cough—Flounders, sir."

"What."

"Well, uh, I'm really—cough—sorry, Mister Flounders, sir, but I'm—"

"What is it."

"Yes—cough—what I meant to say is that—cough—I'm really not feeling very well—"

"WHAT?!"

"I think I need to call in sick today, sir...cough."

A pregnant silence followed.

Shattering the barely audible static on the phone line, a grown baybeetle squealed in Rod's ear, "YOU'LL PAY FOR THIS, *BANKMAN!*" and the line went dead.

These dreams. This job. This life.

Rod Bankman had never in his sixteen years at MWI called in sick, let alone on a Saturday. Having now done so while not the least bit ill gave him an upset stomach, a migraine headache, and hives. "What's happening to me, Slim?"

"Mreeow," replied Slim.

"I...I used to be perfectly normal, Slim. Now...now I'm losing my mind."

"*Mreeow!*"

"Where are these dreams coming from? Why me? Why now?" whined Rod.

"MREEOW!" This time Slim spoke with authority, jumping onto Rod's bed-ridden chest and staring down two inches from Rod's runny nose.

Rod flipped the cat then began flipping through the channels, searching for his sanity. He found it on channel 97, Bizonian Movie Classics. They were showing "Hidden Genius", the true story of Hugh Mackleton. Hugh was the first entrepreneur to successfully turn the misfortunes of his fellow baybeetles into a personal fortune. It was seven thirteen in the morning.

As the life of young Mackleton flashed before Rod's eyes, the Gino's News Symphony interrupted the program, "We interrupt this program to bring you breaking news out of Bullneck City." It was Ted Nedbury, long time Gino's anchorman and voice of the Gino's empire—trusted messenger, fashion conscious, and handsome as all get out. "The footage you are about to see is, to say the least, shocking and devastating."

# BULLNECK CITY

This was nothing new.

"At exactly seven ten this morning in the center of Bullneck City, morning commuters bore witness to a vile attack on our capital city's War Monument One." Ted Nedbury's always sincere, straining head shot was replaced by a shot of the famed Bullneck City skyline. With bloodshot eyes, Rod watched a puff of smoke, barely visible for the surrounding buildings, issue from the mirrored steeple of War Monument One.

"We now turn to live coverage of the bombing with Susan Lakeside and Gino's Mobilecam One, brought to you by Gino's Petroleum Jelly. Good morning, Susan."

"Yes, Ted, and a very good morning to you," smiled Susan in her purple velveteen jumpsuit, knowing that this bombing was her big career break. Rod winced at her stupid luck. With simmering Monument One in the background and lost, concerned faces flashing in and out of the camera, Susan reiterated three or four times what had just been said by Nedbury. Lakeside then began interviewing panicked pedestrians and state officials whose official job it was to repeat official information.

As cameras rolled on the fuming spire of Monument One, Rod's tired eyes saw the entire building tremble, all fifty stories. Was it just a twitch of the cameraman's wrist? The spire trembled again and this time it didn't go unnoticed by Lakeside and Nedbury.

"Oh my God."

"Oh my God."

"Oh my God," echoed Rod. War Monument One housed the largest Gino's Emporium on Nord. At this hour, it would be filled with morning shoppers. As the television audience watched, the full girth of War Monument One, Gino's Emporium included, simply collapsed. All was a confusion lost in clouds of smoke and dust.

Rod's jaw hung open. Susan Lakeside was hunched over with her clipboard covering her face. She was barely visible for the havoc of dust and scrambling baybeetles. Over and over, the changing light from the television reflected off Rod's tongue as over and over the television replayed the collapse of Monument One. Not once did Rod spy a two-headed beast with many arms—like the beast from his dream—blasting through the haze, as over and over he berated himself for expecting to see one.

Speculation as to who was to blame for the terror attack quickly turned to accusation. Muzorans, Muzorans, Muzorans. "The Muzorans," repeated Ted Nedbury, looking directly into the camera, "appear to be responsible." Not since Bellicose Bay, years before Rod was born, had Gibbous Bizonia been attacked by another nation on its own soil.

Hours of the same grisly words and images passed from the television screen into Rod's brain. He flipped from channel to channel lost in thoughts of the dead, their families, the Muzorans, and how all this might open up new markets for MWI and the Buckingham wands. The world would certainly be in need of some magic after this one. Hugh Mackleton of "Hidden Genius" would have known what to do.

The evening of the tragic events in Bullneck City, Rod and his little brother Jake were having at it over family dinner. "Snap out of it, Rod," said Jake, his curly brown mop shaking into his eyes, "It's just not cool to have your sights on a baybeetle's pocketbook when he's already down."

"Oh, don't be prude, Jake," replied Rod, "I'm only being realistic."

"Right, and there is absolutely nothing that you could do to brighten the future of Nord besides exploit new markets for wands."

Prior to arriving at his folks', Rod had spent hours watching the world collapse on tragic television, feeding Slim every time he felt a pang for normalcy. "Maybe you're right," said Rod.

"Of course I'm right," said Jake.

"I mean, maybe you're right in that there is absolutely nothing else that I could do to help out." Rod's thoughts drifted to the bittersweet image of Slim bloated and collapsed atop the overflowing cat bowl.

Jake's irritation with his brother was competing with thoughts of his midnight stroll down abandoned railroad tracks with lightly clad friends Barbara and Jasmine. "Rod, you've got to be kidding me—"

"Now, you two boys stop thees," rebuked Yolanda in her distinct accent, her thoughts drifting nowhere. Yolanda, Rod and Jake's sturdy Muzoran mother, arrived in Gibbous Bizonia arm in arm with Rod and Jake's stringy father Leonard after Leonard's spring break on Isle Solovanana years ago.

"Mom," complained Jake, "This bombing in Bullneck City is the most significant event on Nord since the return of Woodrow Happyhouse—"

"Happyhouse was a nobody," belched Rod.

"—since the return of *Sir* Woodrow Happyhouse, and I just can't believe that in the face of this, Rod's biggest concern is for company profits."

"Jake," said Yolanda, "we are all a leetle deefrent and we are all a leetle scared and we all love your older brother bery bery much."

"That's right," agreed Leonard, his thoughts drifting in and out of the abstract watercolor hung on the wall behind Jake.

Tongue dumplings were going uneaten below the conversation. Yolanda issued the order, "Now eat," and eight of the nine dumplings were promptly devoured.

After eating only vicariously through Slim all day while nursing his hives, Rod was famished. "Is anyone going to eat that?" Rod asked regarding the final dumpling. Yolanda was pleased with the demolition of her dumplings and served Rod herself.

"What I don't get, Jake," said Rod through a mouthful of tongue, "is your claim that this Bullneck City bombing is the biggest event in the last five-hundred years. I mean, how is this attack any different than the attack on Bellicose Bay fifty years ago? Muzorans just hate us and that's that."

"Rod, Mom is Muzoran."

Rod swallowed his tongue.

"I agree that there are many Muzorans that do simply hate Bizonians," continued Jake, "but to say that all Muzorans hate us, or even that most Muzorans hate us, is ridiculous. Had you come with us to Muzora, you'd know. We're all just baybeetles."

"You and I both know," Rod rebutted, "that I had to stay home and iron my curtains. You saw them. But still, why on Nord would you think that a bomb going off in Bullneck City is such a pivotal event? You're always so dramatic."

"Dramatic?!" cried Jake, launching to his feet, arms flapping.

"Boys, boys! Why all of thees beekering—"

"Oh, honey," pleaded Leonard, a little tipsy from his red wine, "the boys are just having a heart to heart—"

# BULLNECK CITY

"My name eez *not* 'honey'. My *name* eez Yolanda Giulietta Pia Brunela Constanza di Lertora Bankman Ceballos and I weel *not* be eenterrupted like thees while my beautiful leettle boys are having on each other's necks!" At this, a quiet landed on the table like an anvil. In lieu of twitching in place, the family ignited into furious table clearing.

Yolanda Giulietta Pia Brunela Constanza di Lertora Bankman Ceballos crammed herself into yellow, elbow-length gloves and attacked the island of dirty plates rising out of the kitchen sink. The boys fell to lounging in the living room, swinging cocktails and fists full of nuts.

The sudsy chatter of porcelain in Yolanda's ears allowed Jake and Rod to continue bickering. Jake turned to Rod, "Ya see, bro', not only did Nord start off as a pretty small planet, but it's grown a lot smaller in the fifty years since Bellicose Bay." Rod looked at Jake with airs on. "Not *physically* smaller, Rod, just smaller in that once strictly separate cultures now communicate with each other at levels unheard of fifty years ago. Our advances in the ways of magic allow us to communicate halfway around the world instantaneously. Baybeetles travel the face of the globe with relative ease. More and more we're becoming one huge, really diverse neighborhood. We are all becoming friends."

"Listen, Jake. You're getting totally off track. The question is, why is the bombing of Bullneck City any different than the bombing of Bellicose Bay?"

"It's different because the Bullneck City bombing happened in the heart of the most powerful nation on Nord—not at some remote outpost—to a monument that was *the* symbol of Bizonian military and economic dominance *and* it happened on live television.

27

Because of the new smallness of the world and the friendship that comes with it, the world has grown less tolerant of this insane violence. Bullneck City will be impossible to ignore. The world is going to be looking at this event under a keen microscope. Remedies to endless war will emerge."

"Oh I'm *sure* they will," cracked Rod, elbowing Leonard.

As the heat began rising off of Jake's head, the silhouette of Yolanda appeared in the living room doorway, drying its hands on the silhouette of a swinging hand towel. Conversation screeched to a halt and Rod, smug, kicked his feet up on the coffee table.

Rod insisted on giving Jake a ride home. The boys were given cuddly send-offs as they climbed up into Babe and Babe rattled to life. Jake sat looking straight ahead, stewing. When Babe's cloud of exhaust was thick enough to obscure Leonard and Yolanda's porch-lit figures, the boys followed Babe's headlights out of the cloud and waved good-bye. "There will always be war, Jake."

"Maybe because you and everybody else keep sayin' so."

Babe swiveled onto NE 63rd. "There has always been war. It has always been this way," persisted Rod.

"You know what, Rod," Jake's heart was burning, "I beg to differ. I don't suppose you have been doing a whole lot of research into this area." Rod's nostril flinched before his face went blank behind his spectacles. He stepped a little harder on the accelerator. Jake, an amateur beetleopologist—Nord's equivalent of an anthropologist—continued, "Well, I *have* been researching—LOOK OUT, ROD!"

A gray cat had darted out in front of the car. Rod screwed his face and spun Babe's wheel hard to the left. Though they only brushed the tail of the racing cat, they now found themselves closing in on an awestruck pedestrian. The brothers screamed simultaneously as the pedestrian's entourage of cats and kittens darted every which way in the headlights. Babe leapt like a cornered beast into another hairpin turn as they shot past the scrambling baybeetle. Babe lurched up and over the curb, crashing headlong into the county's only tree aside from Grace Peck's bingalee. The shaken pedestrian approached Babe in a coarse waddle.

Rod recognized the chocolate brown baybeetle. It was the very same baybeetle from Thursday's drive home and from his dream of flocking butterflies. Rod slammed Babe into reverse. As Babe's tires spun in the muck, this dark fellow in dime-store flip-flops ambled right at them with his walking stick. Rubber burning and engine steaming, Rod dislodged Babe from the tree and thumped her back onto the street. Jake was wide-eyed, unhurt, and engulfed by his brother's streak of madness.

With one hand pressed against the trunk of the tree and one held up in salutation, the dark baybeetle shouted to the brothers as they sped away, zigzagging through the roadway maze of cats and kittens. With shocks of grass flaring from his pockets, the dark baybeetle waved farewell.

One block later, Babe twisted to a halt in front of Jake's house. Rod's tantrum continued, "Get yourself in there and lock the doors before that madman gets here."

"What *is* the deal, Rod? Freaking relax!" Jake was still in disbelief, "Did you hear what that guy back there was shouting?"

"It doesn't matter, now let's get a move on."

"What he was shouting, believe it or not, was, 'Fear not. This tree shall live on.'"

"Good God, Jake, he's even more insane than we imagined. Now out, out, out!"

Jake could take no more. With eyebrows raised, he scooted out of Babe and said good-bye. Rod pulled a muscle in his neck, craning to cover Jake's escape.

Not a moment too soon, Jake shut his front door behind him, allowing Rod to make a break for Slim. With untold damage inside and out, Babe was pained and trundling while Rod continued to milk her for speed. In a final sputter, Babe lost power and Rod forced her to the curb.

Shouting incantation after incantation, Rod got out and looked under Babe's hood, hoping to find a flashing red button to push or a thick golden cord to pull that would fix everything. These he did not find. What he did find was the same filthy mess of alien gadgetry that had always spelled his frustration.

Rod throttled his phone, hoping to score a taxi, only to find himself in another dead battery lurch. Thunder rumbled over a distant waste as Rod locked up Babe and waved his travel wand over her for good measure. Rod then made haste for Grace Peck Apartments on Roadview Drive with only a slight lead on the waddling stranger.

Rod soon realized that his shoes were hard and his socks were thin and that for the very first time he was alone on the streets of Bottom Junction in the dead of night. Never had his senses been so raw as they were now under the burnt orange, starless sky. A fog building on his bifocals, Rod made his way, skulking from hedge to plastic hedge, triggering flood lights and car alarms.

Down the next shady alley, Rod scuffed to a halt and held his breath. The dark, bearded baybeetle and his posse of furry feline followers crossed his path beneath a streetlight. Rod ditched behind a dumpster. With no time to think and for the sake of all that was good in the world, Rod decided to give chase to this silent menace. When the menace reached his damp and despoiled den littered with drugs and shotgun shells, Rod would mark location and eventually notify the Center for Unfashionable Foreigners. Homeland Security was sure to follow.

The dark, hobbled criminal froze in his flip-flops and sniffed the air.

As Rod reached to finger his dead cellular, the criminal resumed his pace and took a sudden left turn. Two blocks away, the street dead-ended into Bottom's Rest Cemetery. The mysterious baybeetle was up and over the neck-high wrought iron fence of the cemetery like it wasn't even there, then he disappeared into the darkness beyond.

Rod snuck up to the fence believing all was lost—his greatest prior feat of athleticism having been a collegiate game of ring toss. A gate secured with rusty chains and a padlock, unopened for generations, was his only hope.

Rod shoved his lint-covered travel wand into the keyhole of the padlock with all he could muster. Having come from a long line of wand industry workers, Rod should not have been surprised when he bore down and the lock clicked open. He remained in pursuit.

Barely visible over the skeleton crests of tombstones, the outline of the criminal's fedora bobbed and then stopped directly behind the cemetery's singular, lonesome rose bush. Daring not disturb the least bit of rubbish beneath his wingtips, Rod edged in for a closer look. There, beneath the distant glow of downtown lights, it happened.

# CHAPTER 3

The evil one abandoned his cane, shoving it into the ground to stand on its own. He removed his fedora and rested it atop the cane. From under a fallen headstone, the criminal removed a small blanket and unfurled it beneath the rosebush. He then curled up around a litter of newborn kittens and fell asleep to the delicate scent of dreaming antique roses.

# CHAPTER FOUR

# Central Nut

Rod awoke to Slim's blue rasp of a tongue licking his eyelid. The hour was ten thirty-five a.m. Rod took one giant swallow, knowing he now had to explain to Flounders why he was four hours late for work. He also had to explain to Slim why they were out of cat food and to the guy pounding on his front door why he didn't give a rip.

"Public Safety," came a surly voice from the hallway.

Pushing himself out of bed and looking for a pair of trousers, Rod shouted, "Just a minute!" He then located the clammy trousers with muddy cuffs that were still on his body. He had passed out fully clothed.

At the door, he greeted a rotund, nearly hairless baybeetle stuffed into a pair of standard denim overalls and a white tee shirt. The embroidered patch in the center of his bib read "Bottom Junction Electric" in small black letters. Below that, written in red cursive script, was the name "Duke".

"May I help you?" asked Rod.

"I'm here to help *you*," said Duke.

Rod's eyelids sank to a half-closed posture, partly under the weight of cat saliva and partly in skepticism, knowing that there wasn't a baybeetle on Nord that could help him right now.

Duke the electrician's recessed features, hardened from decades of impossibly tangled wires, were compounded at the moment by hours of overtime. Duke had no eyebrows and wiry gray hairs sprouting off the tops of his ears. "Boys!"

Duke's boys appeared in the doorway lugging a spherical contraption of brushed steel set with a number of circular mirrored windows. It was the size of a beach ball and stood like a bowling trophy atop a substantial rectangular platform.

"What's that?"

"You kiddin', Mister...Bankman is it?" laughed Duke, scanning his clipboard. "It's a 'lectric eye 'cuz of the bombin' yesterday in Bullneck. We all get 'em. Make sure there's no funny stuff goin' on ya see. Muzorans an' all." Duke's helpers had ushered themselves into Rod's apartment, shifted the coffee table to the side of the room, and begun bolting down the beeping contraption. Duke rummaged in the kitchen for a clean coffee cup and a bite to eat.

Obviously frustrated with Rod's lack of fresh coffee, Duke herded his team out of Rod's place as quickly as possible without bothering to reduce the carpet of wood chips and iron filings the installation had left in its wake. Rod changed his trousers, stubbed the same toe twice on the beeping contraption, and shakily grabbed his phone. He dialed Magic Wands.

"Thank you for calling Magic Wands Incorporated. All departments are now closed, but if you know your party's extension and would like to risk leaving a message and hope that it's found, please enter—"

Rod hung up the phone.

It was Sunday. Sunday, Sunday, Sunday. A Sunday for taking stock. A Sunday for vacuuming bits of old food out from beneath the driver's seat. "Okay then," exhaled Rod.

Rod located a pair of tweezers, a damp rag, and one rubber bootie as he prepared to give Babe the treatment. His second rubber bootie was as elusive as ever, and while turning the place upside-down shadowed by his watchful electric eye, a mustard plume of acrid smoke issued from a tiny protruding orifice in Rod's ceiling— an air quality alert. The less agreeable the plume, the less agreeable the air quality of the day, and this was a bad one.

Rod arrived gagging at the respirator rack and spied the black and white photograph of his grandfather tacked to the plaid wallpaper. It always cracked him up to see the cumbersome old respirators the ancestors wore, the type that obscured his grandfather's face in the photo. "I guess that's what progress is all about though, eh Slim?" Slim had fallen unconscious from the mustard warning blast. "I love Sundays," sniggered Rod, pulling on his trim smog mask and his second bootie.

Outside, the neighbor kids in their cartoon character respirators were setting fire to Humbug Creek with magic wands. Humbug Creek would occasionally ignite under the distress of its own chemistry, but this was ridiculous. Golden sparks and rings of smoke were flying every which way. "Hey you kids! Those aren't toys!" scolded Rod, shaking his tweezers at them.

As their scolding arrived muffled by Rod's mask, all the kids heard was, "May roo tids! Nose barn doys!" The kids looked at each other, shrugged their shoulders, and threw a couple more wands on the fire.

The midday sun filtered down onto Rod through swirling clouds of filth and creek smoke. He had turned his back on the troublemakers and was now standing in his booties, staring limply at an empty parking spot on Roadview Drive. It was the spot that Babe called home. Recalling last night's catastrophe, a wave of grief crashed over Rod.

His eyes lost focus and the world around him faded into a silver, dizzying blur. He teetered in place. Before Rod fell completely over, an explosion issued from Humbug Creek and snapped everything back into focus. "Oh, Babe," pined Rod, and Rod's eyes lost focus again, this time through pools of tears.

Come Monday morning, a subdued dawn filled Rod's apartment. Slim lay sleeping atop a baybeetle carcass next to the electric eye. With the eruption of the alarm clock in the other room, Slim stood and stretched, yawning and arching his back while digging his claws into the carcass. Only with this did the carcass wearing rubber booties come to life and raise its disheveled head. Rod and Slim paused eye to eye.

Rod pried Slim off and wallowed while reflecting on the Sunday that had passed so quickly. First the tacky electric eye. Then the nuisance of children with wands. Then the friendly but hyper Muzoran cab driver and the sight of Babe all alone, helpless on the side of the road with a stiff parking ticket crammed under her windshield wiper. Then, after watching Babe get dragged through town like a piece of meat, Rod abandoned her at the mechanics where complete strangers would have their hands all over her.

This was all too much for Rod and upon reentering his apartment with an armful of cat food Sunday afternoon, he finally fainted. Hitting the living room floor, Rod imploded into a dreamless slumber. Slim ate the spilled cat food and climbed on top of Rod for a warm nap.

# CENTRAL NUT

Neighbor after neighbor ogled through Rod's still wide-open front door on their way to their Monday work demons. This was done primarily in silence, as it was assumed that the new electric eyes were also electric ears. Not until Lou rambled by, offering Rod an overly cheery "Good morning, buddy!" did Rod realize that he had fainted, slept, and wallowed in full-view of the public. Lou was Rod's best friend in the building and a senior nut polisher at Central Nut.

"Yeah, uh, mornin' Lou," and before Rod had a chance to explain away his booties, Lou was down the hall and on his way to the nut line.

In a cab on the way to work, Rod was finally able to settle down and absorb the new Gibbous Bizonia. This is what the newscasters were calling the country—the "new" Gibbous Bizonia or the "post-Bullneck" Bizonia—in the aftermath of the bombing. Rod didn't quite get it. The cloud cover looked the same as did the highways and legions of billboards promoting beauty creams and oral medications. Gibbous Bizonian flags were still at half-mast from the last tragedy.

Rod emptied out his wallet for the drunken cabby and sloshed up the puddled staircase of MWI. Before the front doors had fully squeezed shut behind him, Rod felt the familiar suck on the top of his head from the fluorescent lights smothering the lobby rotunda. "Paper bag, please," requested security guard Carl.

"Sure, Carl. Good morning."

"Mornin', Mister Bankman."

Carl plied his way through Rod's bag, pulling out a catnip mouse and then a small rubber ball. Shoving the light blue ball into his shirt pocket, Carl handed the bag back to Rod. "New security measures, Mister Bankman," and before Rod had a chance to ask for his ball back, Carl had scanned both eyeballs and moved on to the next MWI employee in the unusually long line.

Rod made it to his desk and spilled a sheet of hot coffee over his paperwork and himself when someone wished him a good morning. Screeching, Rod shot out of his chair as quills and wands scattered. Hot Dorothy Tarnuckle had never spoken to him before.

"G'mornin', Duh-uh-Dorothy," stammered Rod.

"What IS this slopwork, Bankman?" shouted Flounders through a megaphone from atop his lifeguard tower in the center of the room. In the absence of threatening follow-up memos, Rod began to wonder about the air of kindness in the office. Everyday baybeetle problems had faded into the shadow of the Bullneck City disaster. Now the only issue that carried any weight in the office was revenge.

All of the radios on cubicle row were tuned into Air Gino's news broadcasts pumping the most recent developments. Did Muzora now possess advanced technologies? How soon should Gibbous Bizonia invade? Despite the general camaraderie, conversation in the office fell silent whenever Pepe the Muzoran caterer wheeled through, offering apples and wraps. Rod worried for his mother and her seat on the neighborhood board.

The quirky workday twitched to a close and Rod emerged from the front doors of MWI into a cold, blowing rain. Only five of his pieces for the Buckingham Project had been rubberstamped "TRIPE" by Flounders. A reunion with Babe was imminent and Dorothy Tarnuckle had acknowledged his existence.

"Taxi!" yelped Rod.

An empty cab pulled over to the flooded MWI curb, dowsing Rod from the neck down as it passed. Thirty feet away, Dorothy Tarnuckle eased into the warm, dry cab.

"Taxi!"

The next cab slowed down for Rod, took one look at his soaked clothes, and sped off. Rod hurled the uneaten half of his sandwich at the cab and watched as it grazed off the rear fender.

"TAXI!"

This time Rod held his bag, minus half a sandwich, in front of his chest to hide his unsightliness. "Where to?" asked the cabby as Rod waded in.

"Gino's Tugliner," said Rod.

"North or South?"

"South."

Thirty-seven dollars and forty cents was all that was left of Rod's Solovanana vacation fund after paying Gino's for Babe's repairs. The exhilaration of the day, including the satisfaction of being back behind the wheel, more than compensated for Rod's dismal finances.

When he reached into his pocket for his key ring, Rod felt a folded up piece of paper. It was Jake's List. Amid the hysteria of post-Bullneck Bizonia, he had forgotten to give it to Jake at dinner as planned. Rod was willing to forego yet another evening of bird watching in order to swing by Jake's. After all, Rod was feeling good.

The front door at Jake's house was wide open. "Knock knock!" shouted Rod, poking his head in. Wiping his shoes on a tattered doormat with a peace sign on it, Rod stepped in and took a look about. He was hit with the aroma of incense and spicy potatoes.

Hearing Rod's call, Jake ran upstairs from the basement hauling a flaccid knapsack in one arm and a sleeping bag rolled taut in the other. Jake tossed his load aside when he saw his brother. "Hey, dude! What's up?" Jake asked with his usual enthusiasm.

"Good afternoon, Jake," Rod said stiffly. "I have something for you."

Before Rod had a chance to hand over the list, a hairy young hebeetle in threadbare clothes arrived without knocking. He raced up to Jake and embraced him in a bear hug. "I'm so excited for you, dude!"

"Yeah. I can't believe it," said Jake, hunched over, arms low, ready for the chase.

"Dude, I've gotta grab some stuff and get out of here, but I'll be back later. We can hang out and I'll help you pack or whatever," said the hairy hebeetle.

"Sounds good. Hey Garth, this is my brother Rod. Rod, this is Garth." Rod jerked back after shaking hands, unable to relate to Garth's unkempt sensibilities.

As soon as Garth disappeared into the house, Rod asked, cleaning his fingernails, "So, you going to get out of town this weekend?" Rod was more interested in the fact that he had never met Garth. The constant flow of roommates through his little brother's life was a fascination.

"Well, sort of."

"How's the dry cleaners?"

"I don't work there anymore."

"Oh really?" Rod's face brightened as he rubbed Jake's List. The hour was ripe for making changes.

"Rod, I don't work there anymore because I'm going to Vivachanga...with Abacus."

"Vivachanga?" mused Rod. Everyone on Nord had heard the name, but it was used exclusively in a humorous or symbolic sense, such as one on Earth might use the term "La La Land". It was a mythical realm often juxtaposed with the "Age of Nature", an age on Nord when there were still ancient forests, running rivers, wild animals, and healthy tribes of nomadic baybeetles. In Bizonian tall tales, what remained of Vivachanga was said to be tucked away on the far shores of the world, beyond even Muzora.

As Jake was a known eccentric, his fantasy had little impact on Rod. "That's nice, Jake. And who's this character with the funny name?"

"You mean Abacus? You've seen him. He's that dark-skinned guy with the beard and the cats that we almost hit with the car the other night. He was wondering if you might not want to come along."

Jake watched as Rod wallowed on the hardwood floor just inside the front door. Rod was delirious and complaining repeatedly about Jake's personality misalignment. Less than twelve hours had passed since Rod was wallowing just inside his own front door. Jake struggled to keep a warm washcloth perched on Rod's forehead.

"Jake... Jake..." Rod croaked.

"Yes, Rod."

"Jake...Jake..."

"Take it easy there."

"Jake...I can see the light...Viva...Vivachanga...no...no...the light..."

"Easy now, Rod."

"It's so close...my...my...the Buckingham Project...the...the light...your misalignment Jake. Jake! What...why...you're not...I can't! Please tell me I'm dreaming. No! Not dreaming! Tell me I'm hallucinating, Jake."

"Breathe deep, brother."

"You're serious, aren't you. Aren't you, Jake. Do you even believe in Vivachanga? This is an ancient myth, Jake. It's all the REZ now. Remote Extraction Zone. Gino's Remote Extraction Zone."

"I do believe in Vivachanga," replied Jake, "and even if Vivachanga doesn't exist, I believe in Abacus and I believe that he needs our help."

"Jake, lots of baybeetles need our help. Who would know that better than me? I work at Magic Wands Incorporated for God's sake. And who on God's Nord is this Albatross character?"

"It's Abacus, and he says that he's a nomad and that his home lies in Vivachanga."

"*Lies* is right, Jake. This guy is all poppycock. Poppycock, poppycock, poppy—"

"This journey with Abacus may be very very important, Rod. Abacus believes that Bullneck City is just the beginning. Not only is war coming to Gibbous Bizonia, but life as we know it on planet Nord hangs in the balance."

"Oh, Jake, Gibbous Bizonia is much too powerful for that. I cannot let you loose on a hair-brained journey with this liar."

"But Rod, look." Jake reached behind the coat rack and pulled out a perfectly formed capital letter Q. The Q was a foot high, meaty, and woven from a pair of dirty shoelaces.

"And?" Rod asked, examining the perfectly tapered ends of the Q's cross member.

"Abacus made it."

"Yes, well, so what?"

# CENTRAL NUT

"He made it in about ten seconds."

"Jake, this doesn't prove that he is who he says he is. I worry about you." The Q was an obvious attempt to play on the legendary prowess of the legendary Vivachangan nomads as master weavers.

"Alright then, how about this?" From behind the same coat rack, Jake brought out a small but highly complex apparatus woven entirely from dried grass. He set it on the worn hardwood and pinched together two loose flaps dangling off one side of the silent device.

Without breaking the silence, the unusual apparatus began to move of its own accord. One of the flaps reached into the air, and soon the apparatus was folding over upon itself in all manner of contortions. Rod scrambled to his feet, the wet rag on his forehead plopping down next to the apparatus. Edging backwards, Rod felt with his hands for a potential barrier between himself and the silent, oscillating maelstrom.

With Jake still in the open, the outrageous contraption rocked up onto two legs, paused, then lifted clean off the floor. It began circling about the entryway just over the top of Jake's upturned face. Jake had let loose a smile and even Rod, peeking over the back of a davenport, could not contain his delight.

The next morning under unusually clear skies, Rod awoke to his clock's usual honking. He buffaloed his way into the shower with his socks on, got dressed, and scared up some sardines, toast, and coffee. In an old family chair, Rod sat holding his loaded paper bag, staring numbly out the window at the blooms awakening on the bingalee tree. The gloom that had settled in Rod's apartment overnight found morning lost to all hope and to all hope of hope. Belinda was stomping with her heels, yelling through Rod's ceiling, calling him a feeble shithead.

Was there really going to be war in Bizonia? Was his little brother really leaving his job at the dry cleaners at such a time in search of the fabled Vivachanga? With a complete stranger? A stranger who was a bad, albeit skilled, imposter? Would he really have to tell this to his coworkers at MWI?

What if something were to happen to Jake? There was no way at this stage in the game that Rod was going to abandon the Buckingham Project and travel to facilitate Jake's unproductive fantasies. Not with the light being so very near.

Seconds ticked away on the cuckoo. The spring-loaded warbler inside burst through the cuckoo's double doors to sing the quarter hour. Tears welled behind Rod's spectacles.

Why me?

Why this?

Why now?

His heart dropping to unexplored lows, Rod's stare fixed on the daydream magenta bingalee blossoms. Just as the last of his happiness was draining from his life forever, there appeared directly in Rod's tear-smeared line of sight a petite hummingbird. It hovered with its head turned sideways, looking directly at Rod through one wild eye. Rod tucked the end of his sleeve under his glasses and mopped his eyes of tears.

"Huh?"

In the empty room, Rod's eyes went wide. Both hands flew to his face, expecting to find his virtual reality goggles clamped to his nose. It wasn't just a hummingbird, it was a hoverbean. And it wasn't just a hoverbean—the diminutive stature, the deep pink glinting off the head and breast, the snowy dorsal with two thin black stripes running the length of its flanks—it was a Foiled Hoverbean.

# CENTRAL NUT

A live one.

As Rod and the hoverbean stared at each other, the tiny bird in a blur of wings flitted to a blossom, probing for nectar with its long beak and even longer tongue. The sunlit blossom played back and forth with the breeze and the hoverbean flew back and forth with it precisely, continuing to suckle as if it were simply the flower's flower.

# CHAPTER FIVE

# Assistant to Abacus

Just as the Foiled Hoverbean disappeared into a hairline streak against the blue sky, Babe and Rod beelined to MWI, narrowly escaping a series of fender-benders along the way. In the aftermath of the hoverbean, Rod was running late and clamored into the office with half of his shirt untucked. At the appearance of Rod, the hive of prattling keyboards hushed to an eerie, electronic buzz.

He was only three minutes early.

Curious noses reared their heads from behind low, padded walls. Cubemates hungry for action darted shameless, reptilian glances from side to side. Rounding into his cell, Rod stumbled at the sight of Archibald Flounders.

Flounders was reclining in Rod's desk chair, waiting in a cloud of smoke with a lit cigar clenched between his remaining teeth. His hands were folded behind his head, lifting his mail-order toupee visibly off the top of his reflective scalp. "Two minutes early, eh?" he said to Rod.

Rod felt the warmth of his body drain through his feet into the pale green linoleum. Giggles in support of Flounders quivered ankle high throughout the department. "If it's not one thing with you it's another, ISN'T it, Bankman."

The brilliant image of the Foiled Hoverbean fortified Rod as he and Flounders engaged in an extended, shuddering glare. Then for the first time in his life, Rod refused to cower to his superior. "And a very good morning to you," he said to Flounders, "Now, would you mind letting me sit down so I can get to work…Archie?"

The department-wide gasp pulled at the tissue of Flounder's eardrums. Workmates sank lower behind their walls, expecting nothing less than shards of glass, plastic, and steel humming through the air from Flounders' immanent tirade. Perhaps, they thought, Rod himself would be seen sailing through the air, bouncing from corkboard to corkboard.

Flounders, however, was dumbfounded.

Rod's chair was heard to creak.

Flounders emerged from his cloud of smoke with head and neck both searing red, his pursed lips strangling the expensive Muzoran cigar. He caught sight of a grunt eyeballing the situation from across the room. Realizing its own peril, the office herd thundered into routine as Flounders steamrolled past Rod and disappeared behind slamming mahogany doors, into his private study.

Spooks from the Spirit Department could be seen circling Bankman's cubicle throughout the morning. A steady stream of memos poured into Rod's computer, each written in priority scarlet. Each was deleted, unread. Hunched over his keyboard, Rod bathed himself in the joy of the day as strange words flowed from his fingertips into the Buckingham Project's myriad components. The end was drawing near. The light.

"Excuse me."

The voice behind Rod was sweet, thusly confounding. His spellbound typing continued.

"Excuse me…Rod?"

"Yes. What."

"Would you like to join me for lunch?"

Rod's active bile rose to his throat. He registered the time in the corner of his monitor. "Thanks, but I've got a ton of work to finish."

# ASSISTANT TO ABACUS

He swiveled to face none other than gorgeous Dorothy Tarnuckle, the most streamlined shebeetle on the seventh floor. "*And…*I'm starving. So let's eat!"

They shared a pastrami with pickles. A dessert of large curd cottage cheese left the yapping couple content and a little drowsy as they waltzed out of Gino's Soup Kitchen. A Dirty Starling was heard to sing above the city ruckus as they happened across Rod's rival, virtual birder Gary.

Gary flourished as he parted his insulting lips. "Jolly afternoon, Gary," said Rod, foiling his coworker's attack. A bit of gibberish slipped from the corner of Gary's mouth. The sight of Rod rubbing elbows with Dorothy Tarnuckle, each with an unopened baggie of Gino's Wafers in hand, confounded Gary's mind.

Despite heightened security, a beam of sunlight found its way to Dorothy's cubicle. There, it illuminated Rod landing a peck on the back of Dorothy's hand. As he walked away, Rod wondered if his luck wasn't a direct result of his morning release of testosterone, the bout between he and Flounders. After clearing his monitor of hot memos, Rod entered into his syntax and his thoughts of Dorothy's saucy wafers. As if this wasn't enough to think about, tonight was Jake's bon voyage party and Abacus was to be in attendance.

Flounders was strangely absent at day's end. Rod gathered his things and was out the door with a shy smile from Dorothy only eleven minutes after quitting time. Two hours later, Rod arrived at Yolanda and Leonard's for Jake's bittersweet bash. Balancing a marshmallow salad on one hand, Rod took a deep breath and raised the tarnished brass knocker.

Thinking better of it, Rod released the knocker without a sound and coaxed the doorknob to unlatch just as quietly. Were Abacus to be taken down, the element of surprise would benefit. Through the crack in the door, he heard spirited laughter and a stranger's voice brainwashing his family. "And then this antelope says, 'These aren't my *horns*, they're—"

"Sorry Abacus. Come on in, Rod!" called Leonard, seeing Rod's fingers curling around the edge of the front door. Leonard, after cutting short Abacus' best antelope joke, rose to his feet along with Jake and Abacus.

"Hey, buddy!" said Leonard.

"What's up, brother!" said Jake.

"That thine beard well-nested be," said Abacus, bending at the waist with one hand held flat against his heart.

After introductions, Leonard raced off, curving around his home's new electric eye, into the kitchen to pour Rod a vodka soda. As Leonard wrestled with a tray of ice cubes, Yolanda butted open the front door cradling a disjointed bag of groceries.

"So nice to meet you, Meester Abacoos."

"Ah, Yolanda of Gibbous Bizonia. You do bear quite some breadth," replied Abacus, pawing Yolanda's outstretched hand. Just in time, Leonard returned with Rod's tumbler and a snifter of sherry for Yolanda. The sherry disappeared in an instant, sending Leonard off again to the liquor cabinet.

"Why thank you, Abacoos. Sorry I am so late," chirped Yolanda, giving Abacus the benefit of the doubt, "I had completely forgotten zee mushrooms and zee wheeping cream. Now you gentlemen relax while I am feenishing off one last thing or two in zee keetchen." Yolanda grabbed her next sherry in passing from Leonard and set herself to secret family recipes.

## ASSISTANT TO ABACUS

Despite expectations, Rod found their new acquaintance, Abacus, intelligent and gentlemanly, even entertaining. Abacus' Bizonian dialect alone held one's interest—it reminded one of medieval Bizonian theater, works produced when Gibbous Bizonia was not Gibbous Bizonia at all, but what the textbooks refer to as Olde Byzontia.

Presently, Yolanda beckoned the boys to the table where platters of meats and vegetables waited under veils of steam. Yolanda blushed when Abacus pulled out her chair for her. Conversation inevitably turned to the subject of Jake and Abacus and their forthcoming journey. "So, Abacus, Jake tells me that you've got some pretty heavy news."

"No. Heavy it is not, Mister Leonard."

"You can call me Lenny."

"Very good then, Mister Lenny. No, the news is not at all heavy. Rather 'tis naught but the weight of the words upon my breath. Quite grave though it is. Tyrone, I do fear, grows in hunger by the moment."

"Tyrone?" questioned Rod, "Who is this Tyrone? Is he..." Rod wanted to ask if he was a terrorist but instead asked, "...clean?"

Abacus laughed and returned to his plate of food. Jake leered at Rod, but the room remained otherwise silent.

Jake had to ask politely, "Abacus, who is Tyrone?"

Abacus merely snorted and had another bite of mutton. Raising his eyes, he saw the puzzled faces of the Bankmans. "Surely 'tis jest?" The family's blank expressions persisted. "For the love of

Dijouti—Tyrone! Tyrone Preposterous! Tyrone Omniscient! Tyrone Outlandish! The Keeper! Tyrone! Do I dream, or is the divine creature unknown unto this household?"

"Do you mean Tyrone Lipscomb, the CEO of Central Nut?" asked Leonard.

"No, Lenny. Certainly he eez referrink to thees actor Tyrone Singlebody from 'Zee Onion Cleavers'. He eez sooo handsome," Yolanda swooned.

"No way, Ma," said Jake.

"Jake! Now don't you go geet freesky."

"Alas, I crave your pardon," conceded Abacus, opening his hands, "Certainly 'tis I with whom error lies, for in my long travels I have grown dull. In the lands from which I hale, due to his deeds and clarity of vision, Tyrone is the respected overseer. We look to Tyrone in times of need. Tyrone is not what one would call an actor nor a businessbeetle. In fact, Tyrone is not baybeetle at all, although he does keep himself extraordinarily clean. Tyrone is what one in Gibbous Bizonia would refer to as 'feline'."

"Feline?"

"A cat?"

"What!?"

Rod was the first to act, "Listen, Alabaster," he said bunching up his napkin and scooting away from the table, "I'm a busy guy, so if you'll excuse me, my pillowcases have been left *in* the dryer, *at* home, *un*folded."

"Rod, his name is Abacus," said Jake.

Before Rod had had a chance to exit, Abacus stopped him cold. "Ho! Rod of Bizonia, take not your leave from us! Tyrone has been placed 'neath a spell that now threatens his very life. The spell is certainly the same spell that provoked such horrendous destruction in Bullneck City."

"A spell?" asked Rod.

"Yes, good sir. A spell."

"Well why didn't you say so, pal? Now you're speakin' my language." Rod settled back into his chair and broke the surface of his marshmallow salad with a giant spoon. "Don't mind if I do. So, Mister Abooboo, let's get down to business, shall we?"

"Most certainly, Mister Rod, sir."

Rod, the family's self-appointed expert in the ways of magic, dumped the serving spoon, folded his fingers together, and asked of Abacus, "Who exactly, may I ask, cast this wicked spell, sir?"

"The precise answer to that question, dear friends, is the sole providence of Tyrone. I am aware only of the urgency of the matter as conveyed to me by my assistant, Anisha of Tulika. Anisha has been in direct correspondence with Tyrone himself.

"Upon my life, Tyrone believes this a spell bent on consuming not only his mortal existence, but our miniscule planet Nord in its entirety. Please now, let us dine and not fret. Good news finds us in that I've full confidence in the success of our forthcoming endeavour. All is well."

Rod was content to let the subject drop and return his thoughts to the morning's hoverbean. For the remainder of the meal, Rod suffered the rudimentary chitchat going on around him while his sighting of the rare Foiled Hoverbean grew in importance moment by moment.

Yolanda invited the table to retire to the parlor for coffee and sweets where conversation eventually spiraled back onto present travails. "Meester Abacoos," Yolanda beseeched, "why eez it that you so much need a Bizonian in zees matter?"

"I am myself uncertain, sweet mistress," Abacus replied. "That of which I am most certain, however, is the integrity of Tyrone. Tyrone hath decreed it necessary the presence in my homeland of a sprite from Gibbous Bizonia. I am therefore myself convinced."

Hanging low over Smartchin Ridge, the immense sun cast laced curtain patterns across the coffee table. Next to Jake, Rod's leg pumped up and down, causing cups and saucers to tremble. The look in Rod's eyes was distant, oblivious to the racket. Was this the perfect moment to share his birding discovery? What if they did not believe, and what if Gary at work were to catch wind?

When coffee began to spill, Yolanda cleared her throat, "Ahem."

"Ahem!" echoed Lenny.

Not until Jake gave Rod an elbow did Rod return to Nord and stop pumping his leg.

Abacus laughed, continuing, "Yes, Tyrone requested a Bizonian, and in your second-born son we found the perfect candidate."

"But why my leetle Jake?" asked Yolanda.

"Ah, Yolanda of Bizonia, I will describe to you the moment...I was devilishly concerned, huddled in a pocket of Loophole Valley, calling desperately for my assistant, Anisha. The hour of our rendezvous had well passed and I feared that not only had I failed Tyrone, but that I had lost my friend and assistant.

"It was then that Anisha appeared not an arm's length away, and she sang to me of a lad with a pennywhistle not far afield. This was Jake. Anisha found Jake hunched over a clump of butter posies, charming the posies with a melody from his pennywhistle. We had found no other Bizonian with such round appreciation for such little things."

As more coffee was slugged down and as more details of the story were unraveled, Rod's irritability spiked. "Listen, guys. This is all very woo-woo and everything," interrupted Rod, overrun with caffeine, "but I've got something *significant* to add to the conversation. This morning in the bingalee I saw...I saw a..." the room was closing in around Rod, filled with a thousand eyes, "I saw...a Foiled Hoverbean."

"Oh, Rod. Not again," said Jake.

"Jesus Beetle, Mary, and Joseph," said Lenny.

"So, anyway, what were you sayink, Abacoos?" asked Yolanda.

"No, really!" Rod screeched.

"Please, Rod, we have company," said Lenny.

The moment that was broken was put back together by Abacus, "What a lovely evening it is. As it is so lovely, I can imagine no better time than the present to introduce to you my lovely assistant." Abacus then proposed some fresh air and a view of the sunset.

Before a sky draped in the salmon gold of dusk, Abacus and the Bankman family clustered around the meandering flagstones of the front lawn. The Bankmans were waiting for Abacus to produce a crude cellular phone woven from a length of fishing line in order to summon his leggy assistant Anisha from around the bend.

Instead, their diminutive houseguest cupped his hands to his muzzle, tilted his beard back, and produced a series of high-pitched clicks and whistles, issuing primarily through his nose. The veins in his neck swelled with the effort. A pause afterward brought nothing but a continued grin from Abacus.

The wait was too long. "I thought you guys loved me!" cried Rod, now in shambles, "My time would obviously be better spent at home, with Slim—who *does* love me—recording my discovery of this once-in-a-lifetime hoverbean. And for *your* information, *this* journal entry will be double-starred *and* underlined," he demonstrated with his index finger, "And just in case you all are lucky enough to see what I've seen, this particular hoverbean is about yea big, has a white back, and two black pinstripes. Just like *this* one," he said pointing to the hummingbird buzzing between he and Abacus. The wind from its beating wings cooled the tip of Rod's finger.

The Foiled Hoverbean zipped to Abacus' shoulder and then down to his nasturtium boutonniere for a sip of spicy nectar. Abacus cleared his throat. "I would now like for you all to meet my assistant, Anisha."

*Napping again on the honey hunt, Abacus lifted his head. A distant shimmer caught his eye through the heavy foliage. Believing it an elephant ear or wing of giant fowl, Abacus scampered barefoot up the nearest tree to get abreast of the situation.*

*The shimmer was neither elephant nor fowl, but a reflection off of stone just beyond the forest. It was never there before. After hiking for three notches of the sundial, Abacus found himself staring up at a baybeetle-built stone edifice. The structure emitted crunching sounds, smoke, and beams of heated light. A rectangular opening was dark and less than inviting, but Abacus braved entry. The interior was hot and sticky. Shapes of other baybeetles, moving in rigid patterns, came into focus through the darkness.*

*Wide belts moved shiny metal nuggets—wing nuts, square nuts, hex nuts—past the diligent workers into brown boxes stamped*

# ASSISTANT TO ABACUS

*"Central Nut". The boxes were wrapped tight with plastic and then thrown into the hold of a cargo truck, also stamped "Central Nut". Abacus hurdled the hatch of the truck to stay with the nuts as the truck wandered away from the nut factory. Abacus and the box were unloaded onto a conveyor belt at another building across town where loads of other boxes from various other factories were converging from all directions.*

*Before being swallowed by the factory, Abacus tumbled away and crouched behind a rusty oil drum. From there he saw the end product of this factory slide down a chute into a clandestine alleyway. The end product was a hideous, two-headed monster, held together by Central Nut and its innocent employees working the line.*

*Abacus could hardly keep up with the fur-covered, mechanical beast as it stepped on anything and everything in its path—garbage cans, hot dog stands, baybeetles. Nothing was safe. The beast, built little by little by the good baybeetles of the city, led Abacus back out of town...directly to his napping grounds.*

*Helpless against the might of the beast, Abacus watched as it uprooted his shade tree, honey-laden beehives and all. The many powerful arms of the beast scooped treacherous craters in the ground, showing no remorse.*

*The beast scraped the carnage of Abacus' loving forest into a thoughtless pile, and with a puff of smoke, it hoisted its booty and lumbered back into town. The beast dumped its load of raw materials directly into the smelters at Central Nut and the process started all over again.*

Abacus awoke with a start from this beastly dream to find himself among unfamiliar furnishings, surrounded by unfamiliar scents. He searched the room for a beast, but remembered the welcoming faces that shared the same roof as he this night. Mumbling prayers to Dijouti, Abacus found his way eventually back to sleep in Leonard and Yolanda's guest room.

Come first light, Anisha jittered morning glories outside the dining room window as Gibbous Bizonia and the Bankman family arose from their slumber. The bon voyage party had carried on late into the evening with cognac, prompting everyone—Rod and Jake included—to sleep at the folks' house. Abacus had been awake for some time, apparently, as the dining room table was littered with miniature forest creatures, each woven from next to nothing. A fruit bat crafted from orange peels took Yolanda aback as she opened the staircase door. The fruit bat flew right over her shoulder and up the stairs towards the showering Leonard.

"Good mornink, Abacoos," sang Yolanda to her houseguest.

"Good day, sweet Yolanda. And how may I be of service?" Despite his courtly demeanor, Abacus appeared distressed.

"You just seet and I am cooking you some coffee, my freend."

"You are most kind, good lady."

Riding drafts of fresh brewed coffee and warm maple syrup, the entire family was soon shuffling about the kitchen. Slim was the last to show, requiring no small amount of beauty sleep. The family shared a bacon-heavy breakfast before Rod bid his final farewell to Jake and left for work.

*Hand in hand with Dorothy Tarnuckle, Rod lay on his back in a field of butter posies. Dorothy and Rod's sights were splayed across the obsidian heavens, awaiting ephemeral streaks of light—a*

*summer storm of falling stars. Rod and Dorothy's hands clenched as the first streak was sighted, a pinstripe etched upon the sky. Each sighting elicited a giggle and a shivering cuddle. Some stars burned so brightly as to illuminate night into electric day. The air was warm and their spirits lifted higher yet with the appearance of two stars, falling through the atmosphere in parallel flight.*

*Drunk with the delicate sights and the barely audible sighs of the shower, Rod and Dorothy were shocked by the meteor that rose off the western skyline. It cried to silence the fiddling cicadas and roosting bullfrogs. Their hands went limp at the sight of the flaring orange body, a wonder of nature, still trolling above them. It became clearer and nearer and louder. This one was bound for Nord itself.*

*As the shrieking blaze completed its crossing of the sky, it tore the top off an ancient sequoia and exploded in a ruby shaft of smoke and debris. The landing was close enough that Rod and Dorothy sprang up to chase it down and examine the crater.*

*At the forest's edge, a pungent fog drifted out to greet them along with a savage cry of pain. First stunned at the improbable disaster, then rushing half-blind through slicing tree branches, Rod and Dorothy sought the unfortunate critter.*

*With the smoking crater in sight, a soldier shackled in battle fatigues and bullet bandoliers erupted from a thicket and pummeled the couple to the ground. Over the machinegun fire he ordered, "Stay down!" as he bled from beneath his helmet.*

*Another orange streak crossed the sky and exploded at the base of another giant tree. The blast shredded its roots and the tree thundered to the ground.*

*"Rod," a horrified, familiar voice whimpered from beyond a barricade of rancid smoke, "Help me."*

*Rod bellowed towards the voice, but his words were drowned out by gunfire and the rumbling of soil underfoot. Pulled away from Dorothy's terrorized eyes, Rod left her in the grips of the unknown soldier. In his panicked search, Rod stumbled over a motionless baybeetle lying face down in a pool of oil. Scrambling back to his feet, Rod heard another cry for help in the familiar voice.*

*"Rod!"*

*Then Rod found him.*

*He wasn't moving.*

*He looked up at Rod, pale and wet, "Rod. Rod. I...I can't move my legs."*

"Jake!"

Hammered out of his dream, Rod lay in the dark of his bed and wept into his ears over the sight of his little brother's body dismembered. The workday had been little better. Slim did what he could to be of comfort. Drained of tears and hopes of sleep, an unsettled Rod placed a gracious hand on Slim's stomach and peeled himself from his bed. Jake was heading straight into a war zone.

By the glow of a leaf-shaped night-light, Slim watched Rod force the cracked leather straps of his chest of heirlooms out of their rusty buckles. A sharp pop of hinges was followed by rippled creaking until the heavy lid of the chest rested against Rod's bedroom wall. The contents of the chest hadn't been disturbed for years.

Beneath musty hand puppets, the neatly folded flag from his great-grandfather's funeral, and an always sticky Mason jar filled with the sands of Isle Solovanana, Rod spotted his grandfather's binoculars. Their rounded case was brittle and chafing. He had always known that his grandfather, another full blood Muzoran, was an avid birder in his day. There weren't any wild birds of note this side of the Rutmus Strait anymore—save for one vagrant Foiled Hoverbean—so Rod had never bothered to breach the binocular case.

Until now.

He folded back the top and tipped the case, allowing the alien contraption within to fall into his left hand. Its weight caught him off guard and there was significant bobbling, a near drop. "Quite odd and cumbersome relative to the virtual reality goggles of the new millennium," whispered Rod, unsure whether he was quoting a Gino's promotion or not. He closed the lid of the trunk, its dust curling into the air, and laid the binoculars on top. Seated on his knees with his hands on his thighs, Rod stared at the binoculars until after daybreak. Only then did he finally, reluctantly roll up into a ball on the floor and catch a couple hours of rest before heading off to face MWI and another day with Jake on the road.

# PART II

# Loose Pawns

# CHAPTER SIX

# Bankman's Day Off

Midafternoon sunrays eased onto Rod, who had passed out from the rocking of the speeding bus.

The bus passed through some long shadows and the strobing of the sun between shadows woke Rod up. Raising his head, he noticed that they had passed under several arcing pipelines. In awe of their girth, Rod followed the pipelines' course as they snaked away from the highway, terminating in the distance at a cluster of perfectly geometric structures. Through a clinging cloud of red smog, Rod saw the spider legs of a network of pipelines converging around the geometric cluster. Rod hadn't realized that he would be passing this close to Bullneck City, the nation's capital, on his way to Isle Solovanana. Rod traced the fabled outline of Bullneck City's skyscrapers—War Monument Two, Gino's Power, the Trust Tower. With a little imagination he could see pigeons circling through the gap where Monument One had once stood.

Shoehorned between a nest of cigarette butts on his armrest and a large, snoring shebeetle's thigh, Rod glanced across the aisle at Abacus, Jake, and Slim. They were all snoring as well. You see, the previous evening as Rod pined over his grandfather's binoculars, a dump truck of uranium bound for MWI hit a pool of slop and overturned, spilling its load across five lanes of traffic. This accident triggered the following chain of events.

The morning after the uranium spill, Rod was pretending interest in his computer, fidgeting with an old octagon-cut wand. He tapped away at the brim of his coffee cup, agitating the coffee's surface but producing no otherwise extraordinary results. He waved the wand across his desk and sent a paper clip tumbling through the air. The paper clip hit the floor with a metallic jingle—Rod wondered what one of the new Buckinghams would have done.

When the office caught wind of the uranium spill, everyone's movements became nervous and jerky. Production would be pushed back for days, if not weeks. Rod's thoughts turned to Jake.

Where was Jake now? Stroking the silken neck of a fine steed as Abacus called for full gallop, the two racing through barren Muzoran canyon lands on horseback? Still breaking waves aboard their clipper ship, plying the Rutmus Strait? Windblown and taking stock of the Bizonian coastline one last time as they ploughed into the unknown?

The spill could theoretically halt the bus lines, throwing Jake and Abacus completely off their itinerary. Rod chanced a call to Yolanda.

Mom informed Rod that the spill had indeed caused a delay and that Jake was currently loitering in the Bottom Junction bus depot. Try as he may to get back to not working, Rod could not get his mind off of Jake. That Jake, always pesky.

Rod remembered Jake as a little baby, swinging around a fat plastic wand, turning everything in the room upside-down. He remembered Jake getting tickled on a big oval rug by their birder grandpa on one of his visits from Muzora. The birds his grampy must have seen! Flamingos, Catchingos, Bobolanas, Roy's Manzanas. How many Foiled Hoverbeans? Any Little Bustards? Honey Buzzards? Rod remembered the bon voyage party. It was nice that the weather and the marshmallow salad had both turned out so sweet. This Abacus character didn't seem like such a bad lout after all.

Rod remembered the time he first saw Abacus there on the sidewalk—well, not exactly *on* it—and shortly thereafter that damn Bullneck thing and more war with Muzora. Though he felt wrong about it, Rod didn't even really *like* war. War with Flounders. War with Gary. War in Muzora. That damn dream last night with soldiers and rockets in the forest. All these *dreams* lately. Where were they coming from? A bursting yolk sack, billions of butterflies, Jake's legs. Jake's shattered legs. Jake. All alone on this small, brutal planet.

It dawned on Rod that he may never see Jake again.

Rod wrangled his sack and without stopping to think, he bolted out of his cubicle directly towards Flounder's study.

Nobody ever did that.

Nobody ever did that, let alone shove open the study's heavy doors and tempt fate. Yet there he was, Rod Bankman, standing in Flounders' open doorway.

In a recess of the darkened room, Rod located the lump that was Flounders. Flounders was squatting, hunched over in a black velvet cape with his back to the door. Yammering insidious nonsense, Flounders moved his hands over a crystal ball filled with dozens of hairy spiders. A red glow from the ball crept up the slate walls and disappeared. The room was otherwise empty, an outhouse cigar smoke haze notwithstanding.

"I realize it's a Wednesday, sir," shouted Rod, "but I don't feel well and need to take an emergency maternity leave, sir. I have a sick family."

"*GET OUT OF MY TREE FORT!*" roared Flounders, twisting his head over his shoulder. Flounders' cape wafted just enough for Rod to see that he wasn't wearing anything but the cape. None too soon, Rod was back in the fluorescent glare where he caught Dorothy waxing her shoes for lunch.

"Dorothy, this is for you," he said handing her a cardboard air freshener on a string. It was in the shape of a rose. Dorothy took Rod's hand in hers. "I'll be back," he told her, "I promise," and Rod kissed Dorothy then and there, slipping her a tin of Iron Sea sardines.

The stench of Babe's burning tires lingered in the lobby of MWI as Rod raced across town to Roadview Drive and the Grace Peck Apartments. Rod dusted under Babe's bumpers and tweezed out her glove box. It took several attempts to contact his friend and neighbor, Lou, who Rod knew to be hot on the afternoon nut line.

"Hello?"

"Lou. Rod."

"Hey, buddy. What's up?"

"Good Lord, Lou. I'm so glad I caught you. Listen. I need to ask you a favor."

"Shoot, buddy."

After jabbering his way around some unusual and mostly unmentionable family emergency, Rod asked Lou if he wouldn't mind watching his apartment for a day or two, if not for a couple of months. Lou said that of course he'd do it and he might even be able to save Rod a little cash by subletting the unit to his oldest nephew Chuck.

Rod tucked Slim under his arm, locked his door behind him, and slipped the house keys with some rent money through Lou's mail slot. Thinking himself mad, Rod entered the mail slot himself up to the wrist, trying desperately to take back his keys and his money, not to mention his life. He didn't see how he would be able to keep his job at MWI after this.

Slim squirmed. Rod's heart skipped a beat. He could always turn around and come back home, Jake struggling in tow if need be. But he had to go, he had to join Jake on his adventure, if for no other reason than to protect baby Jake.

Still crouched with his nose to Lou's slot, Rod reached into his pocket and popped a couple tranquilizers. "Let's do this, Slim," he said. Rod wasn't sure how they were going to pay for their adventure, but acting in concert with such authorities as Tyrone, Abacus surely traveled with a thick billfold.

Rod's taxi arrived at the bus depot in time to catch up with Jake and Abacus. Abacus and Slim had a strange back-and-forth growl-meow, after which Abacus promised Rod cocktails on Isle Solovanana. Now here they were. Bussing. Rod glanced back towards Bukllneck City and its ubiquitous pigeons. What rare species might he be bagging in Muzora in only a day or two? He thought of the array of spicy birds that he would be documenting for virtual birders back home, not the least of which was Anisha.

How long *had* Anisha, that flying shrew, been tracking he and Jake? Though the thought raised Rod's hackles, the dirty pleasure of being spied upon by a Foiled Hoverbean curled the corners of Rod's mouth into an easy smile.

From somewhere above or behind the bus, tiny Anisha zipped to where Rod could see her pumping her wings at blur speed outside his window. Rod tried and tried again to see the demon in Anisha, but, alas, he could not.

Or could he?

Anisha winked and was off to attend to Abacus' shadowy business.

"Three one-ways please," said Rod, Slim clinging to his chin at the ticket window of the Philistine Acres ferry terminal. With his fluffy beard and cat tail moustache, Rod was assumed to be a delegate from the same obscure wizardry association as Abacus.

"Any pets, potions, produce, livestock, sock monkeys, or other controlled substances?" asked the vendor.

Rod and Jake answered "yes" and "no" respectively and simultaneously. Jake kicked Rod's shin and Slim's claws tightened into Rod's face, eliciting a quick reversal. "I mean no. No livestock," said Rod, gritting his teeth. Spilling his peanut butter jar of change, Jake paid up and the four of them tromped off to kill some time across the street at a Gino's Coffee House.

Busting into the Gino's, Rod could taste his element. He was, after all, a coffee house heavyweight. Taking note of a tub of MWI wands on the condiment bar, Rod puffed up and looked from side to side without moving his head. Nowhere on Nord were wands more prevalent than in the cafés of Gibbous Bizonia. The greatest minds in Bizonia would convene in these cafés to sip and discuss the principle issues facing Nord and the nation.

Rod swaggered to the counter, leaned on one elbow, and ordered a three shot tumbleweed latte, adding a wink for the darling, oblivious barista. Jake and Abacus ordered small coffees "for here" and followed Rod's flashy latte to the condiment bar where Rod dusted the top of his beverage with dried panda milk.

"This is the MWI 'Tigerbomb' model," smiled Rod, pulling from the tub of wands a beautiful mahogany wand inlayed with tiger bone. Pulling up his sleeves, Rod circled the wand about his latte.

"Now watch this," he said. Rod waved the dripping wand three times over the bar and released it as if the wand were a winged insect held pinched by the legs.

The wand disappeared.

An army of gray-bearded wizards and keen-eyed witches filled the room. Some gesticulated hazardously with loaded wand hands. Some brooded as they plowed through the *Blanket* morning edition crossword puzzle. Most read quietly as they folded and unfolded *The Blanket: All the News that Matters to Gibbous Bizonia and the World.* The top headlines read "Clint Mosaby Released from Prison: Completes Hat Trick Versus Druids" and "Sally Brighton's Butt Goes Flat: What Really Happened". The front page was bordered on the left by the daily War Column, filled with colorful vignettes from yet another bloody Muzoran campaign.

"Young Jake," said Abacus, "I have witnessed in Gibbous Bizonia a queer phenomenon. Upon the morn' your citizens hide their faces behind large folds of parchment. Around us we see mounds of this parchment inscribed with all manner of evocative imagery. Can you to me describe what is afoot?"

"Those are newspapers," answered Jake, "They're what Bizonians read every day to get the news."

"The news? Are they then reading of new things, I pray?"

"You could say so," said Jake.

"Well then, what is it that is called 'new' today, boy? I am unable to decipher this Bizonian script."

"Let's see here," hummed Jake, "This is called the 'front page' and these are 'headlines', the big stories. This front page is talking about one of our sports idols..."

"Mmm, yes."

"...and the shape of a celebrity shebeetle's backside..."

"Yes *indeed*."

"On the left here," continued Jake, "is the War Column. It's always there and it's never good news."

"If it is always there, for what reason do you call it *new*?" asked Abacus.

"Well, I guess the details are new," said Jake.

"Very interesting, young Jake. New details regarding the new phenomenon we call war."

Rod looked confused.

"I do mean just that, Rod," said Abacus, "The universe is ancient. Nord is ancient. Baybeetle existence has been but a blink in the eye of Father Time. Our current habits of war, of using powerful magical apparatus to kill en masse and at a distance, is absolutely new. Such murderous potential has never been seen."

"What is your point, Abacus?" Rod asked.

"So perhaps it is I who delivers the *news* today," chuckled Abacus, "If what you say is true, these newspapers dwell upon the grisly details of continuous modern warfare—so many deaths here and so many deaths there in the name of this or that affiliation— without presenting the case of modern warfare as a whole. There is no acknowledgement of modern warfare as but a brief phase of baybeetle existence which, as I said, is but a blink in the eye of time. A great story lies in how the current ways of war relate to the beginning of war, its evolution, and the forthcoming end of war."

"The forthcoming end of war?" asked Jake, inspired.

"Indubitably," responded Abacus.

"Don't you know what that would mean for business, Abacus?" said Rod.

Abacus was cool. "Everything in our world changes, Mister Rod. Current business practices, like modern warfare, have a time of conception and a time of demise. A time of changing from one state to another. Do you believe that the forthcoming peace would prove worthy of a headline in the *Blanket?*" asked Abacus.

"You should know, Mister Abacus, that the Muzorans have begun dealing in a very dark magic. Despite our efforts to prevent magical leakage and to keep dark secrets in possession of the Bizonian Magic Circle, Muzora is harvesting tree frogs and puffer fish—dark ingredients for dark purposes. The end of war is nowhere in sight."

"I am well aware, Mister Rod," said Abacus, "of rumors regarding such matters. There is most certainly a chance that the Muzorans are acquiring great destructive force. And it is true that an unmitigated magical conflict between Muzora and Bizonia may put an end to all that we know of life on planet Nord. Indeed, 'tis towards this end of avoiding unnecessary destruction that I to you have come.

"'Tis my belief that this destruction we shall avoid and that Tyrone shall live to breathe again his freedom. We are faced, as a planet, with a choice between Renaissance and Armageddon. The hopelessness of those who push for an Armageddon shall be defeated."

Rod shifted beneath his latte, juggling scenarios as to why he and Jake were really being hauled into this misadventure. Rod still silently suspected Abacus to be softening up he and Jake with peaceful banter in order to mine them for information regarding the Buckingham Project.

Slim climbed back aboard Rod's face.

Rod trudged with his binoculars, Slim, and his two bloated suitcases, lagging behind Jake and Abacus as they entered the ferry terminal. Strange looks at security checkpoints were the worst of it and they all landed aboard the Shining Slipper heavy from their journey. Despite his mounting fatigue, Slim subjected a crowd of seagulls to the chase.

As afternoon leaned into dusk, the Shining Slipper's burly engines began to rumble underfoot. Abacus and company found their seats below deck and watched through salty windows the mooring lines untied. The Rutmus Strait surged into the widening gulf between Rod and his Bizonian homeland.

When water and sky turned the black of night, Abacus excused himself to the top deck of the ferry, inviting his companions to join in the fun. "Do bring a blanket," he advised. Entering the sea air, Abacus folded himself down onto the deck and motioned to chaise lounges for the Bizonians.

"I can't understand why we're up here, Jake," Rod grumbled, twisting in his blanket, wringing Slim between his thighs.

As Rod dialed the poop deck bartender, he noticed Slim staring up at something without preparing to attack. Rod tipped his head back, sneering while wondering what had captivated his little buddy's attention. Abacus and Jake stared along with Slim without a sound.

"What are you guys looking at?" asked Rod, annoyed.

Jake was slow to respond, "What do you mean?" Inside of Jake's head, a question mark appeared. That question mark was his brother. Next to the question mark there appeared a memory.

When Jake was just five years old, Leonard had packed a couple of bags, made a couple of sandwiches, thrown it all into a bright and shiny Babe, and woken up the kids. "All aboard for Loophole Valley!" Leonard was yelling, "The adventure of a lifetime! Come one, come all! All aboard for Loophole Valley!"

Jake ripped on his shorts and grabbed a magnifying glass before sliding down the handrail for a bowl of cereal and a banana on the run. Yolanda failed to see the point in going out to Loophole Valley at all when they had worked so hard to have such a beautiful "leetle" home. Young Rod was still nowhere to be found as Jake crashed his empty bowl into the sink and threw himself into Babe's back seat, as was customary for the younger brother.

Leonard started the engine and ran back into the house to twist Rod's arm. "Looks like it's just you and me, kid," Leonard told Jake as Dad settled back in behind the wheel, "Your brother has some important alphabetizing on the docket."

Jake commandeered the front seat.

As Babe split narrower and narrower roads and the oldies station on her radio began to crackle and give way to pure static, a green splotch of Nord rose above the dashboard. Soon thereafter, Jake and Leonard were hoofing it through the patch of woods known as Loophole Valley—a stretch of land left to the hands of nature due to the sluggish approval of blueprints for a Gino's Magic Carpet factory. In time, Loophole Valley would be conquered, but for now it was a source of immeasurable delight for Jake and his father—birds, rushing water, perky flowers, scampering rodents. There was fresh air above and soft Nord below.

Camp was laid as night spread itself over the treetops. One by one, minute, brilliant lights emerged to glow against the deepening evening sky. "Dad? What are those deelybobbers floating in the sky?" asked young Jake.

Rod hadn't been there.

This journey with Abacus was the first time since infancy that Rod had been beyond the Bottom Junction city limits.

It all made perfect sense.

"Rod," Jake told his brother on the deck of the Shining Slipper bound for Muzora, "We're looking at the stars."

Rod didn't believe it. Stars were the invention of poems and dreams. He couldn't actually see any stars at first, as he had never looked for anything that was so small and so very far away. Once he found them, however, he was in the stars to stay.

CHAPTER SEVEN

# Making Time

*A heavy wooden door loomed, shut fast. Through the small gap beneath the door Slim could smell seven Doberman Pinschers. Brushing his tail against the door, the slippery crystal doorknob turned and the door opened. Slim slinked through halfway as the dogs awakened from their stupefied slumber and attacked as one.*

*With his tail drifting about his toes, Slim settled back onto his haunches and batted his eyelashes. All seven of the Doberman clowns rose off of the kitchen floor and began flailing their legs in mid-air. The dogs ascended and adhered to the ceiling, growling and barking madly. Rod was stuck up there with them, telling Slim that he was a very bad kitty.*

*Slim's path was now clear to the wet food. Tall cans of liver n' fish skin tumbled out of the cupboard on Slim's approach, pouring their contents onto the otherwise clean linoleum.*

*"Bad kitty! Bad, bad kitty!"*

*The cat food was unbelievably moist and reeked of old fat. Perfect. After grappling with his fourth can, Slim's thoughts and gut full of food turned to the outdoors and the ultimate freedom contained therein. This time, a sliding glass door framed in steel blocked his path.*

*Slim extended a singular index claw and ticked his reflection in the glass. The menacing door shattered into beach sand.*

*"Bad kitty! Bad, bad kitty!"*

*Crossing into the wide, wild world, Slim filled his lungs with fresh air. His next chore as dictator was to find a tree to shelter his afternoon nap.*

*Rounding the garden wall, Slim suspended his paw and beheld a new stump. Rubbish. Rubbish, rubbish, rubbish. These baybeetles were beginning to thin Slim's patience. They had now gone and cut down another premium shade tree. And for what?*

*Spears and battle axes straight and strong plus fuel for the smelter. Jolly. How many more baybeetles would be dead by the hands of their own brothers come gentle dawn? Where on Nord would Slim find his nap?*

Slim's dream turned nightmare faded away to the sound of Rod's aggressive snoring.

Abacus was already up and humming, triangulating shadows cast by a cubit-high navigational device. The device, pieced together with coat hangers and drinking straws, sat on a folding table in a patch of sunlight eking through the hotel room's musty window screen.

The Shining Slipper had docked in the Muzoran industrial port city of Hevzladon the previous evening well past midnight. Fires from crumbling smokestacks reflected off the black water of Stool Harbor and filled the air with dense clouds of unbreathable smoke. The stars had again retreated behind the city pollution.

Stepping off the Shining Slipper onto Muzoran soil, the stench of raw sewage and rotting fish crashed into Jake and Abacus like a rogue wave. "Don't worry, Rod. This is the worst of it," Jake said to Rod over his shoulder. "Rod?"

Jake and Abacus turned around to see that Rod was still on the boat, recessed into a corner behind the fire extinguisher. Harrowing

MAKING TIME

Slim was scrunched into his stomach. "Is this…war?" cowered Rod, bug-eyed.

Jake turned back to take another look at the cascades of trash falling from the Muzoran hillsides set to the tune of the grinding wheels of production. "Not exactly, Rod. They're just making everything that we use in Bizonia. But don't worry, my brother. This is the worst of it. Now come on out of there." Jake took one of Rod's hands from Slim. Abacus grabbed Rod's suitcases and the travelers kissed the ferry home good-bye, now foreigners one and all.

Using Jake's broken Muzoran, the Bizonians and the Vivachangan located this ramshackle hotel room with one thin mattress and no electrical outlets. It was now mid-morning and the warmth of the Muzoran mainland was already drying the brothers' soggy Bizonian bones.

After Jake and the hotel's overnight clerk had pieced it together, Jake turned to his companions and said, "It looks like we owe three-hundred-and-seventy mizla, which comes out to about seven dollars and fifty cents. He does accept Bizonian currency."

"Do allow me," said Abacus, probing the contents of an inside blazer pocket. Abacus proceeded to yank out and dangle before the red-eyed clerk a chattering mass of small seashells strung upon a belt of knotted cord. "As they say in Bizonia, you may 'keep the change', my good man. Please tell him, Jake."

Jake had nothing in his shorts pockets except lint and a jackknife. Rod was down to the twenty-dollar bill he had been hiding in his sock for Solovanana cocktails. After paying for their room, all that was left in his sock for the journey, including drinks, was a few hundred-mizla bills and a jangle of Muzoran coins.

Abacus located a bench facing the morning sun, smiling all the while. Despite the storm of industrial madness, Hevzladon retained a very baybeetle charm. Bastions of greenery and bright flowers thrived where it could be managed, and park benches were planted everywhere so that a body could take it easy.

"Steer clear we must of Anthelworp," said Abacus to the penniless, squirming Bizonians. Neither brother could comprehend Abacus detailing their route when for all intents and purposes they were now financial captives on strange soil. Rod found it a fiendish design indeed. Abacus continued, "We must avoid this province of Anthelworp in its entirety, for Anisha tells of the inception of bloodshed there."

It was at this point that Abacus reached down into his vest and produced a scroll bound with a length of braided ribbon. Unfurling the goatskin scroll upon his lap, Abacus clicked his tongue as he drug a long finger over its surface.

From the abyss of their moneyless nightmare—portending not only certain failure for Abacus' mission, but also no way home to Bizonia—Rod stared off into the void, psychologically cremated. Jake did not know if he should laugh, cry, or curse. It was all he could do to engage in meaningless small talk. "What do you have there, Abacus?"

"'Tis is a map of Nord, Jake. The map was given mine family long ago by a chap whose name was Happyhouse."

"Happyhouse?"

"Aye. In name he was Woodrow Happyhouse."

"*The* Woodrow Happyhouse?" asked Jake, astounded.

"Happyhouse was a fraud," moaned Rod.

"A fraud? Know'st then thou of he?" asked Abacus.

Jake interrupted, "Don't mind my brother, Abacus. He tends to be a little...bitter about certain things—"

"Bitter schmitter," Rod persisted.

"—pretty much anything implying that there is room for improvement in Gibbous Bizonia."

"Not uncommon among the inhabitants of any parcel of land," replied Abacus, continuing to click and scan the goatskin map. Seated next to Abacus, Jake peered more intently at the burnt sienna markings on the scroll. Crude but not entirely inaccurate, there lay before him a rendering of Nord predating any map of the world he had ever seen, even as a beetleopologist.

There they were. The Yik Nok Mountains, the Rutmus Strait, Isla Solovanana, the Cliffs of Sahnshili. Most peculiar though, was the name "VIVACHANGA" written in capital letters arching from the western shore of the Bizonian continent, across the Rutmus Strait, and all of the way across the Muzoran continent to its eastern shore where present day Vivachanga would be located, in theory. In other words, all of the land on Nord was designated as Vivachanga with the nations of Muzora and Byzontia noted only in lower case script. The single great body of water that surrounded both continents read "Iron Sea" only in parentheses below the all capital "SISTER OCEAN".

Jake was spellbound. This was all of the Happyhouse myths made real. A storm of questions welled in Jake's heart. The questions were flooding his mouth ready to overflow from his lips onto Abacus when the largest flying insect in Hevzladon roared past Jake's ear. It came to a hover uncomfortably close to Jake's head.

"Anisha," Abacus welcomed his foiled friend. "Let us cease to wonder of the *news* she carries upon her wing." Anisha and Abacus engaged in some nasal chirping with contagious excitement. Abacus declared, "We must now continue our journey forward. The conflict between Muzora and Gibbous Bizonia is spreading all too quickly I fear."

Out of sheer adrenaline, Slim made a lunge for Anisha.

After plucking his projecting nose hair, Rod inserted his tweezers back into his breast pocket next to a thermometer, several writing quills, and an old wand. He then shed his polyester slacks for his Solovanana short pants, exposing his bird legs dipped into white tube socks and wingtips.

"Rod," said Jake, "you can't thumb a ride in those white socks. It's bad luck." Jake, a veteran hitchhiker, knew that colored socks or no socks at all would bring far better fortune. Rod, of course, refused to remove his socks and with back turned to Jake, he grabbed a quill and scribbled an addition to Jake's List.

Three hours later in the murky air of outer Hevzladon, the very tip of Rod's right thumb began to ache from exposure to the Muzoran sun. They hadn't landed a single ride. Eventually everyone's thumbs burned. Slim became limp and Jake's voice was shot from begging Rod to remove his socks.

"See, I told ya it doesn't matter," said Rod, socks glaring as a flatbed pick-up stopped on the road just ahead. Chicken cages were shackled to the bed along with bundles of switches for firewood.

Jake raced to the passenger's window with Slim as Abacus and Rod looked on. The driver and passenger were both light brown and dressed in colorfully embroidered clothing. They began to laugh. Who wouldn't? A ride to Vivachanga? You have got to be joking.

# MAKING TIME

Despite believing the travelers completely off kilter, the door was opened for Slim and Jake. Abacus and Rod climbed onto the truck bed and reached over the chickens to brace themselves on a splintered two-by-four bolted to the back of the cab. Rod bore down into a half squat with white knuckles as the bald tires kicked up dust. He was nearly thrown as the vehicle righted itself from the shoulder of the road. Abacus, on the other hand, was standing upright, holding on with just two fingers, distant for missing his dear friend Anisha.

Hevzladon was stretched narrowly along the Muzoran coast, so pavement shortly disappeared as they went smashing down a pothole road bound for the interior. As Jake enjoyed his sideways conversation with local chicken ranchers, poised Abacus nearly tumbled off the truck, taken aback by the grin buttering Rod's lips. Rod's smile was directed at Slim and his blown back whiskers poking out the front window.

Moments later, both Rod and Abacus actually did tumble off the truck, skidding messily across the top of the rusted cab, onto the hood, and from there onto the gravel road itself. The truck's gritty cloud of road dust caught up with them. From within the grit, one could hear the persistence of the four cylinder engine and Jake thanking the couple for the ride.

When the dust settled, Rod spied his suitcases stacked politely and the pick-up flying down a crumpled side road home, chickens everywhere. Jake stood covered in dust, holding a basket of food wrapped in vibrant cloth. Rubbing his hind quarters and looking back towards town, Rod could still see with his naked eye the hotel where their day had begun.

The next ride appeared three hours later and lasted seven minutes. Most of that time was spent waiting for a herd of goat-like talking boonards to be cleared from the road by their bent shepherd. Despite the looming fate of the planet and Jake's enduring argument against Rod's white socks, Rod would not surrender. He even slipped on an extra pair of white socks to pad his wingtips.

The remaining daylight hours produced several more rides wherein the hitchhikers gorged on more gifts of food and drink and unusual cigarettes. They were asked to join two rock bands in addition to being propositioned for farm labor, group nudity, and positions within the local mafia. Although Jake was intrigued by the bands and the nudity, all of these propositions were roundly refused.

As the sun disappeared, the hitchhikers' thumbs fell from their upright position. Jake grabbed Rod's binoculars and through the darkness sifted upon the day, he looked back to Hevzladon. From their coordinates astride a deserted stretch of highway, Jake focused on an old hebeetle sitting on a park bench with one pigeon on his head and one on each shoulder. The old hebeetle was on the very same bench they had sat on themselves with the Happyhouse map.

They had gone nowhere.

Jake would bury Rod's socks in his sleep.

War raged west of the Chidda Drainage.

Covens of decorated warlocks in herringbone gowns with matching bonnets slurped intoxicating potions in clean war caverns, caverns stocked with superb meat fillets. Frowning but safe from the world, they ate their fill. Young warriors surrounded by gore and death on the front lines gnawed on burned flatbread while deadly shrapnel shot over their heads.

# MAKING TIME

An explosion of proportions unseen in the history of warfare rocked the battleground. The blast left nothing but torn soil, retreating echoes, and a luminous olive haze settling over corpses. Perishing birds and baybeetles would sing their songs never more. A small, dark hebeetle took stock from a strategic hilltop. Just a short ways off, Rod and Jake were alone, covered with tiny thorns and broken sprigs of tumbleweed.

"Bug nabbit, Jake," yelled Rod, "if I told you once, I told you a thousand times, no travelling to Vivachanga with strangers!"

"Rod. You don't even *believe* in Vivachanga."

"Well, you know what I mean—no craziness allowed. Now look at us, smart guy. We'll be lucky if we ever get to see the light of day." As the Muzoran sun shone onto Rod's watery forehead, he searched his orange suitcase for his blue bottle of tranquilizers.

After day one of hitchhiking, Abacus had led their aching thumbs off of the main road to this secluded clearing surrounded by dried brush. The ground was soft beneath their bedrolls and a restful night's sleep was had by all. The stars reappeared. Jake and Rod awoke, however, to find Abacus gone. "Never travel to Vivachanga with strangers!" Rod was now scolding mostly the heavens, his shoulders arched back towards his heels.

For the first time since meeting Abacus, Jake felt that his brother had been right all along.

Abacus was no good.

Jake sat on a low stone, eyes welling with tears, looking at a dead fly between his feet. "I'm so sorry, Rod. I'll get us out of this," he said with determination, "I *will* get us out of this."

"Jake!" Rod gave up his wild curses and was frantically searching his hips—a Buckingham prototype he "borrowed" from work had been tucked into his waistband. "It's gone!"

"What's gone?"

"My Buckingham wand."

After a comprehensive search, only Abacus' walking stick was found resting next to an anthill. There was no other trace of the Vivachangan and no trace of the missing Buckingham. The brothers hurried to collect their things and set their sights on a wicked journey homeward. The kindness of strangers would be their only hope.

At a rustling in the brush, Rod fell to his crusty old wand and Jake careened into a ditch. Rod cocked his wand arm and pulled up a devilish incantation. He would have launched the wand and the incantation were it not for the tufts of Slim's ears aimed right back at him. This was no time for one bad bounce. At the sight of Rod, Slim uttered a tender "mew" from where he perched on Abacus' shoulder.

"Rise and shine, good friends," said Abacus, "I bear the bounty of fair Nord for our delight." Abacus cradled a banana leaf full with berries, nuts, and a variety of spindly tubers. The few ants he held in his hand he tossed into his mouth.

Rod crouched lower into his stance, still unwilling to launch at Slim's expense. A painful prod near Rod's anus straightened him right back up. Reaching back into his shorts, Rod withdrew the Buckingham prototype that had slid south during the night. "It's okay, Jake. You can come out. I found the prototype."

Relieved at the return of Abacus, Jake emerged from the ditch and dusted himself off. He joined Abacus and Slim—both oblivious to Rod's shenanigans—who were preparing breakfast over a fire that Abacus had procured out of thin air. Rod took a moment to gel and comb his scalp before aligning his suitcases and taking his place by the fire. Abacus handed him a hot gourd of coffee.

# MAKING TIME

Despite his suspicions, Rod sipped the coffee and began to wrap his lips around the skewered roots and fruits roasted over an unsanitized campfire. Scrunch-faced, he chewed and spat, chewed and spat, until he realized that the food was all somewhat sweet and savory.

Jake was the first to break into the darker reasons for their journey. "Abacus. You must tell us more."

Abacus said nothing from where he lay on his back, digesting. He raised one lithe arm. Following Abacus' pointed finger to the line of his gaze, the brothers drew their eyes to the sky and searched. They saw a puff of clouds and the edge of Hevzladon's pollutant haze. A Heath's Jibbering Wren creased the air overhead and Rod was forced to ask, "Is it the Jibbering Wren, Abacus, that is the harbinger of this wicked spell?"

"No, my friends. Look." It was then that Abacus raked his arm across the sky to reveal an additional curve of graded discoloration within the pollutant haze. "This...this is what demands our attention."

As a gut reaction to the presence of evil, Rod's fingers shot to his waistband and the prototype. This time he did not draw.

"Yes, that is unusual," said Jake.

"You may follow the path of this nuisance westward as it disappears into the smog of Hevzladon. And you may follow it yon as it stretches beyond the eastern skyline. This is what may be seen of the spell from our vantage point."

"The spell?" marveled Rod.

"But it's massive," said Jake.

"Well, yes and no," said Abacus. The brothers looked at each other, defeated by the immensity. "The spell is, we believe, of a quite singular cause and as such, may be remedied with a quite singular dose of the correct antivenin."

"It almost looks natural," said Jake, puzzled.

"I suppose you could say that it is," replied Abacus.

"Look, bucko. This ain't no twenty questions," said Rod, irritated, throwing down another pill or two.

"Most certainly not, Mister Rod. However, the nature of this spell and the nature of its perpetrator rest beneath veils and veils and veils." Hesitant, Abacus continued, "My friends…there is a beast."

Again, Rod's fingers shot to the prototype.

# CHAPTER EIGHT

# Valgato

"Jesus Beetle! This is so sophomoric!" whined Rod. He was fidgeting with his wingtips, having finally conceded to stripping off his white tube socks as the travelers stood baking on the side of a torrid Muzoran pass. They were covered with sheaths of grime and far from their destination. The day's first and only ride had lasted three minutes and was spent stuffed in the back of a windowless van with seven wet pygmy sheep. It was already well past noon.

Rod stuffed his socks into his pants, bent over, and stuffed his feet back into his shoes. A white pick-up nearly took his head off as it ground to a stop astride the hitchhikers. "*Ou lee doup chow?*" inquired the pretty shebeetle driver, leaning towards the open passenger window.

"Of course! I mean *pou lit zhou* cutie! Let's go guys," said Jake with a mischievous grin.

"*Let's go guys*," mocked Rod under his breath, reminding himself of Flounders. For what seemed the umpteenth time, Rod and Abacus piled into the bed of a pick-up. In this one sat a twenty-something Muzoran hebeetle smiling at the strangers with a row of gold front teeth. Jake and Slim squirmed into the cab next to the radiant shebeetle and off they went.

It wasn't long before Rod noticed something quite out of the ordinary.

They hadn't stopped moving.

No soaring over the truck onto the road. No being dumped like scrap into ragweed. They just kept on moving. Rod never fully accepted the notion that his younger brother knew of magic that he did not.

The air freshened as they distanced themselves from the industry of Hevzladon. The hills greened with forest as they wound gradually upward, deeper into the unknown. Rod perched upon his wheel well throne, engrossed with the sight of so many trees. There were no malls, no factories, no office buildings, no traffic signals, no monuments to war, no parking lots—just trees. Rod couldn't imagine the squirrel problem they must have had out there. As they blew along, their gold-toothed companion would point towards this or that, muttering a confusion of Muzoran. Abacus and Rod would smile and nod.

The forest disappeared and became high desert. The views into the distance, the prickly shrubs, and the short, gnarled trees standing alone fascinated Rod no less than the dense forest. After hours of watching the sky turn darker shades of blue, the white pick-up rounded the top of a parched bluff and rolled into a smooth valley. Burning orange against its deepening sky, the sun threatened the dark horizon.

Concrete shacks began to swoosh by, kept guard by lone roosters and splintered fence posts whose rails had succumbed to the elements. The spaces between the rickety homesteads gradually diminished until the shacks that passed by were butted up one against the other. With no space in-between, their facades formed blocks of unbroken walls.

The pick-up approached a wall of stone perpendicular to and obviously much older than the front walls of the shacks. The wall rose fifteen feet above the tallest shack and must have served as the inner city's fortification in centuries past. The wall crumbled in either direction until it bent out of sight. As they passed through the wall's hand-forged iron gate, the truck's chaotic crunching from grinding over gravel became a low, regular rumble.

With a gander over his shoulder, Rod decided that they were now rolling over cobblestones. Everything Rod had encountered since leaving Gibbous Bizonia had been surreal, extracted from his father's book of nursery rhymes read to him as a child. The book was brilliantly illustrated with sunsets, stars, trees, flowers, deer, and quaint villages whose pathways were lain with what the author termed "cobblestones".

Entranced with the pattern of perfectly fitted stones and wondering who on God's Nord had gone to all that trouble, Rod failed to ready himself as the pick-up came to an abrupt halt. He shot forward against the cab and nearly ruptured his face. Pressing his nose to the cab's rear window, Rod regained his balance and took note of the driver's hemline. Their fetching driver wasted no time in killing the engine and skipping into a homely structure just off the road.

Jake got out and explained that it would be unsafe for Sonia, the driver, or gold-toothed Hector, her protector, to return home after nightfall. Whisperings of war were creeping about the countryside and they had back roads to travel. Otherwise, Sonia would have delivered them closer to their destination. "We're in the town of Valgato, and she's going to leave us here."

Before Rod had a chance to buff his suitcases, Sonia came running back holding a plain envelope. Babbling, she handed the envelope to Jake and kissed him on the cheek. Babbling himself,

Jake tried to push the envelope away. Sonia smiled larger and babbled more sweetly. Jake pleaded. With a final hug, Sonia babbled her last and skittered around the car to jump behind the wheel.

Rod spoke to Jake without moving his lips, "All we have to do is take that 'delivery' and toss it into the nearest garbage can, bro'. We'll never see 'Sonia' again."

"This is the train depot," Jake replied.

"The train depot?" said Rod, examining the leaning, one-room shed. "Well, who cares really. We gotta get rid of those drugs pronto. They may have their eyes on us already." As they waved good-bye to Sonia and Hector, Rod wondered what kind of cockamamie deal his little brother had gotten them into this time.

"These are our tickets to Cherishio, Rod."

"*Cherishio*, eh. So that's how you say 'getting high on drugs' in Muzoran?"

"Not at all, Mister Rod," interrupted Abacus, delighted and stroking Slim, "Cherishio is the final stop on the Leischnogger Express."

"Trains are free in Muzora? Well that's a plus I must say," conceded Rod.

"She bought them for us, Rod," said Jake.

Rod could not understand. "Bought them for us? What were you two doing up there in the front seat anyways?"

"Rod, she's just being kind," said Jake, "I tried to refuse them and I didn't even tell her that we're totally broke."

"I just don't get it..." Rod's mind was under duress, stumped by the generosity of a complete stranger.

# VALGATO

The sun was reduced to a singular thread of red light on the edge of the sky, then vanquished for the night by the turning of Nord. Valgato's palm trees leapt over the tops of grungy adobe abodes. Firecrackers popped and two thigh-high children screamed, scampering barefoot from around the corner. They crashed into a townsbeetle carrying two large jugs of beer but recovered quickly, screeching ever louder. Golden light flowed from an open window.

Rod couldn't believe his eyes, "Did that guy just buy beer through *that* window? Too bad we can't stay and have a snort."

Jake, anxious for liberties, responded by starting across the street towards the beer window. "Our train doesn't get into Valgato until tomorrow!" he said, picking up speed. Jake was speaking with the beer vendor in Muzoran when Abacus, Slim, and Rod arrived, deaf to the conversation.

A round-in-the-belly Muzoran wearing a white, short-sleeved button-up and dark slacks approached the group from behind. With a smile that matched his shirt and his white hair, the Muzoran nodded as he walked right past Jake and laid his money on the window's crooked countertop. Despite Jake's protests, the Muzoran received four enormous jugs of beer. One by one he popped their tops with an opener on a string and handed them to Jake, Abacus, and Rod. The fourth he kept for himself.

"He insisted on buying them," said Jake, "as we're obviously not from around here. And he likes your shirt, Rod." The Muzoran muttered something else to Jake with his arms wide open, "And he wants us to come to his house to meet his family...and have dinner." The stranger raised his bottle by the neck and toasted the strangers. With a belch, the Muzoran extended his hand to Jake and they exchanged greetings. Jake turned to his friends and said, "This is Romiel Sando."

Rod shook Romiel Sando's hand. Abacus' network was more intricate than Rod could have believed. His accomplice, Romiel Sando, was in the most obscure little town imaginable.

After greeting Abacus, Romiel stuck his fingers into his mouth and whistled down a teenager on a bicycle. Lashed behind the bicycle was a chariot. Romiel motioned for Rod, Slim, and Jake to climb in. He then hailed another bicycle chariot for himself and Abacus. Although the pairing would not prevent Abacus and Romiel from scheming, Rod calculated a top speed of eight miles per hour for this get-up—not so fast that he couldn't barrel roll out in a pinch.

Rod's enthusiasm betrayed his dark thoughts as they wheeled at twilight through the gardens that occupied the center of town. All of the colonial buildings surrounding the garden square were built from white stone, thus capturing and amplifying the last light of day.

With every turn of his head, Rod elbowed Jake—"Would ya look at that!"—as they passed troupes of musicians strumming traditional love songs or burros slogging by with their burdens of slouching burlap sacks. But Jake could not be bothered. The convoy of stunning shebeetles young and old had him by the eyeballs. In Bottom Junction he would be lucky to catch anyone at all outside of their home. Here, everyone was out. Jake's chest bristled with heat.

They passed a hebeetle with a small flame on a long pole lighting the wicks of lanterns atop iron lampposts. The lanterns cast an amber glow over the gardens, gardens speckled with blossoms of every shape and color. Jake kept waiting for the warmth in his chest to subside, but it was relentless. The only word he could find to describe this feeling was "love".

# VALGATO

Their lean charioteer exited through a gap in the square of white stone buildings and brought Rod, Jake, and Slim to a halt next to an ancient stone curb. The curb and sidewalk were worn smooth as glass for the hundreds of years of foot traffic. Abacus and Romiel arrived thereafter. After shelling out some mizla to the charioteers, Romiel cleaved a solid wall and led his guests into an imperceptible alley, up a sagging stone staircase.

Three slender cats scattered into the shadows.

Slim and Abacus exchanged knowing glances.

The stairway turned a blind corner.

The farther they climbed up and away from the bustling road, the more the travelers were glad they had Romiel with them. Be he friend or foe, at least he offered the illusion of safety. The splintered network of alleyways provided many proper hiding places for any fiend.

Spiced with fear, the climb was most charming. One could touch both sides of the alley at once with one's fingertips. Candles and tinted lights shone through windows that opened above. They passed a young couple kissing in fever. Ribbons of notes from classical instruments—an oboe, a guitar, a violin—drifted down from locations that could not be pinpointed in the maze.

The croon of a cello, soft and natural, romanced Jake's ears. The melody was strangely familiar, yet from where he could not say. In his rapture, Jake collided with Romiel's shoulder. Romiel had stopped before a wood door beaten but not defeated by the centuries. Romiel cranked a pitted skeleton key in the door's yawning keyhole and as the door creaked open, the cello in Jake's head grew louder and sweeter.

The world inside of the ancient door was in rich contrast to the world of stone shadows outside. An army of tots erupted from the walls and engulfed Romiel with blatant disregard. Over the squelch of the storming youngsters, Romiel pronounced, "Thees eez chirdren and eez grand chirdren chirdren! Very much hello! Hello hello hello!" His hands were busy patting heads and protecting himself from the pummeling affection. The cello continued to sing as Jake's heart continued to bloom. Romiel called into the depths of the home, *"Thulina! Um harta he hehe! Jo alín jhomankí!"*

*"Chieu chieu!"* replied a lilting female voice. The voice echoed from across an open sky courtyard filled with broadleaves, sun chairs, folk paintings, and an altar freckled with candles. Romiel's wife, Thulina, appeared in an apron. Incessantly patting her hair into place, she ran up to the foreigners and greeted each with a customary peck on the cheek.

With a flick of the wrist, Thulina sent off a detachment of tots. The courtyard was surrounded by doors and arches and an ornate second story balcony. The fleet of youngsters reemerged scampering behind the second story banister and stopped to knock on a closed door. The knocking silenced the wafting cello, and with it, Jake's heart, for just when Jake thought he had seen the last beautiful shebeetle, there appeared Romiel's daughter. Yuyu.

Yuyu's heart, at the sight of Jake, stopped too. It was only the reflection in Yuyu's eyes of a shooting star born of a distant, ancient, stellar collision that averted Jake's gaze to the sky above. They both saw it, the shooting star, and another that shot perfectly in line with the first. Again, their eyes locked.

"I'm coming," Yuyu sighed in her native Muzoran and Jake, of course, understood.

"Thees eez the girl chirdren," announced Romiel, "The girl eez the Yuyu," The pair of shooting stars and the name Yuyu would be forever threaded through Jake's heart and soul.

Yuyu reappeared under a cracked archway on ground level wearing pumps and the most amazing blue jeans. She approached Jake smelling of lavender. On tippity toes she kissed not one, but both of Jake's reddening cheeks. "Do you wants somezing?" she asked him in tantalizing Bizonian. She wore glitter in her hair as if she were going to a party.

"Is it fair to ask?" Jake replied in his Muzoran.

Rod had never felt so awkward.

Here he was, a guest in the home of an unknown Muzoran right in the gut of Muzora—the heart of terrorism. His naive brother was right there, enraptured with foxy Agent Yuyu, a smashing young shebeetle. Slim, *his* cat, was licking himself wherever, whenever he pleased. Abacus, using his transparent alias, was feigning innocence while drawing them ever deeper into the bowels of darkness. Rod realized that there were no other bowels.

Romiel was deceptively jolly. Why wouldn't he be? Rod imagined the underworld stream of cash flowing through Romiel's hands. Worse yet, Romiel's "wife" Thulina was in the kitchen reducing a sumptuous gravy for supper. Rod loosened his belt, preparing for anything.

When she was finished, Thulina's courtyard table was covered with pickled dates, whitefish fillet, moist fowl, and the gravy. Using Jake's choppy Muzoran, Yuyu's very succinct corrections, and Romiel's broken Bizonian picked up as a merchant marine, conversation managed to include everyone. Slim was riveted throughout the meal by a pair of Spangled Cotingas roosting on the balcony railing. Rod was thrilled by their presence as well, thumbing through his mental library of nesting habits, mating rituals, and false sightings.

When bellies were plump and Slim's plate was licked clean, a dessert of brown sugar figolino was brought to the table. After serving Jake the last figolino, a whistling teakettle turned Thulina back to the kitchen. In one smooth motion, Thulina grabbed the copper-domed teakettle in one hand, two sets of cup and saucer in the other, and backed out through the kitchen door with her skirt still twirling about her knees.

She placed the teacups down next to Yuyu and Jake's figolinos. Pulling the trigger on the kettle's black handle, Thulina poured hot water from the opened spout. Fresh red rose petals bubbled to the top of the steaming cups. *"Zu dela si."*

Interpreting for her mother, Yuyu whispered to Jake, "Let it steep," brushing his ear with her lips.

When something in his beer reached Rod's most ticklish tendril, he excused himself to the *binachu*, using his new word, *binachu*. He had to bend at the waist to get through the door of the awkwardly constructed lavatory, but inside, the *binachu* was tiled, pink, and clean. Standing there waiting, Rod was overcome by the strangeness of being alone in a room for the very first time so far from his only reality. Was life carrying on as usual back in Bottom Junction, or had the town been turned upside-down?

From the *binachu*, Rod found his way upstairs to his room and took off his shoes. The bed sheets felt cool and calming, but he couldn't get to sleep for the bursts of laughter below. When the

VALGATO

laughter became unbearable, Rod launched himself onto the balcony in his robe and slippers. Everyone at the table was half-drunk, waving for him to come down and join them.

"Dress!"

"Geet dress!"

"You geet dress!"

They were getting ready to go out.

"Waddaya mean we're goin' out?" a disbelieving Rod cried from the balcony.

"Aw, come on, Rod," jeered Jake.

"'Tis naught but an evening," said Abacus.

"I can imagine beautiful things happening tonight," said Yuyu in perfect Bizonian and Jake's heart stilled once more.

Rod made it down after polishing his shoes and knotting himself into the paisley tie he had selected for their travels. He wore a pouty face, as if being drug off to school for the first time. It was explained that not only was it common to get a late start in Valgato—it must have been twelve thirty in the morning—but tonight was special. It was the climax of the high season, the final night of the Festival of Mysteries.

"Thees month we are to celebrating the infinite mysterious nature of the life," said Romiel.

Rod knew there were still a couple of unsolved mysteries—UFOs and hairy baybeetles with giant feet that showed up in grainy photographs—but "the infinite mysterious nature of life"? Please.

"Why should I, Romiel Sando, exist in thees baybeetle body with my hairs growing and falling out all over the place? Why thees, when I am made of nothing but tiny particles or maybe not particles, but just energy? Because I am such a cloud, how eez it I am even

99

able to controlling anything—even the moving of my finger?" He wiggled his finger. "Why does any of thees have to exist at all?"

Rod wiggled his finger and wondered.

"Where did we come from?" continued Romiel, "Yes, our ancestor baybeetles and perhaps the original baybeetle, but where did all of the life on Nord come from? If our origin does come from one universe big bang or from one God, where did thees big bang come from? Where did thees God come from?

"Where are we? In the Valgato, yes, but where eez thees? Muzora, yes, and yes on planet Nord, and yes in the Meelky Way Galaxy, but where eez the galaxy and where eez the universe?

"Now eez time when we stop and we wonder why our mysterious world eez in such a hurry hurry hurry," as Romiel rambled, Rod sighed and looked to his wristwatch.

"Even when we are standing still," Romiel looked down to his shoes, affirming that they were solidly in one place, "we are moving five hundred mile an hour around the meedle of our spinning leetle planet. Our planet also eez moving, tens of thousands mile an hour around our sun. Thees entire solar system eez moving much faster than that around the meedle of the galaxy and the galaxy eez moving faster than thees around somezing else! We are already so ridiculous fast! Why hurry?"

Rod looked up from his wristwatch, searching for another clock in the room.

"With thees extraordinary ridiculous of everything, our emotions become just as ridiculous. Joy and love and fear and hate are all equal ridiculous. Why not choose joy and love over the fear and hate?

# VALGATO

"That eez what we are celebrating—the ultimate mystery of the life and the desire to joy and love that thees mystery does allow us. Do you see? Each and every moment that we are experience every single day eez infinite mysterious and miracle. To make sure we do not forget, we celebrate. The more we learn about life, the more mysterious it become and the more lively our celebration become."

Romiel paused, reflected, and added, "The only thing that I think I know for certain eez that *thees* eez where I am supposed to be."

"Valgato?" asked Rod, giving up on nailing down local time.

"Well, just *here*," Romiel said, looking at his shoes again and pointing down with both hands, "Maybe I am in city of Bullneck, maybe Solovanana…even though I may not think so, I am exactly where I am supposed to be *all of the time.*

"Then there are, of course, those mysterious leetle dots of light."

# CHAPTER NINE

# Rod's Landing

Hoisted into the air, Rod bounced atop the shoulder to shoulder crowd. With a petunia tucked behind his ear, he flailed a heavy jug of bubbly. Red lipstick was smeared on his cheek and across the full of his mouth. From his privileged vantage point, Rod saw a tiny lad on the edge of the square ignite a fifty-foot-high wooden tower covered in hundreds of fireworks. The tower flickered, floundered, then erupted in a rainbow of flame. A silver rocket burst from the third tier of the tower and swooshed through the air on trajectory with Rod's forehead.

Everyone saw the rocket coming and scattered. Even those holding Rod aloft dispersed into the crowd, leaving Rod hovering in space. The rocket singed the end of Rod's necktie as he fell, and as his tailbone was about to receive a critical blow from nursery rhyme cobblestones, the angelic hands of Valgato came out of nowhere to buffer Rod's landing. A circle of children in a mad polka were aiming to stomp out the blasting silver rocket as it screamed off of their marshmallow knees.

Beneath pinwheels of rushing sparks spinning on the tower, Rod passed his jug to a stranger and raised his voice to Romiel, "Isn't that illegal?"

"What part?" asked Romiel as another rocket shot into the drunken crowd to be chased down by the youth. Seeing the ridiculousness of it all, Rod chuckled. Then he laughed at his drunk chuckle.

A two-legged bison ten feet tall, with horns taller yet, was tossing live sticks of dynamite into the masses. "Look at that buffalo costume, Jake!" yelled Rod, "Jake?"

Jake was nowhere to be found.

"Abacus! Where's Jake?"

"If you answer 'Where is Yuyu?' methinks there you shall find Jake," Abacus said with a look.

"Where eez the Yuyu?" added Romiel, "I think the better question eez, 'Where eez a drunk goat in summer clover?'" Rod twisted as Romiel continued, "But no worry. I am owner of socks and sweet meat shop here in the Valgato. I know everybody."

Rod was astounded, "You mean I can buy socks and sweet meat at the same store?"

"Oh yes," said Romiel excitedly, "Sometimes you can buy sweet meat that eez cold even on a very hot day."

"Fantastic!" replied Rod. Valgato was a mystery indeed, and Jake had gone missing within the baffling configuration of Valgato itself. Not only was the doorway to Romiel's *binachu* only waist-high, but the town had built stairways everywhere. Some led under the street to a dark network of ancient subterranean tunnels. Some led to footbridges that crossed overhead—spans that cost tons of stone and years of labor only to serve one small, nondescript door, perhaps unused. Many stairways led nowhere, to dead ends of solid wall.

What were once obviously great arches in spectacular buildings peaked just inches above the sidewalk. Mostly buried, the remaining spaces beneath the arches were filled in with brick. There was not a right angle or a straight line in the whole city.

# ROD'S LANDING

Plowing through bodies, Abacus, Slim, Rod, and Romiel ducked through the swinging shutter doors of *Da Shoomp Shouvar*—the Greasy Lamp—Romiel's favorite watering hole. A tipsy hebeetle with a handlebar mustache fell backwards through the doors and out onto the sidewalk, nearly busting a buttock, but saving his mug of ale.

Three bar stools were vacated, as Rod and Abacus, escorted by Romiel, were nothing if not guests of honor in this celebration of the mysterious. If Rod and Abacus were guests of honor, then Slim was king—the foreigners were welcomed by shouts and whistles and toasts to *"Vigunchi! Vigunchi! Vigunchi!"* meaning "Kitty! Kitty! Kitty!" On the top shelf behind the bar, whiskers and ears drawn back, Slim sniffed down some of the finest bottles of spirits on the planet.

Once settled in, Rod leaned through the bubbly on his breath towards Romiel. "Romiel?"

"Yes, Rod."

"I'm really confused. I'm so uptight and pasty that everyone here must know that I'm Bizonian. Here I am, the enemy, and everyone in Valgato is treating me like a prince. I don't understand how Muzorans could do something as horrible as bomb Bullneck City."

"First of all," replied Romiel, "they *say* that it was the Muzoran who bombed the Bullneck City. But who really knows? Anybody could have done it. Anybody could have paid piles of money to anybody else so they would arrange for it to happen. The TV can say whatever it wants. The truth eez hard to find, and I am thinking you will not find it on the news. I am sure the TV eez making all us Muzorans look pretty bad.

"But anyway, let us say it *was* the Muzorans who bombed your War Monument One in an act of war. Throughout the Nord history, those who decide to go to war are usually just a leetle piece of society—small, isolated groups such as the governors or the fancy businessmen who can buy these governors. These small, radical groups usually do not represent the sentiment of the general population, the common baybeetle. Thees you can see by the kindliness of the Muzorans you have met. Unfortunately, in the end, it eez the common baybeetle that pay the biggest price for war—they live in fear and they die by the thousands.

"For the sake of argument, Mister Rod, maybe we should try to figure out why even one leetle fraction of Muzorans might want to bomb Bullneck City, to do thees 'terrorism' as you call it."

"Let's do that," said Rod.

"And you listen to me," Romiel looked stern and shook his finger, "I do not say that the right or good thing eez to blow up the building and kill the baybeetle. We must think only what can make a good baybeetle conduct thees horrible business."

"A very good idea," said Abacus, "The clock, it hath struck upon the bell and our time together, it is short."

Abacus was intent on finding a line to the hex that was bringing Tyrone to his death.

"We can imagine," said Romiel, "a room where two baybeetle brothers must live with each other. Thees eez their world, thees one room. They may not ever leave. Every day, there appear in thees room two loaf of bread. The two loaf are the same in every way and so are the brothers. The brothers are the same size, have the same appetite. The two loaf are the only food in the world, and every day the first brother right away eat one-an-a-half loaf of bread, leaving only one half of loaf for second brother.

"How many days you think the second brother will sit still and be hungry when his companion eat and eat and eat? How many?" Romiel wagged his finger, "No. Not very many days. He will get angry and frustration at the obvious mistake and maybe bomb his brother."

"How does this relate," asked Rod, "to Bullneck? To the war?"

"Yes, Rod," answered Romiel, "You see, we live on a very very small planet and we can think thees planet to be the room of the two brothers. And the two brother, we will say, are the two country Gibbous Bizonia and Muzora."

"Hmm."

"Yes, and the two loaf of bread, they are all of the many many beautiful and useful resources that are the gifts of our leetle Nord. We need thees natural resources both to survive and to enjoy our mysterious leetle life.

"Living the way that you do in Gibbous Bizonia, you consume, consume, consume. Big car, big house, big everything, and everything eez used and throw it away. Even the size of the Bizonia baybeetle eez always bigger, bigger, bigger.

"Everything we consume comes from Nord, from nature in one way or the other. So to fill its need, Bizonia uses not only its loaf—its own natural resources—but Bizonia must seek the loaf of other country."

"So what you are saying, Romiel," injected Abacus, for Rod's sake, "is that Gibbous Bizonia is eating Muzora's loaf."

"Exactly. And it eez very obvious to us Muzoran that Gibbous Bizonia will do anything to get thees loaf." Romiel paused and took a deep breath. "Forever on Nord, we have been told that our nations are going to war for thees reason or that reason. Going to war because God has told us that our neighbors have the wrong God and we should kill them or somezing else crazy. The truth eez, we go to war for the other country's resources—maybe the gold, the slaves, the oil, or maybe the land itself. Our neighbor eez always having something and we are always wanting it for ourself.

"Maybe more crazy eez after they win the big resource war, the big baybeetles who win the riches of war do not share with the rest of their countrybeetle. They go sell the riches and get more rich. Anyway, thees eez how things work on Nord sometimes.

"When Bullneck City happened, we in Muzora were sad, but we could not help but think that such an event was inevitable. Gibbous Bizonia has been poking its fingers into other baybeetles' business for many many years. Some even think that the Gibbous Bizonia bombed itself for an excuse to go to war with Muzora. Many Bizonian baybeetles make a lot of money—*a lot* of money—when your nation goes to war."

Rod knew this to be true. The military industry was responsible for a huge portion of the Bizonian economy.

"Everything would have to change," continued Romiel, "but if the baybeetles of both Muzora and Gibbous Bizonia used minimal resources to survive and enjoy life, if each ate only their own loaf, then neither Muzora or Gibbous Bizonia would have any reason to bomb Bullneck City. That eez what I believe." Romiel took a slug of beer from his mug. "Yes, world eez a leetle crazy and you Bizonians are a leetle crazy. My baybeetles, Muzora baybeetles, also a leetle crazy!" to which Romiel burst into his mad laugh and slapped Rod on the back. "BUT, we are all good baybeetles. We all come from good leetle babies. Even old hebeetle like me, I come from cute, leetle baby baybeetle. I think thees war that eez happening today in Muzora, I believe it has many potential to make the world better for chirdren and babies."

Abacus was intrigued, "War? A boon to children? How you jest, Romiel."

"Oh, of course I hate hate hate thees war and all war. What I am believe eez that finally all of Nord eez getting smart enough and together enough so that thees war maybe eez being our last Great War. Baybeetles will see how gruesome, selfish, and pointless eez the war. It eez an unfortunate way to learn not to make war, but it eez happening. When all eez finish with thees bloody mess, we will have better place for chirdren, hopefully forever. We have to figure out that no war eez worth the loss of one baby baybeetle."

Romiel knew that the pendulum on planet Nord had changed direction and was swinging away from the peak of warfare. However, like a battleship at full steam whose momentum carries it forward though its propellers have been thrown into reverse, the momentum of peak warfare still carried fearsome potential.

The musicians on stage in *Da Shoomp Shouvar* rang clear. They were a band of balding and hairless elders fronted by elegant Shantra, a siren of many wisdoms. Shantra hoisted Slim up off of the shoulders of the hobnobbing bartender and draped the *vigunchi* about her silken neck. She placed a red rose in Slim's fangs and tail to cleavage, the couple seduced the room with animal paces.

"*Vigunchi!*"

"*VIGUNCHI!*"

Shantra sang of Rod knew not what, but to judge by the gentle tones and gestures, it was a song of love or sweet bestiality. "I still don't get it," Rod said to Romiel, "even if Bizonia does have its eyes on Muzora's loaf of resources, Bizonia is giving a lot of Muzorans jobs. You should see the factories in Hevzladon! And Muzora is a beautiful country with beautiful baybeetles. It's warm and sunny. Can't Muzorans just be happy?"

"I had a dream," said Romiel, "about Muzora."

"Here we go again," sighed Rod.

"A beautiful, healthy serpent with beautiful colors was inside of a glass box. All of the beautiful, white baybeetles of Bizonia were passing by outside of the box, amazed by the beautiful, colorful serpent. Before I awoke from the dream, the beautiful serpent transformed into a very very angry Muzoran, still trapped in a glass box."

"Dreams can be kind of silly," said Rod, "What do you think it meant?"

"The Bizonia baybeetle comes to look at the Muzora country and the beautiful Muzora baybeetle and thinks to himself, 'How beautiful. Yes, how beautiful,' and thees eez not a lie, my friend. Look at thees Shantra. Look at the mountain and the desert and the Valgato and the everything bird, sky, river. Very beautiful. Like looking at the beautiful serpent. What the Bizonians do not see, maybe refuse to see, eez that underneath thees beauty there lies great frustration. No big Bizonian money. No big Bizonian house. No big Bizonian vacation.

ROD'S LANDING

"These jobs that Bizonian factories bring to Muzora, they do not provide for a good life by Bizonian standard. Very long hours for very low pay. The Muzoran cannot buy what he makes. He sends it all to Bizonia. The Muzora baybeetle becomes more mechanical and the Muzora landscape gets more pollution.

"The Muzora baybeetle, like the beautiful serpent, eez as if behind a shield of glass through which Bizonian compassion cannot penetrate."

Rod swiveled his barstool away from the bar, giving himself a shot of both the dance floor and the front shutter doors. A pair of pickled stragglers crashed into *Da Shoomp Shouvar*, knocking one of the shutter doors clean off its hinges. Rod could see through the doorway now, straight into the night.

In the middle of the road outside the tavern, a couple in love was locked in a kiss. Though the girl was a bit of a trollop, Rod did have to admit that the two looked kind of cute, albeit vulgar. An uproar from his fellow patrons turned Rod back around.

There was Romiel, preaching to the crowd with his arms raised above his head. In his raised hands was Slim, whose powers of social lubrication were, apparently, extreme. Romiel held Slim at the hips and shoulders in stretched display, all four legs at full extension. When Slim spread wide all twenty-six toes and extended his claws, the crowd went wild.

The meaning of Romiel's carnival calls were lost onto Rod, but in the beauty of the moment, Rod wept with joy. Choking on his words, not taking his eyes off of Slim, Rod wailed to Abacus, "Buddy, even if this is the end of the line, it sure is a hell of a way to go."

# CHAPTER TEN

# Love Is an Ancient Alphabet

$F$ar flung from *Da Shoomp Shouvar*, Yuyu and Jake could still hear cheers of *"Vigunchi! Vigunchi! Vigunchi!"* and the clanking of bottles. "What do you think of my city, Jake?" asked Yuyu.

*"Zhou tsi bolumva!"* answered Jake, his heart pounding. In a world that held little faith in love, when Jake looked upon Yuyu, he had no doubts.

Yuyu giggled, "You *love* it?"

"Yes. Very much. We showed up at the right time."

Yuyu's response was barely audible over a cacophony of church bells. "Festivals are difficult to avoid in Muzora. When we are not busy celebrating, we are busy preparing for the next festival. Follow me." Yuyu pulled Jake by the sleeve into an unmarked subterranean passage.

The tunnel opened into a bog of baybeetles beneath a smoky haze. There was a band playing in there and just as Jake and Yuyu entered the fray, the song ended and the crowd roared.

"Is that it?" asked Jake. It was two-thirty in the morning.

"It is only just beginning," replied Yuyu as Jake tripped over a couple rolling on the barroom floor.

Yuyu yanked Jake up towards the even thicker crowd surrounding the bartender. Jake, the intriguing foreigner, was cloaked in fiery stares from the congress of exotic ladies. Everyone was chatting breathlessly, laughing while sloshing drinks all over themselves and the establishment. Slapping a cold bottle in Jake's hand, Yuyu raised a cheer.

A circle of strangers joined the toast to the Bizonian. *"Harvs tut Bizonoun!"* Bottles were raised high in a bunch when the jester leapt from off the top of the bar, his stomach landing on the crown of raised bottles. He crashed through.

*"Show me the mo-ney. Gotta get me some lovin' ho-ney…"*

"I can't believe they're playing 'Show Me the Money'," yelled Jake into Yuyu's ear.

"Why not?"

"It's weird. I'm in some tiny town, somewhere in the middle of Muzora, and I'm listening to Ace Redworm. I could be in any bar back home and hear the same thing."

"Jakey, Bizonian culture is all over Muzora. And it's a great song," Yuyu pushed up into Jake, "You have so many creative individuals in Gibbous Bizonia. It is a wonderful thing."

"The idea of Bizonian culture being everywhere stresses me out though. We're so violent and egotistical. We use disposable everything."

"It is true, Jakey, that neither Gibbous Bizonia nor Muzora is perfect, but to build a wall between your culture and ours would only make matters worse. The relationship between our countries must grow."

"But we're taking over the whole world, Yuyu!"

Yuyu cupped Jake's shoulder and spun him around to face her. "That is why we are all lucky to have so many brilliant, worldly baybeetles in Bizonia—like *you*. Your country will get better and better."

"Maybe."

"And because word travels fast and because everyone everywhere *loves* your culture, as Bizonia improves, the world at large will improve with you. This is the key, Jake."

# LOVE IS A ANCIENT ALPHABET

Something deep inside of Jake unlatched. Not only was Yuyu beautiful, but she was wicked smart and spoke a mean Bizonian.

The band in the cavernous bar was playing its heart out when Yuyu spotted her lifelong friend Claudia. Yuyu and Claudia kissed each other and Claudia kissed Jake. Jake was having no trouble adjusting to this Muzoran custom. Yuyu whispered something into Claudia's ear and suddenly it was time to make a few turns about town. Claudia exhumed Jake and Yuyu from the bar's randy catacombs and the threesome hit the skewed streets of Valgato.

The streets of Valgato were old and narrow, designed for horses, mules, and baybeetles. Although narrow, they were broken open by plazas at every stone's throw. Most nights, one could find an empty bench in these plazas to enjoy the flowers, or a fountain that had been bone dry for decades. Tonight the plazas, benches and all, were packed.

As Jake and the girls wandered, strange scents would emerge from the distance, sometimes growing more rancid, sometimes more delicious. Sometimes at the end of a scent there would appear a hot kiosk stationed by sweaty chefs passing out handfuls of food. Yuyu and Claudia delighted in all of these snacks. Jake, however, was squeamish. None of these Muzoran delicacies, ranging from cricket larvae to rat tails, struck him as anything he would like to put in his mouth.

Jake closed his eyes and Claudia placed just one pinch of her snack on Jake's tongue. The food moved. Chewing grudgingly, Jake noticed that Claudia's cup was a writhing mass of tentacles. The tentacles were cleaved into segments, but still moving of their own accord. Jake swallowed, ignoring the creature's rubbery texture while Claudia laughed and Yuyu vacuumed ice cubes at the bottom of her cup with a thick, yellow straw. Claudia finished off the tentacles and they settled onto a curb to watch a passing parade.

Chains of glossy-eyed dancers glimmered, dappled in sweat and sequins. The crimson-robed dancers moved in loose but hypnotic synchronization, three steps forward and two steps back, to the clacks of crude, wooden percussion. Small children dressed as goblins ran dragging lines of rope behind them, ropes baited with pots and pans. Their clatter rose well above that of the fireworks and church bells. Other youth ran in circles, wearing complete body armor of dangling tin cans whose clatter rivaled even that of the pots and pans. Teenagers with enormous braided palm frond beaver tails were sneaking up behind baybeetles and thunderclapping the cobblestone with their oversized beaver tails. The unwarned would leap into the air with the explosion of sound.

Amid the manic disorder of the celebration, they were led by Claudia and her lewd nature to the lover's promenade. Stars in their eyes reflecting the skies, teeth and cufflinks gleaming, couples sashayed hand in hand, around and around a grove of makka trees. Nestled in the grove was a whitewashed gazebo, luminous with the flames from bent iron sconces.

As the musicians under the canopy floated ballads into the night, Claudia elbowed Yuyu, twice. Yuyu remained coy however, tucking her chin behind her shoulder and glancing up at Jake. Though her stare burned through several lines of Jake's defenses, Jake was paralyzed. The significance of the promenade seemed greater than the distance around the makkas. Not yet willing to wager his bachelorhood on a lap around the promenade with Yuyu, Jake deferred his attention to his shoes.

Sensing the stalemate, Claudia grabbed Jake and Yuyu. Under Claudia's dangerous supervision, they were led through more tight streets and even tighter alleyways. There was no hint of the patriotic street grid to which Jake was accustomed in Bottom Junction. Strangely, regardless of which direction they moved, they always ended up back in the central gardens, the heart of the celebration. "*Gronau Esquito*," said Yuyu, "the Garden Baybeetle." This is where Jake had absorbed his first impressions of Valgato from inside his chariot with Rod and Slim.

"Eet eez a black hole," said Claudia with a devious grin, referring to the garden.

Buffeting through the crowd in *Gronau Esquito* was slow and amusing. Yuyu and Claudia told jokes in Muzoran that Jake could not possibly understand—and this made him laugh. Pressing up against Yuyu as crowding and opportunity dictated, Jake was in Heaven. More lost in mystery than the rest of the party, he was more so in Heaven.

As a flaking, flowered statuette of an archaic deity floated by on the shoulders of dignitaries, Jake was grabbed from the rear. Through the smallest of openings pried between an ice creamery and a cobbler, Yuyu drug Jake away from the street's commotion. Up this narrowest of alleys, Jake found to his surprise that they were alone. Together. For the first time this lifetime.

"Yu-Yuyu," Jake studdered.

"Yes, Jakey?"

"Where's C-C-Claudia?"

"She has sent us off," replied Yuyu, her dark eyes reaching into Jake's soul, "I am wants to show you somezing." Yuyu only carried an accent when she so desired. Taking his hand in hers, also for the first time, they rose three steps into the glow of a distant porch lantern. When Yuyu stopped, she turned to Jake, twisting gently back and forth. "Thees eez zee Alley of zee Kiss."

Jake was overheating. He imagined his teeth falling out, bouncing off of Yuyu's breasts and onto his shoes.

"Here is where many years ago," Yuyu said looking up, "two young lovers whose love was deep, but forbidden, united their lips from balcony to balcony across this alley." Yuyu reached out to Jakey's chest with one hand, inhaling. With her other hand, she brushed back her hair.

Jake was finally defeated.

Beneath the balconies of lore, Jake reached around the small of Yuyu's arching back. She reached up behind him, clutching for his spine. Jake's other hand brushed across Yuyu's shoulder and through her soft curls. He embraced the curve of Yuyu's neck. Their faces drew together, tilting just so. Their eyes closed, slowly. Slowly, wishing to see the other's lips closer, and then closer. Closer still.

Splayed out on a couch in a crowded disco.

Back to front, pressed up against a lamppost near the reservoir.

Pinned into the smallest enclave just out of reach of the thrashing mob.

Their lips would not surrender.

In a chariot.

In the *binachu*.

Rolling on the concrete floor of a chicken coop.

Broken up by an officer of the law.

Oblivious to the attention given them by the townsbeetles, Yuyu and Jakey eventually stood in an embrace, rocking from side to side in the middle of the street, some street, sharing a kiss for the ages. Hours passed, their feet not moving an inch.

The sky began to lighten and the bashing throngs began to thin. An uproar of cheers from inside a tavern next to where Yuyu and Jake stood caused their eternal kiss to take pause. They thought the cheers were for them.

What they saw through the broken shutter doors of *Da Shoomp Shouvar* was not leering, cheering old hebeetles. What they saw was Romiel, announcing to the crowd with his arms raised high above his head. In his hands he displayed Slim, in a full toe spread. There was Rod, at the bar, weeping tears of joy onto Abacus.

"I'm thirsty, Jakey," said Yuyu, "and there's water in Joy's room. Would you like to see her room?" Yuyu's friend Joy was away with the family at another celebration and Yuyu had been left with a key to Joy's house. Jake greeted Yuyu's invitation with more than his usual enthusiasm.

Yuyu and Jake were both afraid that their giggling would give them away as they broke into and sneaked through Joy's house, past Joy's aunt who had stayed behind and was now passed out on the couch. They made it into Joy's room without being discovered and helped themselves to the ceramic pitcher of water that Joy kept on her bedside table.

"I like to write poetry, Jakey. Would you like to hear one of my poems?" In the candlelight of Joy's bedroom where the only place to sit was on Joy's bed, Yuyu wetted her lips and began reciting her poem from memory, one hand over her heart, one on Jake's thigh. Had he cared to try, Jake could have followed the poem word for word. As it was, all that Jake followed were sweet Yuyu's lips, the meaning of her syllables lost in the sensual roll of a gentle Muzoran growl.

When she had finished her poem, Yuyu fell back onto the sheets and without speaking, she called for Jake. With Jake as her cello, it took hours, but together they wrecked Joy's bedroom.

Upon waking, neither Jake nor Yuyu knew how they came to arrive on Joy's bedroom floor, their bodies warm and seamlessly swirled together. Lying there in the morning light on cool terra cotta tiles after the nearly sleepless night, Yuyu proposed climbing a mountain—if they could find enough of their clothing. The mountain was called *Da Bufa* and it overlooked Valgato from the outskirts of town, from the high, open desert.

"The most phenomenal experiences are born of love. Don't you think, Jakey?" Jake just hummed a low note, responding both to his daydreams of Yuyu and to Yuyu herself, still by his side, sunning on a flat boulder. They were both thirsty again in the warm air atop *Da Bufa*, so they leaned together and kissed.

There wasn't much to be heard of Valgato from this height, save for the church bells—always the church bells. Behind them, a free cow mooed into the thin air and to no other cow in particular, as there were none in sight. An orange and black butterfly landed on a dry succulent.

# LOVE IS A ANCIENT ALPHABET

Earlier, after failing to escape from Joy's house without the cross-armed disapproval of Joy's aunt, Jake and Yuyu twisted through the streets of Valgato until there were only twisted alleys. From there they twisted through the city walls until there were only twisted canines on twisted ropes growling and barking, protecting their own. After the last twisted hound, there was nothing but a twisted dirt trail that led them up and away into the desert, away from the meanings of baybeetles. There on *Da Bufa*, they were younger than their years, sharing fits of laughter over the simplest flavors of conversation.

When they reached the exposed stone summit of *Da Bufa*, the city of Valgato became insignificant. Inside the city walls, the city was everywhere and meant everything. Outside of the walls, its meanings meant nothing and this butterfly, this one butterfly, meant everything. The butterfly was miraculous.

Jake and Yuyu both laid back and stared up into the heavens. "I mean every day someone falls in love who wasn't expecting to," continued Yuyu, rambling, "and I just can't wait for the world to be at peace." She was as certain of this outcome as she was certain that Jake's lost boxer shorts would eventually resurface at Joy's house.

Jake wanted to feel this way too, about world peace, but he couldn't imagine having the same certainty. He was hopeful, but not certain. He wondered if he was on the same planet as Yuyu, seeing the same sky as Yuyu, the same sky he had always seen. "Yuyu, when you look into the plain blue sky, can you see that it is still kind of moving? A little fuzzy?"

She delighted over the word "fuzzy" and said, "Well sure. Do you mean those little dots of light?"

"No. It's just kind of fuzzy."

"Yes, I know. Those are the little lights."

"I don't get it."

"You can't *get it* because they are always moving very quickly. Like this one!" she waved her finger excitedly through space, "And that one! There are too many!" Layered with sleepiness and confusion, Jake tried to grasp what Yuyu was saying. He continued to stare off into the redeeming sky, imagining with all his might a sea, between he and the blue, of tiny white dots of light. "And that one!" said Yuyu.

Jake's eyes blurred in and out, seeking Yuyu's sky, hoping she wasn't just teasing. Rolling his head in her direction, Jake saw sincerity in Yuyu's countenance, so he tried harder to see.

Suddenly, straining, it happened.

Jake saw a singular point of light flying through his field of vision for the smallest fraction of a second.

That changed everything.

"I think those little lights are doing something," said Yuyu.

"I can't believe this," said Jake.

"What can't you believe, Jakey?"

"I cannot believe that there are tiny dots of light. Everywhere."

"Oh, yes. Like that one!"

As the free cow bellowed from ever deeper within its cud, Jake and Yuyu continued to stare hazily off into space watching the sky and the lights. In the giddy, enlightening nonsense of the day, something else up above in the heavens caught Jake's attention. Up there among the oodles of flying dots was the slight curve of graded discoloration—the hex that Abacus feared may destroy all that was good on small planet Nord. Jake pushed himself up to his feet.

Following the discoloration westward, in the direction of Gibbous Bizonia, the smudge noticeably tightened. It came to a head as a cyclone would draw itself into a vicious point and took the shape of the tapered end of a fox's tail. Jake spun around to the east, in the direction of the vast unknown. If Vivachanga existed, it was to be found over there. Again, the discoloration was seen to draw to a point in the shape of the tip of a fox tail. The vague silhouette of a mountain drew the spell to a point. *Da Bufa* was a teabag compared to this distant peak.

"Yuyu?"

"Mmm, yes."

"What mountains are those?"

Yuyu arched into a yawn before rising. "Those are in the *nooshtah* Jake. They don't have a name."

"What's the *nooshtah*?"

"The *nooshtah* is so far away from everything that nobody goes there. There is no reason to go there." Thinking about small, simple things did not come easy after their indulgent evening—let alone large, complex, beguiling, and fearsome things. Jake's head was now full of large, complex, beguiling, and fearsome things.

Jake did not want to leave *Da Bufa* and face his departure from Yuyu, but the discolored hex in the sky beckoned. His dedication to Abacus and to their mission left Jake no other option than to begin the precipitous descent back towards Valgato's myriad streets and alleyways, back to the black hole of *Gronau Esquito*.

As he and Yuyu crossed the threshold of the open desert back into the honed stone of the city, Jake stole another glance of the buzzing desert sky. Not only was there the usual fuzzy blue out there, but now there were miniscule flying lights and a tainted haze that threatened to destroy the world. Jake wasn't sure if it was last night's bubbly or a bit of advice from the mysterious dots of light, but he also saw, written across the sky from horizon to horizon, the words "*All patience is is stillness*".

What patience had to do with either love or the end of the world, Jake had no idea.

# PART III

# The Mission

# CHAPTER ELEVEN

# The Express

*The mime wanted Rod. Not the guy next to Rod, but Rod.*

*With nothing to lose, Rod dislodged himself from the crowd and lay prone in front of the mime and the jeering masses. The mime looked down on Rod like a big cat over a sleeping dog.*

*After dissecting Rod's fragility, the mime started to juggle sharpened machetes over Rod's abdomen as if Rod were no more than decaying wood. A sloshed hebeetle on the other side of a concrete block wall trumpeted and trumpeted on his tarnished trumpet as if he were the one to awaken Rod, the sleeping, decaying wooden dog. The tone was hideous and would crank on for hours. Dawn broke an ominous mist upon the eastern sky.*

*Rod jerked to his right at the sound of Abacus howling to a bouquet of sleek Muzoran shebeetles. Abacus howled as he leapt to the top of the concrete block wall, waving a sexually lewd figure woven from drinking straw wrappers. Rod shouted at him, but the church bells slammed into a demon melody, overwhelming Rod's cries.*

*Slim was embarrassingly drunk. With a hoisted tail, he peed onto Rod's left shoe.*

*"Romiel, I don't know," Rod slurred after the mime had had its way with him, "This place is beautiful. Hanoshi! If only Jake were around."*

*Arm in arm in arm in paw, Rod, Romiel, Abacus, and Slim stumbled home. The police made Rod erase the name "Dorothy" inside of a heart that he scratched into freshly poured concrete with a twig. Then they make him clean the rest of the sidewalk with his bare hands and a cup of lukewarm coffee.*

*After four weeks of citywide celebration, Rod and company were the last ones left standing and Rod had lost his necktie. The streets of Valgato were eerily empty. Where was Jake? How could he be missing? How could he not be missing?*

Rod awoke pulverized. Luckily this dream, this nightmare of juggled machetes, nicked neckties, and drunken kittens, was just that—a dream. Or was it? The sun shone through Rod's bedroom window like a thousand bleating lambs. The lambs pierced the detached lining of Rod's brain as he tried to wash away the nightmare and the nightmare of his hangover. *Hanoshi.* Just ten more minutes of sleep then Rod would roust Abacus, Jake, and Slim and take leave of Valgato.

An hour-and-a-half flew by with Rod sweating cigarette smoke and alcohol, but there was no sleep to be had. The tune of a madman's drunken trumpet outside Rod's open window and the thundering of church bells would not allow it.

Rod wished he had never learned the word *hanoshi*. Muzoran for "beautiful," every time he said *hanoshi* someone handed him a fresh beer or a tub of liquor, grateful to hear a Bizonian giving the Muzoran language an effort.

Like pulling old bubble gum from hot pavement, Rod pulled his head from his pillow and sat on the edge of the bed. He pushed on his glasses. He took them off again, rubbed them with his nightshirt, and shoved them back on his face. Even with prescription lenses, the world around him was bleary and shifting. Someone had hosed all of the shapes and colors from the room. His eyes fell to the floor and his head began to pound.

## THE EXPRESS

On the floor Rod saw a scattered bag of catnip. Slim was passed out with his tail in a knot, his cat breath reeking of alcohol. Next to Slim, tightly woven from drinking straw wrappers, was an oversized model of the male baybeetle genitalia—three balls and a stinger. Rod lunged for the door and the *binachu* that he prayed existed outside of his imagination.

Racing over the dizzying mosaic of mismatched floor tiles, Rod passed Abacus' quarters. Abacus was shirtless, being fed toast and berries in bed by an unfamiliar shebeetle. "Good day, Mister Rod!" he shouted to the streaking Rod. Abacus wasn't missing Anisha too awfully and Rod was ready to burst from both ends, so he did not respond.

With the threat of a hygienic catastrophe increasing with every step, Rod passed another open bedroom door. The bed was undisturbed from the previous night and Jake's rucksack lay against the wall. The next open door was Yuyu's room. Her bed was undisturbed as well. Finally Rod reached the *binachu* door. He fell through the door, fell to his knees, and although he yelled for Jake, all that was heard were dragon cries, boiling mud pots, and several flushes of the toilet. Rod limped back to his bedroom with a spotty face.

"*Dut flooja!* Good mornings!" said cheery Romiel in passing.

"Where's Jake?"

"Thees I do not know. I imagine he eez with the Yuyu."

"Where's Yuyu!" Rod demanded, panting. His internal efficiency graph could not tolerate the thought of missing the train to Cherishio.

"I have not one idea, Rod. You would like one cup of coffee?"

"What TIME is it!" Rod gasped as he was hit by another wave of nausea and lower intestinal disarray. This time he did not make it to the *binachu* and his hygienic catastrophe came to fruition right there in front of Romiel, narrowly missing Romiel himself.

By the time Jake and Yuyu arrived home after climbing *Da Bufa*, Rod was cleaned up in fresh clothes, but experiencing the emotional distress of birth, puberty, and a midlife crisis, all distilled into the window of one half an hour.

"It's okay! It's okay! The train doesn't leave for another half an hour," insisted Jake.

"I don't think I can take another half an hour," Rod growled. Of course Romiel was connected and two bicycle charioteers materialized at the bottom of Romiel's alley the moment they emerged onto the cobblestone sidewalk.

Hand in hand, Yuyu and Jake floated into one of the chariots. Romiel sidled into the other, motioning for Abacus, a recuperating Slim, and Rod to join him. Rod, however, felt he should chaperone and scrunched in next to the floating love birds. Rod turned to begin the small talk but found Jake and Yuyu already engaged, their foreheads pressed together, smiling and whispering.

They reached the train station shack with hangovers redoubled from bouncing over cobblestones and found that the train to Cherishio, the Leischnogger Express, was behind schedule. "Thees eez so *unusual*," said Romiel with a smile and a wink to the counterbeetle. They had their tickets torn and ambled onto the boarding platform, a strip of dirt behind the station. Jake and Yuyu disappeared from sight, crouching behind a stack of hay bales.

Trains came and went, loosening what few spikes still held the rails to the ties. Few trains slowed, even fewer stopped, and none bore mention of Cherishio. "*Quio sant alloo pa Monzluma, Danzluma, luf Nonzlumaaaaaaaa!*" would yell the porters, hanging from open passenger cars. All of this waiting was like sandpaper on Rod's pancreas and an acidic broth crept up the back of his throat.

Once everyone was at peace with the idea of remaining on the dusty boarding platform forever, there appeared a primordial, pugnosed steam engine chugging its way to Valgato. Black with soot, clearly the engine was born deep within the gut of Nord. "*Quio sant alloo pa Pantuga, Limonchee, Helontha, luf Cherishioooooooooooooo!*" horned the mustachioed conductor, performing the impossible stunt of leaning his giant torso out of a window the size of a postage stamp.

"Cherishio. That's us," said Jake, mostly to himself. He held Yuyu's hand and looked up with eyes weary, teary, and anxious for what lie ahead.

Yuyu leaned over and whispered into Jake's ear. With a kiss on the lips, the pair sent a dream into future encounters and they stood up to join the others flitting about the platform.

The train bound for Cherishio slowed but did not stop. Several cars passed as the travelers and their Muzoran hosts stood waiting. Several more cars passed and the caboose came into view from around the bend. The cranky whine of metal on metal grew louder as the caboose loped past the party, but still did not stop.

"Are you staying?" asked Romiel, his hands clasped behind his back. Rod, Jake, and Abacus shot nervous glances to Romiel, Yuyu, each other, and the train that was moving farther and farther away. Abacus shook Romiel's hand, gave Yuyu a kiss, and began to run. Rod did the same, followed by Slim, tail waving as he ran. Somewhere ahead, the train sounded its whistle and began to pick up speed. Yuyu and Jake kissed in front of Romiel and squeezed each other tight. Tearing himself away, Jake thanked Romiel and took off at a sprint. A giant hand stopped Jake from behind. It was Romiel, who gave Jake a fatherly bear hug.

At top speed, Jake threw his pack to Rod and made a leap for it. Hanging on with just a thumb and index finger, Jake looked back to Yuyu. She was wearing an immense smile, standing with arms spread wide. Blowing kisses and waving, Jake watched through his blowing hair and burgeoning tears as Yuyu was reduced to a little white dot of light, and then to a memory.

The adventurers settled into a pair of vacant benches facing one another in Car 17. The benches shared a window tinted on the inside with smoke from tens of thousands of cigarettes, on the outside with smoke from coal fires that had fueled the Leischnogger Express for tens of thousands of miles.

Car 17 was occupied by large Muzoran families, small families of livestock, and vagrant minstrels bellying down the aisle, singing sonnets for a coin. Vendors selling peanuts or chewing gum would pass through chanting his or her sales shtick in a loop.

Once Rod felt safe, he relaxed and spent less time polishing Slim's urine off his shoe and more time focusing on the discomfort of his hangover. Highlights from the previous evening oozed from the misshapen pores of his mind. Slim's exaltation by the masses, fine bubbly, being treated like family, being treated like a lipstick magnet. Could it be that Muzorans were actually pretty decent after all? Gibbous Bizonia's constant war with Muzora was looking more and more absurd. Shocked at even considering the possibility of peace between nations, Rod drifted off into the train's low, steady wobble where he dreamed the impossible.

Rod dreamed he was walking home from his job at the dry cleaners with a two-headed beast on a leash. Rod and the beast dropped-in and bought a pair of trousers at the thrift shop before heading to their tiny home where Rod ate his rice and beans.

Chained in the back yard with crumbs from Gibbous Bizonia's loaf at its feet, the beast strained at the end of its leash. It was drooling over Muzora's loaf, visible at a distance. Rod watched through the kitchen window, washing his only spoon.

All of the neighbors were lined-up, laughing at Rod and his little house while their own homes grew larger with every breath. Smarmy neighbor Chet was trying to cut through the beast's chain with a hack saw. Rod felt a pang when every one of his neighbors bought palettes of disposable eight-slice toasters. After counting his savings and brushing his long, curly hair, Rod walked across town to Gino's Emporium, pulling the straining beast behind.

When they arrived, the beast was angrier than ever, clawing the ground with its many clawed hands, snapping at Muzoran immigrants. Gino's Emporium didn't allow pets. If Rod was going to land those new toasters, he would have to let the beast go, to devour what it may of the world.

Just as Rod's left hand was pushing open the door to Gino's and his right hand was letting go of the beast, Romiel Sando flew in from above, grabbing both Rod and beast. Romiel took them to a land where all the homes were small, two-slice toasters were passed down through generations, and Dorothy Tarnuckle waited in a sundress with nothing but time on her hands. The beast added some spice notes to its rice and beans and forgot about Muzora's loaf entirely.

Jake chose the bench that faced back towards the caboose, so as not to let thoughts of Yuyu fade in haste. Remembering Yuyu's exorbitant kiss in a stolen canoe, he wondered if perhaps there wasn't a God after all. Staring off through the blemished window, Jake could still see the crumbling fortress walls of Valgato and beyond them, *Da Bufa*. He began to play with the focus of his eyes and once again caught sight of a tiny, moving pinhole of light. These lights were definitely out there—or *in* there.

Was it possible to focus outwardly in order to see something that was inside of his own head? How was it impossible? Wasn't everything that he saw in the outside world ultimately just a projection upon his own mind? Little stinking white dots. Zillions of them. Jake's thoughts wandered in and out among the tiny white lights. "Perhaps now is the time," he wished into the lights, "for the dreamers to take *their* turn." With this thought, Jake gave in to his fatigue and lapsed into dream.

Jake dreamed he was in a coal mine, working long hours alongside other geniuses and dreamers. He and his coworkers were doing what baybeetlekind had been doing since its inception— providing the means for their existence.

Jake dreamed that after eons of technological and economic development, the world above the mines had become congested with supercomputers and festering piles of money. The means available to their species had runneth over, but everything was in all of the wrong places. Planet Nord was dying because of it.

# THE EXPRESS

The geniuses and dreamers in the coal mines had workable plans to rectify Nord and its baybeetles. They saw a Nord that was healthy, beautiful, and peaceful. They saw a content baybeetle race no longer in a state of constant war, no longer engaged in meaningless work. There were more than enough means available above ground to fulfill the dreams, but the dreams continued to drown in the sweat of the coal mines. It was time for the means to serve the dreams.

Through half-closed eyes, Abacus basked in the aftertaste of a full night's binge. These Muzorans did nurture a merry heart and he had gotten a little crazy. "All work and no play makes for a very greasy chimp," Abacus' father would say.

Abacus looked across to Jake and Slim, curled up into each other. Rod was dreaming with his head cocked on Abacus' shoulder. Such a plight for these three Bizonians. Jake in his genuine concern for Nord, its beauty and variety. Rod in his genuine concern for his little brother and in his buried desire to enjoy life. Calm Slim. Each in his own way was yearning for peace, or at the very least, a way to avoid the next Great War—a war that may have already begun. Rod released a watery grunt just inches from Abacus' ear.

Removing his shoulder, Abacus buttressed Rod's head with his walking stick and slipped into the aisle. A few cars down the line, Abacus reached the caboose. The door at its tail was unlatched.

Hands gripping the rusty rear guardrail, Abacus watched as the Express kicked up dust and dry leaves that traveled along with the Express in its wake of disturbed air. Like the dry leaves caught in the draft of the speeding caboose, Abacus had seen the baybeetles of Gibbous Bizonia keeping pace with their manic society, their always changing fashions and devices, their magic run amuck. Few Bizonians ever noticed that they were caught in this draft, for like the storm of leaves and dust behind the train, everything in the draft moved together. Nobody knew or even cared in what direction they were moving.

Abacus was born and raised in a culture that had existed essentially unchanged for tens of thousands of years. He was well off the tracks which carried the speeding train of modern Bizonian society. Just as a leaf on a tree growing off the tracks of the Express would think the behavior of leaves caught behind the train an unworldly anomaly, Abacus found the behavior of modern Bizonia an unworldly anomaly, and not altogether healthy.

Brooding over this, Abacus watched the land trail away towards the horizon from which they had come. When he tired, Abacus returned to his seat and plopped Rod's head back onto his shoulder. Rod's mucus shifted accordingly.

Shifting his attention from Rod's mucus to the downy tufts of Slim's ears, Abacus was led to his concern for his cat friend and respected overseer, Tyrone. What dark magic was it that would entrap Tyrone, a harmless figurehead of free, intelligent beings? Had the nasty spell afflicting Tyrone spread to engulf broader expanses of Vivachanga since he, Abacus, last trod there? Where was his tribe of nomads now? Had the spell taken any of his kin?

After witnessing the galvanized chaos that was the nation of Gibbous Bizonia, Abacus began to wonder if his appointed mission wasn't pure folly. What power had Tyrone that could possibly stop onrushing Gibbous Bizonia? Perhaps his mission was merely a gift given him by Tyrone—the gift of diverting one's eyes from the suffering of one's own tribe.

A Great War, potentially the most ruthless excrement of the mysterious spell, was unavoidable. Muzora was acquiring the secrets of ultimately destructive magic and Gibbous Bizonia was not afraid to use what darkness it already possessed. What future could be worthwhile in the aftermath of such global massacre?

Nord was doomed.

In his mind, Abacus saw a small, hard seed. In the fast-paced mayhem of Gibbous Bizonia, how were seeds to find still, fertile soil—the seeds that rested within each and every baybeetle, the seeds of visions and dreams, the seeds of each soul's purpose? How were these seeds to take root and grow? Gibbous Bizonia would never change. If Bizonia never changed, Nord would be driven to its demise.

His thoughts spiraling around dying seeds, Abacus sank into sleep, into the light of darkness. He dreamed he heard the crying of an unsprouted seed. The seed was wailing in the dark about the hell that was its darkness. "Why are you doing this to me?" it cried, "I curse you for depriving me of light!" The seed's name was Abacus.

Abacus recoiled as he jerked awake. Rod's head bounced and he was nearly aroused from his stupor.

"Think of the light," Abacus said to himself, his heart racing, "Speak of the light." Nord was in a bind, but spending his energy crying over the darkness was akin to a seed spending its energy crying over the dirt in which it was buried. Wasn't he, Abacus, thinking like a still buried seed lamenting the black soil that would provide it with life?

The material world was constantly being created by the nonmaterial world, the world of words and thoughts. "To think that I should pollute the river of language," Abacus mused. A contest of words had been in motion since baybeetles had first learned to speak. There was no right or wrong in this contest of words, however, with their thoughts and with their speech, baybeetles were all creating their own reality. Life was a series of self-fulfilling prophecies.

With or without the next war, Nord was a heaving seed, ready to crack. The planet had only recently been unified by trade, travel, and communication. If one were to tell a tiny seed, blind in the darkness, that it was to become a giant sequoia, towering and drenched in sunlight, would the seed believe? Might not the limitless ingenuity of baybeetles, even in Gibbous Bizonia, allow for seeds to take root despite limitless adversity?

Thinking and speaking negatively towards a world yet to be born made no more sense than lambasting a newborn baby for crying or for not understanding magnetism. Nord was on the brink of a growing season and growth always involved destruction—the cracking of a seed, the shedding of the skin. If everyone allowed the next Great War to happen or if they were helpless against its unfolding, perhaps this would not be the end, but a painful beginning. Perhaps the Great War would be the pain of birth, the painful cracking open of the seed, the seed destined to grow into a beautiful, peaceful, content Nord.

"Vivachanga is everywhere, even in Gibbous Bizonia," whispered Abacus. With this comforting thought, Abacus' heart warmed and he joined the others in hypnotized slumber.

Though his unknotted tail remained tender, Slim was grateful for the train ride and the opportunity to let his thoughts flow. It had been a hectic journey leaving little time for reflection. As his stiffness of tail abated, Slim deepened his contemplation of a recent, profound dream.

In this dream, Slim could feel the warmth churning in his heart. He was able to stoke these heart flames until his chest was burning with love. Standing on his hind legs with his head tilted back and his front paws stretched towards the sky, Slim thrust his heart fire straight up through his head and he took flight.

Slim's dream flight was perfectly streamlined until he began to over think things. He began to wonder how and why he was flying and whether or not he could sustain his flight. He began to exert unnecessary effort. This worry and effort, this loss of confidence, only diverted Slim's flight trajectory, slowing him down and eventually bringing him back down to solid Nord.

This was the end of the dream, but only the beginning of Slim's analysis.

Slim was aware of the fact that in the vacuous reaches of outer space, where the effects of gravity were least evident, an object set in motion with initial effort continued at speed along its path indefinitely, without any additional effort. On planet Nord, where the effects of gravity were most evident, all of the friction that came with gravity resulted in what one called life. Due to all of the ambient friction on Nord, no longer was initial effort sufficient to maintain physical motion indefinitely. But Slim was not easily fooled. It was not due to friction or the force of gravity that Slim's flight was snuffed.

Simply because the coagulating influence of gravity had become massively apparent over a miniscule portion of the universe—on planet Nord—this by no means canceled the universal law of initial effort. The material universe was created by the nonmaterial universe and the law of initial effort transcended the material universe. Slim was beginning to confuse even himself, but he could not help but to reason that when one had a heartfelt vision and the courage to set it into motion, all one had to do was let it be.

There was no need to over think it.

There was no reason in worry.

The worrisome thoughts in our pea-sized conscious minds paled in comparison to the wisdom of our vast subconscious and the wisdom of our heart.

Satisfied with the quality of his analysis, Slim joined Abacus and the others in Dreamland.

They slept through several towns. At each town the train grew shorter, dropping the dead weight of unoccupied passenger cars. The Express dropped down to just the pug-nosed engine and three cars at Twig Station. One hour later, upon departure from Revone, the Leischnogger Express consisted of no more than the engine and Car 17—no caboose, no livestock, no musicians. The derelict operation parted the increasingly sultry Muzoran countryside, deeper into the *nooshtah*, the unknown.

After burning the last of its fuel, the Leischnogger Express coasted and eventually came to rest in a bank of sand drifting over the end of the line. "*Cherishiooooooooooooooo!*" called the conductor.

Our travelers and one old, gray hebeetle, who had fallen asleep with a leaning bag of peanuts on his lap, were the only ones to reach

# THE EXPRESS

Cherishio. They were all awakened by the shouting of the conductor. The old, gray hebeetle took one look out the window, rolled over, and went back to sleep on a cushion of spilled peanuts.

The Bizonians were surprised and a little concerned by the solitude of their arrival. They gathered their belongings, took rich breaths of sea air, and stepped outside of the mechanized world.

"I'll hail a cab."

"Mister Rod," said Abacus, "you will note that there are no roads here."

"What's all this dirt?" asked Rod.

"It's sand," replied Jake.

"What's that noise?" asked Rod.

"That noise is the ocean, Mister Rod," replied Abacus.

Rod had been too young to remember his family trips to the coast and by the time he reached early puberty, his paperwork and grooming rituals would not allow for frivolous weekends. "WHAT *TIME* IS IT?" he bellowed.

# CHAPTER TWELVE

# Beyond the Iron Sea

Small and relaxed, a prandali stared unblinking into an aurora of flame, tiny feet unwavering on a white-hot shelf of coals. All around the prandali, other prandalia were emerging one by one. Born of the flame and to die with it, the prandalia began to dance. Enthralled with the moment, pirouettes and cartwheels were executed effortlessly. From a distance, the bloom of orange-glowing prandalia, for its sheer numbers and complex movements, was easily mistaken for combusting gases racing across split timbers.

At the peak of its madness, the prandali in question scissor-jumped to the edge of its charring shelf, deep within the fire. Looking down, it saw a sheer face of incinerating wood. The prandali thrust both hands into the air and without hesitation, dove with a twist into the unknown. A rage of heat from below shot the arching, glowing prandali skyward. A fraction of a second later, the luminous prandali was extinguished, frozen black in the balmy air.

"Amen!" shouted Abacus into the cozy silence around the campfire. A lone dog in the distance let out a deep howl.

Abacus launched to his feet, dancing around the fire. One would not have guessed that Abacus used a walking stick in the city. By the looks on their faces, Abacus realized that the brothers were baffled. He sat back down on his driftwood. "The first prandali," he said, eyes widening with a grin.

"The first what?" asked Jake.

"The first prandali. The performance, the life and death of the prandalia has begun. Did you not see the first dancer erupt from the campfire?"

"That was just a spark," said Rod.

"*Just* a spark?" Smiling, Abacus looked down and shook his head. For those who claimed dominion over Nord and all of Mother Nature, Bizonians certainly had a lot to learn.

The dog howled again as the fire popped and a shower of prandalia shot into the air, disappearing over the campfire. Abacus shot up and waved his hands in the air with a holler.

After deboarding the Express, the foursome had wandered the sands in search of Cherishio proper. Only by following Abacus' nose for seafood did they eventually meander through the cluster of mud huts that was the municipality of Cherishio.

Rod was exhausted and ready to lie, cheat, and steal his way into luxury. Located at the end of the world, the best lodging that Cherishio had to offer was a clean dirt floor. Rod insisted that they keep looking for the upscale neighborhood—maybe they could land a couch or a hot tub, or something besides a stick of wood to use as a pillow. This search only left them lost and entangled in jungle, bitten at by ants and barbed vines. Conceding to what Abacus and Jake had been suggesting all along, a campfire on the beach, Rod returned his vile of cologne to his back pocket along with his hopes of landing a five star massage.

The night was warm and exquisite with starlight. Even Jake had never imagined so many stars visible to the naked eye. Within minutes of deciding upon a spot, Abacus had kindled a fire and prepared the mollusks given them by the inhabitants of Cherishio. "In Vivachanga," he said, "we greatly appreciate an appearance by the prandalia. Their presence portends the revelation of truth."

BEYOND THE IRON SEA

Abacus' gaze deepened, penetrating the white heart of the fire. An entire family of prandalia perished into darkness. Knowing that all eyes were now on the prandalia, Abacus added, "Some of them make sweet love as they ascend."

The brothers looked at each other. Rod noticed that even Jake did think their guide a few peas shy of a pod. In the scant, rich light, Abacus was seen to cock his head towards the sky. Looking to planet Manx shining red among the stars, his attention swung intensely back into the fire. "Jake. Rod. There are some things you must know.

"We baybeetles are not who we think we are."

Jake and Rod were silent with fear.

"It was from our beginning as humble, unexpected guests on Nord," Abacus continued, "that we baybeetles turned and began to think of ourselves as something special. We began considering ourselves as superior creatures, above the rest of nature. In reality, we were, and we remain, lost in space.

"Before the arrival of the baybeetles, planet Nord had served the cycles of nature in robust fashion for eons. Everybody was eating everybody else, as they continue to do today, but the overall system was never significantly altered for the worse by any one species. Now, one single species of animal, the baybeetle, is degrading the entire planet all by itself. Forests that have stood for millennia are being shaved down to the ground. Sister Ocean is losing all of her fish. The air is thick and species are being driven to extinction by the tens of thousands.

"All the while, as we spend generations huddled behind divisive walls, the truth has remained unchanged." Abacus' eyes brightened and lifted to the brothers' faces. "The cats are letting us stay."

Slim nodded, solemn.

In the firelight, the color of the three baybeetles' skins were indistinguishable one from the other. "You see," continued Abacus, "you and I come from the same source. Although we have grown to differ in our outward appearance, our ancestors are the very same baybeetles. The story of our origin has been passed down through the ages to me, and I am here to share it with you.

"It all begins hundreds of thousands of years ago with an accidental incident.

"A pod of suckling baybeetles was maturing in the weightlessness of outer space, as baybeetles have done for time immemorial. These sucklings were readying to detach themselves from their pod and become the weightless, angelic travelers that they were always meant to be. That is when the pod got caught in the gravitational pull of planet Nord.

"The fetal baybeetles were lucky to have survived their womb-like pod's collision with planet Nord. Luckier still, they landed in a warm, incubatory climate. Their new world was rich with honey."

With these words, Rod's head began to reel, remembering his traumatic dreams. He had dreamed the collision, the honey hunt, the beast.

"As beasts great and small closed in around us, us dazed and tender creatures," continued Abacus, "the cats dropped from the trees. The cats knew of our true, angelic nature and protected us with their ferocity and respected reputation.

"The cats knew that the maturing of these baybeetles would be slow and arduous under the influence of Nord's gravity. They would be potentially dangerous to themselves and to the planet as a whole.

"Despite this, it was decided that these Nord-bound baybeetles shall live."

Upon reflection, Jake replied, "Abacus. This is complete bullshit."

Rod was wondering if a womb-like pod wouldn't by necessity contain a central yolk sack.

Abacus took a slug from the skin of wine given them in Cherishio and passed the bloated hide to Jake. "Life on Nord remained harmonious, Jake," continued Abacus, "during these early days. With help from our animal friends, we learned to survive without destroying our forest and without creating economic divides between those of our own kind. Violence was confined to verbal lashings and an occasional blow to the thorax. We were possessed of celestial minds and we were passionately curious about our environment.

"What difference does it make, Mister Jake, whether baybeetles arrived on the wings of an errant space pod, as the product of evolution from a single ancient amoeba, or with the sudden, divine creation of the entire universe? Nord, home to us all, is burning."

When the first Muzoran laid foot on the other continent—the land that would one day become Gibbous Bizonia—he thought it just one of the many small inhabited islands off the west coast of Muzora. This first Muzoran in the New World was named Ernest Byzontho. Ernest was a lean fisherbeetle from a quaint fishing settlement just outside the walls of medieval Hevzladon.

Ernest's morning had started off like any other, with a bowl of sardines and mango, before shoving his dinghy off into the breakers. Ernest's dinghy soon encountered uncanny ocean swells. No match for the sea, the dinghy ran astray, landing Ernest on an unfamiliar coastline.

Ernest pulled his empty craft up onto the sand. He would have to wait out the shifting seas by taking rest under his hat and mending his nets. Head down with crusty fingers, Ernest began to check one knot at a time. His work was slow, not only because he kept lifting his gaze to read the tides, but because he kept turning to look inland, not knowing why.

As he twisted and spliced cords stained green from seaweed, Ernest grew stronger and more cheerful. With a sense of energized abandon, he dropped his labors to explore the coast and talk to the locals.

Before reaching the nearest village, Ernest came to a river pouring into the sea. There was no bridge. Through the gap in the forest left by the course of the river, Ernest saw a distant, tree-covered hill. The hill was perfect, not one branch on any tree out of place. He had never seen such a thing. Every other hill in Muzora had either been covered with dwellings, denuded of trees, or both.

Having reached the impasse that the river provided, Ernest took one more look at the perfect hill and started back towards his dinghy. This time, as he walked along the edge of the coastal forest, he was looking for a sign, any sign, of baybeetlekind—a path, a hut, a column of smoke, even just a footprint. By the time Ernest reached his boat, he had seen none of these things. He was standing on a living remnant of the Age of Nature and he knew it. It felt wonderful. Ernest waited for the seas to fall and paddled back home to share the news of a pristine paradise, an uninhabited New World.

There were, of course, many Muzorans in Hevzladon and beyond who took a keen interest in the New World. Competition in Muzora for scarce natural resources had already become fierce. Shortly after the Sigman Fur Trading Company and Gino's Tobacco established outposts in the New World, Ernest Byzontho himself stole a wife and settled there as well.

At the ribbon-cutting ceremony officially naming the new land Byzontia in honor of its discoverer, a six-gun salute and brass band were abruptly silenced when at the edge of the clearing there appeared a small party of nearly naked baybeetles. They wore nothing but loin cloths, feathers, and seashells. They carried a slaughtered boar as large as a stallion while balancing baskets of fresh produce on the tops of their heads. The strangers smiled, placed their offerings on the ground, and went to work digging an oven to cook the boar.

When Ernest greeted the strangers, he discovered that they were deranged and unable to speak the Muzoran mother tongue. Despite the fact that these strangers were savages, a grand party was had by all.

Raised in a compassionate household, Ernest befriended the naked strangers and would go with them on extended picnics throughout the island's interior. On his third picnic, the strangers led Ernest to the apex of a hill with a view. Byzontia, the New World, was no small island. "So many resources, so little time," whispered Ernest, blushing with the honor and the responsibility. On the same outing, the strangers brought Ernest to their settlement. These strangers were no lost detachment of deranged Muzorans, they were a civilization, natives long established in the New World.

These generous natives proved easy enough to kill off.

Their lack of advanced weaponry.

Their susceptibility to disease.

The few natives who survived made very nice slaves, so the ranches and plantations of Byzontia thrived. There was such abundance in the New World that a few generations after the discovery of Byzontia, its Muzoran transplants saw no advantage in retaining their social and political ties with the motherland. They warred for independence, created their own language, and sold off the spoils of the New World to the highest bidder. The new continent was stripped of all things good and in time was no longer recognizable as the pristine wonder found by Ernest Byzontho. The dams on the rivers alone had disrupted the entire cycle of life.

Reared in these muddled, horse-drawn days of Olde Byzontia, a young hebeetle brooded by candlelight in his stone bedroom, discontent. "'Tis lovely," he mumbled sarcastically, "that mine own baybeetles have wrought such a vulgar fate upon this land's native population. We have destroyed the natives down to the very last teaspoon."

This young hebeetle was a fearless, idealistic young fellow.

His name was Woodrow Happyhouse.

The Happyhouse family had been proprietors of a successful Byzontian rat farm since the times of Woodrow's great-grandfather, Jeremiah Happyhouse. Woodrow was groomed to inherit governorship of the rat farm and its slaves, and his time to take the reins was drawing near.

Woodrow, however, had other ideas.

Woodrow was interested in freedom.

In the process of milking Byzontia's resources to turn the nation into Nord's top military and economic power, the continent was run under and there was no longer any freedom to be found. Since infancy, however, Woodrow had been entranced by tales of the mythical paradise of Vivachanga, a land that was the last vestige of the long forgotten Age of Nature. These tales of Vivachanga and the

Age of Nature were kept alive only through the lyrics of melancholy folk songs, songs kept alive only by a thin film of folk musicians who had become as strange as the songs themselves.

The folk songs told of peaceful tribes living in a harmonious world rich with species, both plant and animal. It was sung that freedom—the concept of going where, when, and how one pleased—was so commonplace in Vivachanga that its natives did not even have a word for it. Woodrow felt that it was his destiny to try and find this Vivachanga. He would either find it or prove that it did not exist.

Woodrow wreaked havoc on the hearts of his family by denouncing his claim to the throne of Happyhouse Rat Farms. He then grabbed a bag of oats and traveled across the Rutmus Strait to the land of Muzora where he wandered as a vagabond. Woodrow acquired the Muzoran tongue and sought clues as to the possible whereabouts of Vivachanga. He found that with the Muzorans, as with his Byzontian countrybeetles, Vivachanga was all but forgotten.

It wasn't until he reached the dusty recesses of a hamlet of guitar luthiers that Woodrow finally encountered a lead in the form of an ancient healer. The ancient shebeetle sat Woodrow down and said unto him, "Strike into the unknown, white boy, and there you shall find Vivachanga."

Although Woodrow had hoped for a trail map and a guide, these wise words would have to suffice. Woodrow paid the woman with a bottle of tequila and was out the door.

Woodrow returned to Olde Byzontia and nearly destroyed his mind and body constructing a seaworthy vessel, the ship that would carry him into the greatest of unknowns—the Iron Sea. Although nobody in Woodrow's time had dared the venture, it was believed that beyond the Iron Sea one would plummet off the edge of Nord to drift in space to the death. Woodrow, however, sensed that Vivachanga *must* be out there.

Promising rewards of glory and a Vivachangan bride, Woodrow was unable to coerce even the lowliest criminal into risking a plummet off the edge of the world. Woodrow would sail alone. With more scorn than fanfare, Woodrow smashed a bottle of cheap Chianti against the hull of the Santa McClovery and at high tide he shouldered the craft into the sea.

Acting as both captain and crew, Woodrow ran madly from stem to stern, helm to galley, poop deck to crow's nest, barking orders all the while. "Reel in the flying jib!" "Let fly the spanker!" "Oil the captain's teak!"

After six days and seven nights of Woodrow's unceasing vigilance, the Santa McClovery began to take on water. Liquor and food rations were running dry. Woodrow mutinied and nearly walked the plank at the tip of his own dagger. Standing on the deck in dawn's first light, bloodied and bandaged after a lashing from a giant squid in the dead of night, Woodrow began to weep.

It was for the wash of tears that Woodrow could hardly distinguish land from sea.

He wiped his eyes.

When Woodrow became certain that he saw on the horizon not the brutal, unforgiving end of the world, but the smooth ocean horizon ruffled by a string of toobler trees, he fell overboard with joy. The rails of the Santa McClovery weren't so high, however, that Woodrow couldn't vault from the flukes of his dolphin friend, back onto his vessel.

After a change of wardrobe, Woodrow began to celebrate with the last of his rum. The rum was strong at the bottom of the barrel and Woodrow got wrecked. Unwittingly, he smashed the Santa McClovery to pieces on the only rocks within miles on the otherwise white and sandy coastline. Drunk, wet, weary, and elated, Woodrow staggered ashore in the shadows of the toobler trees and passed out with a mouthful of sand.

Were it not for the diminutive Vivachangans who found Woodrow's bedraggled body, he would have perished overnight, eaten by armies of sand crabs. When Woodrow opened his eyes to see a circle of small, chocolate brown baybeetles leaning over him, silhouetted against the forest canopy, he was simultaneously thrilled and panicked. Panic was promptly consumed by the beauty of the Vivachangan ways and the beauty of the land.

Not only did Vivachanga exist, but Woodrow had found it. Not only had he found it, but the tales were true. The land was in pristine condition, virtually unaltered by the baybeetles who lived there. The Vivachangans were peaceful, strong, and graceful, just like in the folk songs. They had next to nothing in the way of personal possessions—a singular stick pushed into the ground would be a family's home—but they were more content than any other baybeetles on Nord. They remained content even after Woodrow accidentally trampled seven homes in the throes of his welcome party.

Years passed.

Woodrow taught his friends to speak Olde Byzontian.

The Vivachangans taught Woodrow how to provide for himself efficiently and in ways that did not destroy the natural balance. The greater portion of most days was spent on sport, art, worship, and leisure. Woodrow had no means nor desire to return to the enslavement of Olde Byzontia. An explorer at heart, Woodrow would use his lax schedule to strike out into the Vivachangan wilds and be gone for days and weeks on end, nibbling as he went.

Freedom.

It was on just such an outing that Woodrow happened across a hebeetle making his way through the woods, muttering to himself in a backcountry Muzoran dialect. Woodrow approached this individual only to learn the most absurd and intriguing news. This was not a stranded, disturbed adventurer like himself, but a fur trapper from the Muzoran village of Zapuco, a day's walk from where they now stood.

Shocked and homesick, Woodrow followed the path described by the Muzoran trapper. Two days later, he found the quiet, thoroughly Muzoran village of Zapuco. The citizens of Zapuco treated Woodrow to meals and a soft place to sleep, despite thinking him dangerously delusional with his stories of the purely mythical Vivachangans. Sensing his hosts' discomfort, Woodrow excused himself from Zapuco after three days of confusion and made haste to his Vivachangan brothers and sisters.

In his search for Vivachanga, Woodrow had inadvertently proved that there was no drop-off at the edge of Nord. He had sailed around the world, traversed the Iron Sea, and found Vivachanga on the far side of Muzora. The profundity of Woodrow's discovery was relentless. Dreams of oranges and coconuts bombarding his Byzontian homeland stole his sleep. After much soul searching,

# BEYOND THE IRON SEA

Woodrow decided to bid farewell to his beloved Vivachangans and return, over land via Muzora, to Byzontia.

Once back in Byzontia, Woodrow wasted no time in grandstanding his discoveries. "Nord is round like an orange or a coconut!" he cried, "We are tiny, anchorless, afloat in the vastness of space." For his efforts, Woodrow was found guilty of subversion and sentenced to seven years in a leper colony.

Three years into his sentence, Woodrow was knighted by the Byzontian throne for discovering the Remote Extraction Zone and opening up new markets for big time Olde Byzontian swindlers. Sir Woodrow was sent home where he spent the remaining four years of his sentence under house arrest, still considered a threat to the status quo.

Happyhouse's fate from this point forward would be cloaked in mystery. Some say he married in Muzora and spent his days as a tormented artist striving to paint the perfect loaf of bread. Others say he went mad in a small corner of Byzontia, editing and re-editing his memoirs, perishing in poverty. A loose but well-educated pocket of youth in modern Gibbous Bizonia calling themselves "The Guild" claimed that Woodrow returned to live out his days in Vivachanga, to be recounted in myth as the elusive White Giant.

Whether he stayed to the end of his days in Vivachanga or not, it is certain that Woodrow made the return journey there on at least one occasion. Woodrow's love and concern for his Vivachangan family prompted him to drag a chest of goods to Vivachanga, a chest that he left in the care of Abacus' direct ancestors. Among the goods in the chest were Abacus' sheepskin map of Nord and an assortment of other bound scrolls.

By the light of the beach campfire, Abacus reached into his vest pocket. Rod tensed. This would surely be the moment when Abacus at last drew his musket. Unarmed, Abacus revealed another scroll. He handed it to Rod to read aloud. "I have yet to acquire the gift," Abacus confirmed, "of moving the written word from parchment into mine throat."

Rod took Abacus' scroll in his left hand, pinching and pulling at its satin ribbon. With a light cackle, the parchment unraveled to the howling of Cherishio's dog. The dog was louder, nearer. Rocking the document, penned in meticulous block letters, towards the bonfire flames, Rod began. "Ye friends of Vivachanga. A warning.

"The society of Byzontia from which I hale hath fallen from balance. It hath come to be at odds with the natural environment of our dear Nord. Honourable Vivachangans, thou hast yet to be encumbered by what shall come if Byzontia stays its course.

"Byzontia lives alone by choice upon its rock, turning shoulder to what exists in the rest of the known world. Turning shoulder even to its own Mother Nature—she who does coddle us and she who shall mete out our punishment.

"We of Byzontia destroy Nature herself in folly. Meaningless gadgets mold we from crushed and bleeding Nord. These gadgets, our Mother Nord, fail and become rubbish, rubbish that comes to rest in our plagued gutters. Upon the acquisition of these gadgets, we base our wealth and status.

"The destruction of Mother Nord transpires beyond the walls of our cities, Vivachangans, walls you do not yet know. The Mother is torn apart and run under far from the view of the city dweller. The Mother is then carted inside our walls to be disguised as products to be turned into rubbish. Our city dwellers know not the price exacted upon their own Mother for the goods they do consume. This situation of which I speak is so simple and yet so distressing upon the mind.

"If my Byzontian countrybeetles fail to embrace the fact that they inhabit a round, limited planet, the beauty that is Vivachanga is sure to be challenged. The challenges to Vivachanga will be the axes, the hammers, the roads, the chariots, and the smelters of Byzontia. This is kinda long don't you think?"

"C'mon, Rod. You're almost done," egged Jake.

"Okay, okay...the roads, the chariots, and the smelters of Byzontia. The baybeetles of Byzontia shall arrive in your lands wearing smiles upon their faces. Yet, as they know not the consequences of their pillage, their smiles shall flatten and their eyes shall narrow when the Byzontians are denied the spoils of your land. Beware the war machines of my compatriots, friends. There is great, dark magic at play.

"Take heed and may this warning, this map, and these goods serve you well. May the gift of language serve as a bridge to the heart of Heaven for all of Vivachanga and indeed for all of life upon this precious, precious Nord.

"Signed, Sir Woodrow Happyhouse. That was a real pain to read in this light, I'll have ya know."

"What does it say on the back?" asked Jake, folding the scroll, drawing attention to a scribbling in longhand on the back side.

"Hmm. Let's see here," said Rod, "Since I'm on a roll, it says...I have seen a baby Beast. It carries two heads upon one body. One head holds a benevolent countenance, yet its words instill fear and conjure untruths. The other head wears the angry scowl of war and destruction—it does not conceal its voracious intentions. The eyes of both heads sink fermented and blind. In both comforting and instilling fear, the Beast pushes baybeetles into emotional paralysis. In this paralysis, we see no trouble in consuming our own freedom and our own happiness."

"Whoa," said Jake, struck dumb after Rod's reading of the Happyhouse parchment. "Abacus, you have mentioned something about a beast before. Were you referring to the same kind of beast that Happyhouse saw?"

Abacus looked sick. "Young Jake, this passage on the reverse of Woodrow's warning has never, until tonight, been deciphered and given voice. This passage was assumed 'til now to be nothing more than ornament." Abacus again examined the longhand, harried script on the back of Woodrow's warning. "In fact, for many years both sides of the document were believed to be nothing more than filigree. My culture has no written language, no need for holding words with ink."

"Have you seen a beast?" asked Jake.

Abacus hesitated, "Until now, only in dream. But I do not disbelieve."

"Do you think the beast is the one who cast this spell?" asked Rod, reliving the beast in his own dreams. Rod handed the wine skin to Abacus, who took a pull.

With his bare hand, Abacus grabbed a flaming log that had fallen from the fire and tossed it back in. "As I said before," he answered, "Tyrone is the sole proprietor of this knowledge. For you and I, the correct course of investigation is not to unravel what beast cast this spell, but rather to unravel who or what is creating the beast itself."

BEYOND THE IRON SEA

∾⊚

For seven years and counting, in basement bedrooms and cluttered attics across Bottom Junction, The Guild had been gathering to conduct its high business. As a founding member of The Guild, Jake would be there, as would Garth, Jasmine, Barbara, Zander, Raven, and a circle of others—some roomies, some not— dressed mostly in second-hand. Ten to twenty members of The Guild along with ten to twenty six-packs would show up at most meetings. The Guild, short for The Guild of The Shift, was composed of forty-three lifetime members, all told. Sir Woodrow Happyhouse was the reason for the Guild's existence.

Jake and the rest of The Guild spent their energy researching the life and times of Sir Woodrow Happyhouse, believing that the discoveries and insights of Happyhouse would prove profoundly beneficial for all of baybeetlekind. The Guild believed that the repercussions of Happyhouse's existence were only just beginning to manifest themselves on small Nord.

The Guild stressed open-mindedness. Before the return of Happyhouse to Olde Byzontia, there were many in Woodrow's time who never would have believed that Nord could be round. There were the few, however, who did not *disbelieve* in the *potential* roundness of Nord. These few could not have known if Nord was flat or round, but at least their minds were open to the possibilities within the unknown.

When Happyhouse did return to Olde Byzontia from his round-the-world journey, proving Nord to be at least a cylinder if not a sphere, those who believed that Nord could only be flat were shown to be more foolhardy than their open-minded counterparts. The Guild refused to unquestioningly accept the "truths" given them by their elders, the media, and other institutions. They refused to join the ranks of the foolhardy without a fight. Perhaps certain concepts deemed "unbelievable" or "impossible" even in the Space Age would prove to be absolute truths at some point in the future.

The Guild of the Shift chose its name from what they coined "The Great Shift in Consciousness From Flat Thinking to Spherical Thinking". When discussing the Great Shift, The Guild identified ongoing changes in the baybeetle mind which were occurring as a result of the discovery that Nord is round.

Baybeetle thought had been evolving for more than a hundred thousand years. For the vast majority of this evolution, most did not care about the shape of Nord. At best, they believed Nord to be flat, stretching endlessly beyond every horizon or ending in great drop-offs at the edges of the Iron Sea. This flat pattern of thinking led to the belief that one could set out to conquer others in any direction and continue to conquer in that direction without circling the planet and conquering one's self from the rear.

Little thought was spent on the idea that Nord's natural resources might have a very distinct limit. Little thought was spent on the idea that all baybeetles were one great family, bottled together on Nord, afloat in the cosmos.

According to members of The Guild, Gibbous Bizonia—the dominant nation on modern Nord—had indeed begun to conquer itself from the rear, both physically and metaphorically. That Muzora, Bizonia's archenemy, had acquired knowledge of the darkest, most destructive Bizonian magic was only proof of this. That the Age of Nature had long passed was proof of this as well. In the eyes of The Guild, the destruction of Nord's natural systems was not only "conquering one's self from the rear" but in that, also a form of suicide.

The Guild stressed that the shift to spherical thinking or simply "The Shift" *is* drastic. Relative to the eons of flat thinking, the world had only known it was round for the blink of an eye—a few hundred years. The roundness of Nord still rested only superficially upon the collective baybeetle mind. The consequences of life on a round planet still lie utterly uninvestigated.

The Guild stressed the importance of waking up to the great hope that came with the current era in Nord's history. How could one not find hope in the world when the world had only recently become small and understandable, albeit dirty? Before Happyhouse it was easy to think of other groups of baybeetles as distinct from one's own. As the new realization took hold—the realization that Nord was only very small and round—the lines between tribes would begin to blur. Similarities between baybeetles would become greater than their differences.

The Guild stressed the infinite nature of the mind and, in turn, the infinite number of options available for action or inaction at any given moment. It was stressed that peace, communication, and simply waiting were all viable options—personally, politically, and otherwise. Flat thinking had evolved only to the point that standoffishness and violence were the dominant options for conflict resolution.

Despite its general state of warfare, Nord *had* seen periods of general peace between baybeetles. The Guild believed that once the realization of roundness took hold, these periods of peace would expand and multiply as the multitudes of nonviolent options for action were given more serious consideration.

The Guild refused to place blame on any one individual or group of individuals for the ridiculous violence and destruction of their age. Were they to hold captive the entire process of history? A history that was responsible for the creation of all of the minds and all of the decisions of modern baybeetles? Overall, baybeetle evolution had earned high marks for moving everything along as far as it had.

The Guild held as truth that the world could change overnight, be engulfed by a wave of energy so large that any tiny Nord would be but a sardine at the mercy of the Iron Sea. Here sat Jake with a hebeetle from Vivachanga who possessed a document and a map penned by Happyhouse himself. Were Jake ever to make it home— past the travails of Tyrone, past war in Muzora, and past Yuyu's loving arms—The Guild would of necessity create a media sensation to resurrect the peaceful spirit of Happyhouse. Jake chose to travel light, but now regretted having left his camera at home in his nightstand.

"If you have noticed," said Abacus, his pronounced cheekbones sharp in the firelight, "geese or ducks in a flock tend to land upon the water simultaneously, regardless of the complexity of their formation in flight." Rod nodded in agreement. "We must therefore be alert. In Vivachanga we say that when baybeetlekind falls from its natural divinity, the gods descend from the heavens to lift us back up. I should suppose that as a flock of geese lands, so do the gods. At any given moment, with the creation of any given song, the gods may surround us and surge from within us to remind us of who we really are and why we are really here.

"You see, my friends, I have told that the cats know of our true identity. We call ourselves the baybeetles, but the cats call us the

Mreeow, the Dreamers. We are only here to observe, enjoy, and dream."

Later that night, after conversation had died along with the bonfire flames, Rod was unable to sleep, let alone dream, under the influence of so much wine and information. As his companions slumbered, Rod squeezed himself out from under his quilt, skivvies tight. He ambled through the warm sand towards the coo of the ocean. The powdery sands grew firm and moist beneath his toes. To keep tabs on their modest encampment, Rod turned around and took three backward steps.

The pressure from Rod's footsteps disturbed minute creatures permeating the damp sand. When disturbed, the creatures gave off a glowing yellow light before slipping back into the dark of night. Rod knew nothing of the creatures and stood motionless, enraptured with his three glowing footprints—the three footprints that proved his natural divinity beyond any shadow of a doubt.

# CHAPTER THIRTEEN

# The Snow Chicken

Believing the spell and their journey no more than a dream, Rod awoke groping for his bedside table. Finding only a baby sea turtle—no remote control, no alarm clock—Gino's News Morning with Ted Nedbury and another day at Magic Wands Incorporated were both dropped from the equation. Rod's initial panic was followed by the contentment of watching the sea turtle's determined flippers brush over the sand. Rod sat up next to the fire pit heaped with the ashen corpses of prandalia and watched the sun rise out of the sea.

Abacus, of course, was already up and poking the sleeping Jake with his walking stick. Once finished with Jake, Abacus turned to poking the pile of ashes, bringing last night's fire back to life.

Before Rod had pulled his socks all of the way up, Abacus offered him a coconut of hot coffee. "Best that we soon take to our heels," said Abacus. The troupe packed up and set out on bellies full of shellfish.

Walking along the beach, Rod and Jake couldn't avoid an obsession with Slim and stared at him compulsively with no taste for common courtesy. They did not wish to make the animal feel uncomfortable, but after the campfire stories there was now an intrigue, an ambiguity as to who was the master and who was the pet. Slim had been reminding them that they were the Dreamers, the "Mreeow", for years, and they had never even known.

Rod's slacks were rolled up above the knee, exposing tan socks imbued with the magic to cling to Rod's smooth, featureless calves. In one hand, Rod dangled his wingtips. In the other, he heaved his yellow suitcase. Abacus, eyes nested deep beneath the brim of his fedora, balanced Rod's other suitcase on top of his head. Jake looked a mess of hair and Slim looked fabulous, as usual.

To their starboard, as they walked into the unfiltered sun, was the rolling ocean, home to an endless array of alien life. To their portside, a wall of jungle. "This is our destination," said Abacus, jutting his chin towards a cloud-obscured peak rising above the vegetation. "Near the summit of Mount Rancancan lies the cave that is the lair of Tyrone Preposterous, Tyrone Omniscient."

The peak was so close, yet insurmountable.

Jake remembered the distant peak in the *nooshtah* he and Yuyu had seen from *Da Bufa*. It was Mount Rancancan. Rancancan was a terminus of the spell that carried itself across the sky, all of the way back to Gibbous Bizonia.

They walked without speaking, their concerns massaged by the ongoing waves of Sister Ocean. There was nothing to do but walk. There were no other baybeetles in sight. No sign of them, not even a footprint or a cigarette butt.

"This 'sand' as you call it, is somethin' else," said Rod. Jake and Abacus looked at Rod and at each other. For incalculable reasons, they were all smiling.

Porous nubs of stone spat up through the sand, giving flat waves diversion as they crashed and wrapped around the nubs. The nubs grew in number and in girth until they were everywhere, cradling standing basins of sea water in their craters.

"These are called tide pools," Jake said to Rod. Everything that Jake had taken for granted about the natural world was new and extravagant to his older brother. "When the tide moves in, these rocks are almost completely underwater."

"When the what moves in?" asked Rod.

"The tide. The ocean level rises, so the water line moves way up the beach."

"Just cut the crap, Jake."

Soon cat and baybeetles were forced to skip almost exclusively from stone to stone. Rod put his wingtips back on after his virginal pain from testing the jagged volcanic rocks with just his socks on. Rod's wingtips had no tread, so three steps into it, Rod slipped off an anemone right into one of these alleged "tide pools".

"Bid thee for now farewell to your tide pools and the rest of your Sister Ocean," said Abacus, "In we go." Rod clenched his binoculars as Abacus turned their path towards the untamed jungle. Crossing the threshold from sunshine to deep shade, they commenced to bushwhacking.

It was well before midday, but the jungle was already hot and humid. No one had washed in fresh water since leaving the sanctity of Leonard and Yolanda's, so the jungle stuck easily to their filth, frosting Jake, Rod, Abacus, and Slim with layers of insects, spider webs, feathers, and flower petals.

While Slim and Abacus moved as naturally as spirits through the growth, Rod and Jake were busy clubbing and clawing their way uphill, Rod's wet sock squishing and sucking with every step. In their struggle, Rod and Jake failed to notice the roughly hewn monoliths that littered the jungle around them. Some were carved into faces.

Every wall of jungle they pushed through greeted them with another wall of jungle on the other side. There was no relief for the Bizonians. Jake had discovered his share of brambles and wicked undergrowth in Loophole Valley, but those gauntlets were well-groomed compared to this foray into Vivachanga. Rod had known nothing but city sidewalks, linoleum, and parking lots. This beating left him reassured in his belief that anyone who was interested in locating and exploring the remains of the natural world was poorly educated.

Like moles tunneling up to surface daylight, the bushwhackers peeled aside a particularly sticky cascade of vines drooping from the canopy. Their heads jerked back as one as they shielded their eyes from the sudden brightness of the sun. Everyone's dilated pupils constricted against the light as Abacus assembled a tale. "Welcome to the teeth and bones of the Sheel city of Lugan," he said.

From atop their bluff, the terrain below opened to reveal a city of towering, crumbling temples. Centuries of abandonment had turned immovable blocks of stone this way and that—creepers and iguanas took root in the jumbled network of cracks and crevices. The jungle was rising to conceal the city of Lugan from the eyes of beasts for the rest of time.

"These settling remains were once brightly painted and filled with the Sheel themselves," said Abacus, surveying the limestone ruins bleached chalk white from exposure.

The brothers dropped their hacking sticks in awe. The Sheel—whoever they were, for even Jake had never heard of them—

certainly did know beauty. With little effort, the clean lines of the city and its structures could be imagined as they existed before being reclaimed by the Mother Nature.

The site upon which the Sheel chose to build their monumental city was naturally magnificent. Its elevation afforded generous views of the ocean and the broad, white beaches. From this height, the beaches stretched in either direction until becoming little more than white hairlines separating land from sea. Lugan had been built low enough however, that the grade of the city's footprint was a gentle, unencumbering slope. Behind Lugan, the wilds became steep and treacherous as they bent up towards Mount Rancancan. Throughout the ruins were purple-flowered jacaranda trees, some taller than the most formidable of the cockeyed, stair-stepped pyramids.

Abacus hopscotched down a path of stones, each stone more than half-buried. The path had endured the years, as had the gutter bordering the path that carried ants and a trickle of water. Stone rectangles the size of your hand were placed end to end to form the sides and bottom of the gutter. Despite these fragile details of the city's infrastructure that had survived since prehistory, the bulk of the city's primary architecture had lost great chunks of its original integrity.

By the time Jake and Rod caught up with Slim and Abacus, Abacus and the cat were seated atop a cut stone seven feet high. Abacus had tuned up the next chapter of his tale. "As you can see," he said, indicating the once immaculate constructs of Lugan, "even the elements of this world which we assume will last forever are subject to the power of change."

Again lamenting the absence of his camera, Jake produced a purple notebook and a writing quill. He started sketching the layout of Lugan, the bent lines of its buildings, and the corroded relief carvings scratched into every surface. Any beetleopologist worth his salt would have done the same.

Jake had his intrepid Uncle Frank to thank for spurring his interest in beetleopology. Uncle Frank, Leonard's older brother, spent most of his life working in the REZ as a backhoe operator and gutterman. When Rod and Jake were young boys, Uncle Frank would show up from time to time on the Bankmans' doorstep and live on the couch for weeks on end. In his stained jeans and grizzled nose, Uncle Frank would tell stories about his experiences in Gino's Remote Extraction Zone.

Sketchbook in hand, Jake remembered one such story where Uncle Frank described an ancient city the likes of Lugan—a city of stone palaces fallen into ruins, overrun by the jungle. As he grew older, Jake never stopped wondering if such ancient cities really existed, despite Leonard and Yolanda's claims that Uncle Frank was a nut.

Eventually Jake made up his own mind—Uncle Frank *was* a nut, but this did not necessarily mean that he was a liar. Thus, Uncle Frank's stories of mysterious civilizations sparked Jake's curiosity and his dedication to beetleopology, the study of the ways of baybeetles past and present, far and wide. The ruins of Lugan were Jake's dreams come true.

Jake looked up from his work to see Abacus waving him in from atop the highest pyramid in the ruins. Rod and Slim were already half-way up the nearly vertical ascent of one-hundred steps, each step measuring the height of three modern stair steps.

When Jake arrived atop the pyramid, Rod was unconscious from fatigue, lying with his head cocked against a stone table. The stone table's etchings were voluptuous and involved. "Yes, that which may seem forever etched upon this Nord," spoke Abacus, his previous monologue uninterrupted, "may have been created for only a very discrete, time-bound purpose."

The view from the top of the temple pyramid included all of the beauty visible from below, but much, much more. With his back turned towards the sea, Jake located a waterfall buried in the jungle behind Lugan. The water flowed from the falls into a canal that formed the central axis of the ruins. From the canal, the water flowed back into the heavy foliage separating Lugan from the seashore. Facing the ocean, Jake could see the beach where they slept and the approximate route they had taken to reach Lugan. Wisps of smoke rising from the trees to the west were the clay ovens of Cherishio.

"This stone table before us is an altar," said Abacus, "It holds a central position in this Sheel city and is embossed with the crowning achievements of Lugan. The city of Lugan was ornate and imposing, but it is told that the thoughts etched upon this altar meant more to the Sheel than did their capacity to engineer and build. It is told that Lugan existed not for its own glory, but as a means of acquiring knowledge."

"What happened?" asked Jake, "How did they all die?"

"The Sheel did not die, Jake. They did, however, find it prudent to abandon the way of life that involved these immaculate cities. Perhaps they were the victims of an agricultural disaster that forced them to return to their traditional ways of hunting and gathering. Perhaps the Sheel in their opulence and pageantry became the target of attacks waged by the 'have nots' of their time who were not allowed to share in the wealth and luxuries of the Sheel. It is even possible that the Sheel of Lugan left their city voluntarily when its purpose of extracting information from the cosmos was fulfilled. We do not know with any certainty what transpired towards the end.

"What we do know is that the descendants of the ancient Sheel are still with us. They are most certainly aware of our presence here already." Rod lifted his head from the foot of the altar. Abacus sensed his anxiety at the idea of being silently observed, again. "Not to worry, Mister Rod. The Sheel are a coy sort, very humble and kind. They will likely not present themselves to us. However, if we travel well and are lucky, they might bake us a birthday cake."

As they sat and rested in the shadow of the ribcage colonnade atop the pyramid, Abacus handed them each a fist full of berries and a conical leaf half-full with cool water. Rod removed his grandfather's binoculars to wipe his neck clean of sweat and insects.

Abacus picked up the Rod's stray binoculars and began to fiddle with them, looking into the big ends—the wrong ends—and flipping the binoculars upside down and back upright again. "Fascinating," said Abacus, "how the tiny pictures painted on the inside of these tubes never turn upside-down. What in the name of Dijouti are these bechonquilars for?"

"They're *binoculars*," said Rod, "and they're for bird watching. Here." Abacus handed the binoculars back over to Rod who then placed the big ends over his eyes and began adjusting the big center knob, flipping the contraption upside down and back as Abacus had done. Seeing that the little paintings *didn't* turn upside-down, Rod wondered how these were supposed to help anyone get into non-virtual birding.

"Mind if I try?" Sensing his brother and Abacus befuddled, Jake took it upon himself to demonstrate. He flipped the binoculars around, placing the small ends against his eyes. Rod and Abacus both hummed in contemplation. Jake focused one eyepiece on a cusp of canopy, then rotated the other eyepiece until it too was in focus. He handed the binoculars back to Rod.

Rod removed his spectacles and replaced them with the small ends of the binoculars. Looking through the device, Rod was overwhelmed by grotesque, magnified images. He began whipping his head back and forth with the binoculars, disoriented, rudderless, and placing everyone in peril. He wretched and regurgitated his berries onto the precious Sheel altar. Rod handed the binoculars immediately over to Abacus who remained content looking through the big ends at the tiny, mysterious paintings.

As a departure from his brother's activities, Jake asked Abacus what information this Sheel altar contained that was so very important. "It would be difficult to say, Jake," answered Abacus, "for interactions between the Sheel and the rest of the world are few and very far between. When in my life I have had the pleasure of facing a Sheel, the very last thing upon our minds is such a serious question. We usually just tell a few jokes and tongue the weather.

"The Sheel, like most Vivachangans, monitor the pulse of the planet and I do believe that they shall come out of hiding at the appropriate moment to teach the world what it needs to know. It is my hope that this moment is coming soon, for there are always fewer Sheel who comprehend the symbols preserved upon the Altar of Lugan.

"The Sheel have lived for thousands of years overcoming the challenges of nature, but modern Nord threatens to eliminate the hearts and minds of the Sheel forever. The Sheel are a forgotten tribe. My baybeetles, the Tulikans, are a forgotten tribe. The entire land between here and where the sun rises—call it Vivachanga—has been forgotten by those who call themselves the inhabitants of the 'first world'. How the modern, industrial world justifies calling itself the 'first world' is a mystery to us. If we were to indeed draw lines, Vivachanga, our Mother Nature, is all that is left of the true first world. Industrialized baybeetles might call parts of Vivachanga the 'third world' if they call it anything at all.

"Nature is forgotten. Vivachanga has become one great quarry, one great oil field, one great logging operation. As the land of the Sheel is taken from them and the land's beauty is stripped away, the history of the Sheel is stripped away as well. The Sheel abandon the ways of the forest and are absorbed into the modern way. Their language and their stories, the knowledge of their forefathers is forgotten. They forget how to heal with plants."

Sliding off the last bleached bone of Lugan back into the wilds, Abacus herded everyone to the waterfall behind the ruins. In the cool spray, Jake, Rod, and Abacus showered to the lifting hum of a swarm of Foiled Hoverbeans. Strange to be among so many hoverbeans with no Anisha in sight. Slim licked his entire body five times over.

A thorn scratch here, a stick in the eye there, they returned to beating their way through nasty thickets. "I don't like it here," sniveled Rod, now melancholy from memories of their travel on painless busses, trains, ferries, and chariots, "Are you sure we're on the path?"

"Why yes," answered Abacus, "We travel a path carved by mouse and muskrat."

Looking down at his bloody shins, Jake asked, "Aren't there any larger game trails around? Elk, goat, pig…"

"No no. Most assuredly not," said Abacus, "We may, however, attempt the streambed. Water is low, so I do believe it navigable if one minds the fragility of the terrain." Several painful moments later they stood with a wedge of blue sky above and a tumbling of stones and water underfoot.

The streambed proved itself the lesser of two evils. Bloody scrapes from thistles and spiny bramblewort stalks were replaced by blunt, heavy blows and twisted ankles—deeper pains but with less frequency. At first, the challenge was to bounce from stone to stone, doing one's best to outwit loose, teetering stones and stones that spat you off their wet green slime and into the stream itself. The farther they worked up the stream, the lighter the flow of water and the larger the obstacles to be overcome.

By the time the stream's dribbling of water could only be heard and not seen, they were climbing over boulders, some higher than the baybeetles were tall. Tree trunks fallen across the meandering rift only made matters worse. Abacus and Slim always seemed to manage, but Jake and Rod were in constant need of a boost or a hand from above.

With Jake's interlocked fingers providing a waist-high foothold, Rod groped in vain for the top of a behemoth. Moving a foot up to Jake's shoulder and then to his head, Rod was finally able to reach over the top of the boulder to pull himself up. Seeking the next handhold, Rod froze. His free hand hovered motionless over a nest of deadly copper trigger wasps, a mass of sunbathing dragons, meaty and metallic. In one of his rare cat-like moments, Rod eased his frozen hand away from the wasps and scaled down the face of Jake to relative safety.

"I thought ya had it there, bro'" said Jake.

"I do not like it here, Jake," said Rod, not so much sniveling now as making a throaty statement. Forewarned, Jake took a calculated boost and examined the nest himself. Together, Rod and Jake yelled for Abacus.

Keen of hearing and quick as a bug, Abacus backtracked towards their calls. In a minute he was looking down on the frightened brothers and holding a fistful of the copper trigger wasps. "How may I be of assistance?" he asked, shoving the wasps into his mouth. "So zesty."

When the beaten crew reached the stream's headwaters, drawn before them was a bristling lake spanning all direct routes towards Mount Rancancan. Beads of sunlight pulled on fluttering silver veils crowded the lake's surface. A thousand shades of green licked the shore. Rancancan presided over it all, casting its choppy reflection onto the glittering lake—another page from the book of nursery rhymes and fairy tales.

Abacus wove a quick canoe with three oars and a mainsail. Slim questioned its bouyancy at full occupancy, but it was either jump aboard or be left behind.

Breaking the lake's surface were a host of warty islands, small and mostly bald. Scant tufts of grass wilted upon their shores. A Wood Duck, watching the circular retreat of his own ripples, paddled to get behind one of the warty lumps as the unorthodox travellers sloshed by. The male Wood Duck was soon joined by a female, nibbling on passing fleets of algae. The warty island between the ducks and the travelers began to move. It retreated behind the Wood Ducks.

A second warty island moved directly in front of the canoe and soon the islands had the canoe and the ducks surrounded. The woven canoe's oars were already soggy and a flying fish had pierced the mainsail, so speedy escape was not an option. With the crew's fear taking hold, sturdy Abacus took over.

"Uncommon peril is part of the life of a sailor," said Abacus, "Everything is under control."

"Snake!" screamed Rod. Rocketing to his feet, he nearly overturned the tippy canoe. The thick, gray snake reared its head and heaved daggers of lake water from its dark, empty eye sockets. Rod ducked, panicked, and jumped overboard.

"A herd of elephants walking the bottom," said Abacus as Rod slobbered back aboard the rubbery, separating canoe.

"A herd of elephants!" exclaimed Jake, "Are they going to attack us?"

"Perhaps. Our chances hinge upon their emotional well-being." Just then the canoe was bumped from below. Jake stopped his questioning, gave up on his unraveling oar, and started preparing for a losing battle.

Though no one was paddling, the canoe began to pick up speed. The remaining oars were shredded and torn from their hands by the force of the passing water. Someone or something had seized control of their disintegrating canoe.

"We're gonna die!" yelled Rod.

"Of course," Abacus said, raising his voice but seemingly unconcerned, "but do not worry for our transport. We are simply engaged in a bit of your...what do you call it? Hitchhiking. Much smoother than our first attempt, would you not agree?"

Their elephant escort deposited its passengers and what was left of the canoe on the far pebbled shore. It raised its warty head out of the water, flapped its billboard ears, and disappeared to go join its mates. Days at MWI were not like this.

The baybeetles joined an arc of other beasts on the pebbled shore who had come to water themselves in the shallows. Three baboons sipped side by side with a quartet of muddied boar, dozens of jungle raccoon, and one adult female zambula.

On all fours, Abacus joined the zambula—a large, elegant, albeit lethargic ruminant—and began lapping at the lake's surface. The zambula's two calves took a break from their romp and scrunched in next to Abacus for a drink.

When mother zambula had slurped her fill, she raised her thick head with knurled horns and licked her shiny, black nose. Her calves licked Abacus' nose and bolted off to run circles around their mother, now swinging her wide belly as she hoofed off towards the wooly jungle.

"Quickly," said Abacus, "we must not let them get away." Slim and the others scrambled not to lose the zambulas and with them the easy travel of a zambula trail carving through the forest.

Abacus had chosen well. Although keeping eyes open for droppings and more snakes, everyone was able to loosen up as they hiked the zambula trail. Abacus sang sweet, unfamiliar verses in unfamiliar tongues. Slim sniffed catalogues of new scents, ears drawn back and eyes crossed. Jake was lost in the unique beauty of their surroundings, examining the shapes of leaves he never knew existed.

Summoning his courage, Rod acclimated to his grandfather's binoculars. Without them, he had heard the calls of Short-Toed

Larks, Great Snipes, and Drunken Warblers, but with his naked eye, he could only see what might or might not be the quivering silhouettes of these avian rarities.

With the binoculars reined in, Rod found that he could peer through the shoots and branches to locate his feathered friends proper. Now he was absolutely burning with birds. His head spun with the species he was bagging and logging on graph paper with annotations of stars, underlines and double underlines. A Cranky Morning Pile here. A Bean Goose there. "Snow Chicken," he announced, scoping the bird's mottled gray-brown and white plumage, "Another 'Virtual Birding Quarterly' winner."

"You must be mistaken, Mister Rod," said Abacus, "The Snow Chicken, also known as the Rock Ptarmigan, has not visited itself upon these lands for centuries. I do believe that you have logged a Willow Grouse, my friend. The robust beak on the specimen will tell you."

It was true. Although similar in appearance to the Willow Grouse, the Snow Chicken did sport a more delicate beak.

"Beyond that," continued Abacus, "the Snow Chicken is the harbinger of peace upon the land."

"Like the Dove?" asked Rod, "The symbol of peace?"

"No no. We call the Snow Chicken by the name Dijouti, the Ptarmigan of Peace. When Dijouti comes to these lands, there will be turmoil and great rejoicing. Turmoil as the steadfast crumbles. Rejoicing as the new rises from the ashes of the old."

"You mean like a Phoenix rising from the ashes?" asked Rod.

"No no. It shall rise from the ashes like a Spangled Woodcock."

# CHAPTER FOURTEEN

# Saffron and Answers

The farther they traveled, the more Abacus seemed to gain his bearings. Where they now walked on the zambula trail, they were within falling distance of an ominous, misplaced rock formation. The formation was so poorly aligned and top-heavy, that the sooner it toppled over, the better. "These stones," Abacus said, "They are what is called the Heart of the World. The stones indicate that we are very near the special place."

All Abacus could talk about was the "special place" they would visit on the way to Tyrone's enclave. Wishing the special place to remain a surprise, he would reveal no details.

"If that is so," declared Rod, "I believe I'd rather just take myself to the special place. It sounds like a place where one would prefer a little privacy." Rod huffed on ahead of the others, quite a chore on the steep pitch. Abacus, Slim, and Jake quickened their pace to stay with Rod until Rod grew hot under the collar and told them all to go away.

"As you wish, Mister Rod, but *you are already there*." As he spoke, Abacus motioned to the hanging limbs on the evergreen krundle pines that surrounded them.

*You are already there.* This is what Yuyu had whispered in Jake's ear behind the hay bales at the Valgato train depot. They were the very last words she shared with Jake. The only way to know peace, she told him, was to know that you are already there. Already in Heaven. Huddled on a peak in the heavenly *nooshtah*, all that the

Bizonians could see in the tree branches were tawny clusters of twigs and pine needles collecting on spider webs and caterpillar nests. The collecting debris was so abundant that even the thickest krundle pine branches were bent towards the ground.

Jake caught a bright orange flash on one of the clusters. "Oh my God."

Rod dusted off his glasses to see what Jake had seen. "Oh my God," he echoed.

It *was* a special place.

It was not debris that was weighing down the sturdy limbs of the forest, but untold millions, perhaps billions of monarch butterflies at rest. It was as if a blizzard had dropped couches of snow on the trees and then fouled them all with sheets of cinnamon.

"They are still just waking up," said Abacus, "The night air does put a chill on. The monarchs sleep in bundles and must warm to the day." As they watched, the outer crust of butterflies did warm to the day and started dripping from the branches to take wing. The drips turned to shimmering orange showers. To the ends of the forest, butterflies were raining from the trees. The song of millions if not billions of butterfly wings filled the air. It was the sound of whitewater.

The awakening monarch butterflies pooled on the knoll's peak until they burst into a river that flowed downhill around every tree and shrubbery. Wading through the river of insects, careful not to crush the coupled butterflies mating on the forest floor, one could not avoid getting stuck to a few. The wandering baybeetles would be visited by a butterfly on the chest, a butterfly on the shoulder, and two butterflies on the head, all at the same time. Slim was having the hunt of his life despite the alarming speed and maneuverability displayed by the flower petal insects.

# SAFFRON AND ANSWERS

Rod, Jake, and Slim found a love for Abacus' special place. Never had they seen anything so strange and beautiful in all their lives. Jake decided Yuyu must be right. Nord must be Heaven after all. What more could one ask for? Taller trees? More beautiful butterflies? A deeper ocean? A sky more blue? Older tortoises?

With their heads swimming in the sea of monarchs, Abacus suggested that they sit, rest, and eat among the butterflies. "Follow me," he said, plowing deeper into the woods and butterflies. Ribbons of steam began to rise through the flow of monarchs.

The steam grew thicker and more fragrant until they arrived at a natural hot spring, deep enough for a sit. Everyone except for Slim dressed down to their birthday suits. Everyone including Slim lowered their hips into the pool of golden water. Flakes of fool's gold were suspended throughout the hot spring, reflecting the light of the sun. "The Sheel have recently passed through this place," said Abacus, rubbing a leaf, "and we would only know this were it intended for us to know."

As the weightless soak soothed everyone's bones, an iridescent flying lungbeetle circled the crucible of spring water then dove headlong towards the deep end. The lungbeetle broke the pool's surface and held its trajectory, submerging itself in the roiling water. The swimming lungbeetle hid beneath a rock on the pool's bottom.

"If only I could fly," dreamed Rod, eyes glistening as he watched a dragonfly that had taken over the lungbeetle's air space. The dragonfly circled and dove headlong towards the spring water. Unlike the lungbeetle, the dragonfly was not a swimmer and crashed ferociously on the surface of the water. The soaked dragonfly peeled itself from the pool's surface and repeated its performance, crashing and splashing, head first.

"Do have a look," said Abacus, "Just on the far bank you will observe the sleeping flummox. The flummox takes up residence only in the most delicate of ambiance." All that could be seen on the far bank, besides a patchwork of ferns, were hanging vines that lounged from the branches of stunted chelota trees. The very tips of the leafy vines tickled the surface of the water where it flowed out of the steaming pool.

"The flummox is there, just among the other hanging vines," continued Abacus, "Perfectly camouflaged, it appears as a vine itself, its toes brushing the water's surface. The toes touch the moving water for hydration and to prevent atrophy. Its head and body are to us just a twist in the vines of the legs.

"Many creatures in these precious lands sleep for most of their lives and the flummox is no exception. Only once every three years does the flummox awaken. This it does purely to elude predators by creeping to the next idyllic location.

"Just below the flummox we see the lemon cherub, fully submerged." In the spot Abacus had indicated, there was only the exiting stream of spring water with omnipresent eddies coddling tiny pockets of air bubbles. "The lemon cherub sleeps for decades, hunting as it sleeps. Its body is there, the greasy stone.

"The lemon cherub exhales tiny grease bubbles into the water one at a time. The bubbles travel with the current, taking their sweet, salivary time to burst at the surface. One loses interest in watching and waiting for any particular bubble to burst, so the eyes move back to the next exhaled grease bubble. Thus, each bubble seems to last forever, yet the total number of bubbles never increases despite the cherub's steady breathing. In this way, the lemon cherub's prey is hypnotized and lured to its destruction." The flying lungbeetle poked its head out from beneath the lemon cherub, but it could not escape the lemon cherub's grasp.

Rod refused to believe these lowly fables of Abacus.

"That insect over there," Abacus motioned to a resting monarch, "has eight legs, flies with paper wings, weighs less than a hampshire leaf, and migrates thousands of miles over the course of its lifetime."

Amazed by such stone cold lies, Rod nabbed a handful of the huckleberry and clover salad that Abacus had tossed together. After gobbling the dripping handful of salad down to his fingers, Rod reached for the pocket of his poolside pants. From the pocket, Rod withdrew a snow-white paper cloth, elegantly embossed with seashells and abstract design. It fell about his hands as would a drowsy, long-haired kitten. Rod wiped off his fingers, dabbed the corner of his mouth, and threw the crumpled napkin to the ground next to his pants.

"Are you going to eat that?" asked Abacus, looking at Rod.

The huckleberries and clover were both gone. He, Rod, wasn't about to eat the flummox, the greasy lemon cherub, or the lungbeetle remains left uneaten by the lemon cherub. Concluding from Rod's blank stare that he was not going to eat it, Abacus reached over and ate Rod's crumpled napkin. "They're so perfectly dry."

"You just ate that," said Rod.

"Why yes. It was either that, or weave from it a tiny hammock, but the fibres had already lost their integrity and I would hate for a chipmunk to fall through on my account. Were you to leave this napkin upon the ground?"

"Well, I was either going to leave it there or just throw it away when we got home."

Bizonian logic. Everything disposable. Abacus could too easily see Rod's used napkin moving from his waste basket back home to an open prairie turned landfill. "We are talking about saving the world, Mister Rod. Saving what remains of the natural world, which we obviously love, and saving our own natural happiness."

"Hm?"

"We are talking about the prevention of the next Great War, are we not?" continued Abacus.

"What are we talking about?" Rod was confused, as usual.

"We are talking about preserving or, Dijouti forbid, actually improving the quality of life for the baby animals in the world. Full-grown animals too."

"It's just a napkin."

"Ah, one napkin—although they usually come in a stacks—appears insignificant within the scheme of the cosmos. You wipe your lips and toss it aside. Everyone else is performing the same napkin trick, so you think nothing of it.

"Let us, however, tally the natural resources required to produce just one paper napkin. We must think about not only the physical dimensions of the napkin itself, but the size and shape of everything that was required of Nord to deliver that napkin into your grubby paws.

"The napkin may well have started as an ancient tree in an ancient forest not unlike the forest upon this very knoll. The tools and machines that were required to chop down the tree were forged from ore extracted from bottomless mines drilled into the face of Nord. Another allotment of ore was required to produce the mining machines and so on and so on. This is not to mention the tools and machines required to build the roads into the forests to get to where the ancient tree lived.

"Once the tree was felled, it was then transported by a motorized vehicle—requiring its share of resources to produce—to a lumber mill. The mill itself was built from more felled trees, quarried stone, and mined ore. Great numbers of tools and great amounts of mechanical energy were extended towards reducing the tree to the napkin via processes that most of us know little about.

"More trees were chopped down in order to make boxes both large and small to package the stacks of new napkins. Once the boxes were filled, the finished napkin began to travel. More vehicles spread the boxes of napkins far and wide around the planet. We can only imagine where the gasoline to fuel these napkin processes came from or how many machines were required to extract, refine, and transport the gasoline.

"If these napkins were to be made from what you call recycled materials, one must still consider the vehicles, roads, tools, machines, and packaging involved in producing the recycled napkin. If we do not curtail our overall rate of consumption, no alternative products or alternative sources of energy will save us.

"In short, the environmental cost of one napkin is far greater than a small slice of a tree."

"I thought you said we were talking about stopping the Great War," said Rod.

"We must imagine," continued Abacus, "that every time we engage in the act of consuming a napkin or any other product that gets used and put into the garbage, precisely the same act is happening thousands if not millions of times over on the face of

Nord at that exact same moment. The *cumulative* mass of resources required for that moment in time becomes indeed massive.

"Once we consider the number of napkins used per day or per week, let alone per month or year, the demands on the planet are quickly pushed beyond the mind's ability to comprehend. Here we are considering only a tiny product, the napkin. Imagine the toll taken by a magic wand, a mansion, a jet fighter, or by some other piece of high magical technology that must go through dozens more processing phases than a simple paper napkin."

Rod considered the other napkins and wands he had sequestered for the journey. Then he thought about all of the napkins and wands he had used in his entire life. He was still alive. "I still don't believe that I'm destroying the planet. And I definitely don't believe I'm causing war," he said.

"We baybeetles are pleasure seekers, Rod. I find, and apparently you do too, Mother Nature and her wonders to be quite pleasurable. She can be ruthless, but these moments are few when compared to her continuous stream of goodness. Mother Nature is soothing. She makes us happy. She provides us with nourishment. She provides us with plants that contain remedies for our physical ailments. When we need to be alone to be sad or angry or overjoyed, she gives us space. She contains the wisdom that we need to survive and be content. She gives us peace.

"That singular delicious napkin—due to the loss of Mother Nature that it requires—may truly be the one napkin that removes from us the possibility of peace. That napkin may be the straw that breaks the camel's back and launches us into the next Great War, if it has not already begun."

A lone ladybeetle with small, sensitive ears watched from a distance as the travelers shifted in and out of view through butterflies and the steam misting off the water. She found a leaf hidden from the heat of the day, folded it in half, and let one small drop of dew gather and fall upon her tongue. Then she's gone without a sound, licking her cake-covered fingers.

"Hmh. I'm really not seein' it," said Rod.

"Another way of looking at it," added Jake, excited to share his thoughts, "is not so much that your act of consumption is starting wars, but by *not* consuming you are helping *prevent* war by making your own life better. Wouldn't you say that the happier or more content that you are, the less desire you have to do harm to others?"

"I guess," said Rod.

"Are you happy, Rod?" Jake asked.

"Well, sometimes."

"Exactly. Happiness is not so much an 'on' or 'off' proposition. Happiness exists upon a wide spectrum. You can be miserable, content, ecstatic, or anywhere in-between at any given moment."

"Well, yeah. So?"

"So, when you forego one tiny act of consumption, you effect the entire chain of events that are required to create that napkin. You save one little chunk of Mother Nature and your own happiness. You have bumped your feelings just a tad in the right direction.

"Perhaps by not consuming, you save the tree where a family of rare birds live. There is no reason that saving them should not make you happy. The survival of the tree for the tree's sake should make you happy as well. It is not a myth that trees and other plants provide the air that we breathe. As it is, just enough oxygen blows into Bizonia from here to keep us alive and using more napkins.

"Another angle on not using the napkin," continued Jake, "is to think of it not as saving the world in one great swoop, but as saving it little by little. The first rung on the ladder out of Hell is not going to resemble Heaven at all. You're still gonna climb that ladder though."

"Let's say," said Rod, "that I do forego using paper napkins. It's just me. One single baybeetle. There is no guarantee that even one other baybeetle would follow."

"You would be surprised, Mister Rod," said Abacus, "there is power in small acts, power that is at your fingertips right now. Not only is there power in an act itself, but there is a vibration that radiates from this act. Many things in this life happen in waves, and as one baybeetle does, others do too. Foregoing consumption is not only useful and peaceful in a physical sense, but also in a symbolic sense. Not using the disposable napkin is symbolic of an awareness, of an attitude of understanding."

"For argument's sake," chimed in Jake, "let's say that only a few of us give up a little bit of luxury and the baybeetle race fails outright to provide a healthier planet for baby animals. Wouldn't it be nice to know that you gave it your best shot? The other option being that you knew what was going on but just let life die and become sad for everyone? Including yourself?"

"Very nice, Jake," Abacus commended, "Might I toss one last morsel onto this tirade?"

"If you must," sighed Rod, chin-resting-on-hand-ish-ly, staring-up-at-the-ceiling-ly.

"What the rest of the world calls 'natural resources'—the trees, the rocks, the water, the air—these are what my baybeetles call 'gods'. Everything is alive and everything is God. We do not destroy our gods lightly."

"I still don't believe you guys," said Rod, hands-on-the-hips-ish-ly, "This is the most beautiful place that I have ever seen. You can't possibly be telling me that the planet is in danger. Just look at that pair of Sociable Rubnecks over there, for Beetle's sake." Indeed there were two gorgeous, bright red Sociable Rubnecks with blunt beaks bobbing up and down in a savage bingalee tree.

"Very good then," conceded Abacus, "Let us log our Rubnecks and make some time shall we?"

After dressing next to the hot springs, Rod drew their attention to a metallic reflection in the forest. Abacus led the way to a raised wooden plank holding a vintage tin cake carrier.

The Sheel had left them a birthday cake.

It looked a pile of wet hair, but was light and fruity to the palette.

Rod sat alone on a stump, watching debris hiss past on the edge of a chapped wind. He was thinking out loud. "If everyone in Muzora gets their turn and starts consuming as much as we do in Bizonia, then the planet and her resources will disappear in a puff of smoke."

Abacus had led him here, to the next rounded knoll in the foothills of Mount Rancancan. The knoll where Rod sat had once been another winter shelter for multitudes of migrating monarchs. Where for thousands upon thousands of years there had been three and only three hilltops suitable for the spectacle of migrating monarchs, now there was but one. This knoll and an adjacent knoll had been logged for timber.

Clearcut.

"Who would do such a thing?" Rod asked himself as a disheartened monarch landed to share his stump, "What will happen to you, my little friend, when your last hilltop, your ancestral home, is logged into oblivion?" The wonderful show he had just witnessed in the special place would pull the greatest magic trick of all and disappear forever—another miraculous species eliminated from the universe at the hands of the baybeetles.

Jake had always told Rod that baybeetles were responsible for such irresponsible and deadly actions, but Rod's motto had always been "Out of sight. Out of mind". Now Rod was in love with a place and a species that both faced extinction.

Blank and entranced by a dry patch of ground, layers of Rod's hardened thought processes fell loose, melting before him. He felt dizzied. "How can we treat you or any other species this way?" Rod asked his monarch companion, "We can't even imagine what it's like to be a butterfly. Who are we to say that nothing of any merit transpires inside of your butterfly mind? How big is a thought? Who is more worthy of the richness of the forest, you monarchs or us baybeetles?"

The sum of baybeetle worthiness, or lack thereof, lay all around Rod in the form of rotting krundle pine stumps. "You are such delicate creatures. Once the more delicate creatures become extinct, who will be next? Baybeetles themselves? Isn't eliminating species from the face of Nord akin to pulling random parts out of a complex engine? We might be able to get away with yanking this or that part out, but it won't be long before the machine begins to implode. Who would do this? Who would cut down your trees, little friend?"

As Rod sat baffled by the crude behavior of his species, a thin sheet of pink paper, obviously a triplicate, cartwheeled and stuck with the breeze to his shin. There was something familiar about it. Flattening it on his knee, Rod found out why.

It was a materials requisition form. The request? Twenty thousand board feet of virgin krundle pine. The form was stamped "TOP SECRET" in red ink. At the top of the page was the Gino's corporate letterhead. Handwritten in the subject line, "MWI: Buckingham Project".

Rod read it again and again until tears blurred the words beyond recognition. He and everyone he had ever known back home simply did not get it. What they didn't get was that with everything they consumed in Bizonia to fulfill a need—even if this "need" was for a seven- or eight-slice toaster—they were causing destruction of the natural world, the beautiful and healthy natural world. The reason they didn't get it is because the destruction was taking place far from their madcap cities. Out of sight. Out of mind.

Though his bones were heavy, Rod broke from the stump and scraped himself up to the hill's ridgeline. He felt a drop of rain. Hot and dirty again from trudging through the arid clearcut, Rod spread his arms and tilted his head back. There was a steady, cooling rain, but not a cloud in the sky. Afternoon blue was thick in every direction. As the cloudless rain poured, Rod knew enlightenment.

The remainder of the day's hike towards Mount Rancancan was spent in wonder and wordless grief. Under a darkening sky, deep in a crease of the forest, Abacus brought their trail to an end and called it camp. He prepared gourds of dandelion tea, dipping water from a creek that eventually fed the elephants' lake somewhere below. A Sooty Owl hooted as Abacus handed out the gourds of tea.

"Hey, Rod. Can I use your stirring stick?" asked Jake.

"If you mean the Buckingham prototype, you're going to have to take that back, little mister."

"May I use your *wand* then please?"

Realizing that he had said the words "Buckingham prototype" out loud in front of Abacus, Rod jumbled about, delivering the Buckingham to Jake and desperately trying to change the subject. "*God* I love camping. Don't you, Abacus?"

"Oh yes. My baybeetles do not call it camping though. We call it living."

Rod faked a laugh and smacked Jake on the arm. Half of Jake's hot tea splashed to the ground.

"May I borrow the wand as well?" asked Abacus, "My tea could use a jostling."

"No!" shouted Rod, reaching through the campfire flames to snatch the Buckingham out of Abacus' grasping fingers, "I mean, this one is probably dirty." Rod could still lose faith in Abacus. "I think I have another one around here somewhere."

As Rod patted himself down, mortified Jake grabbed the prototype back. Rod lunged and Slim hissed, but Jake managed to deliver the Buckingham to Abacus.

"Thank you, Jake," said Abacus, examining the Buckingham in the firelight and assuring Rod that it appeared quite clean enough for him.

As the Buckingham entered Abacus' gourd, Rod watched from the dirt, paralyzed. His chin was smeared with ash and saliva from his failed lunge. When Abacus made a sudden move with the Buckingham, Rod whined and covered his eyes.

After shaking off the last drop of tea, Abacus handed the prototype back to Jake. "Mmm. Your magic wand certainly does stir tea quite well, Mister Rod."

Rod opened his eyes to find Jake waving the prototype back and forth hypnotically in front of Rod's nose. Rod's shaking hand ripped the prototype from Jake. In response to Abacus' compliment, Rod became downright smug. He knew the Buckingham was special. "Call them what you will, Jake, but they *are* magic."

"Making stirring sticks—your 'magic wands'—disappear into a garbage can next to the cream and sugar does not make them magic," said Jake, "it makes them garbage."

"They are *very* magic, little snot. MWI makes the best stirring sticks of all time. We don't call them 'wands' for nothing."

"Prithee, Mister Rod," Abacus intervened, "may I see what you call the 'Buckingham prototype' once again?"

Rod was cornered.

He handed the prototype back to Abacus.

Although his standing at MWI was now in jeopardy, the Buckingham was still Rod's pet and he would never want its secrets to fall into the wrong hands. Abacus pored over the wand with increased scrutiny, admiring the varnished krundle pine shaft with ebony inlays and the twelve-sided shark skin grip.

Taking aim at the constellation Minerva with the stirring stick prototype, Abacus called an exotic incantation into the shadows. *"OOLAZOO BATOOM!"*

The brothers both fell off their log when there appeared in the darkness a glowing fog. The fog was twice as tall as any of them and twice as long as it was high. Unlike the wisps of smoke from their campfire, which held form for a moment only to evaporate into nothing, the fog that was this *thing* continued to solidify. All of the yammering critters of the night grew silent when the solidifying fog made a grunt and a snarfle.

The lines of a creature continued to harden and brighten until the creature snapped into crisp, solid form. It had a long neck and an equally long tail, both covered in fine, flowing hair, as was the rest of its muscular body. The creature's head was defined by massive, blood-red eyes with orange flames for eyelashes. The tips of its bottom fangs were blackened by the flaming eyelashes as the fangs curled up to nearly touch the eyes.

The entire flop-eared beast radiated pearlescent green and reflected gold and silver from the firelight and the moon. A great, blue tongue began to lick at the tremendous front claws. The raking of the tongue over the claws shot electric sparks into the brush, igniting spot fires.

The familiar hum of a giant insect zipped down from above the campfire, parting the spiraling flecks of glowing prandalia. Assumed lost or mauled, Anisha baited the enormous beast with shrill peeps. The beast looked up from its claws, noticing the campers for the first time.

No one moved as Anisha swayed back and forth in front of the fire, her beak pointed directly at the pearly green dragon. Anisha licked her chops with a dagger tongue. In a singular blue-tongued scream, the dragon rose into the air on oceanic wings. A fury of hair and smoke, it shot like a bullet into the black greens of the forest, maneuvering untouched through the brambles.

Anisha followed in hot pursuit.

The brothers' heads were convulsing with adrenaline. When they started breathing again, Abacus was laughing, rocking loosely atop his log. "Not to worry, my friends. She won't hurt anybody—the dragon that is. As for Anisha, sometimes she plays rough." Abacus continued to chuckle, slapping himself, wiggling his fingers in the air.

Rod could not take his eyes off of the Buckingham. "How on Nord did you do that?"

"Do what?" Abacus asked.

"Where on Nord did that dragon puppet come from?"

"Dragon puppet? Your sense of humor *is* improving, Mister Rod."

"It wasn't *real*."

"But of course it is real. Can you not you smell that thing? *Oolazoo batoom* surely does bring a smelly one."

"I knew it!" Rod squealed, "I knew the Buckingham was special! Back at MWI we're still working on getting the Buckingham to dissolve instant coffee in boiling hot water, but Abacus! What you just did is, well...I can't wait to shove a smelly one in Flounders' face."

Abacus handed the ornate Buckingham back to Rod and nabbed a charred, gnarled twig that had been kicked from the fire. Without incantation, Abacus shook the twig at a pinecone.

The pinecone beeped three times before turning into a fairy godmother sprinkled with saffron and answers. She winked at Rod, snapped her fingers, and disappeared in a bolt of lightning.

"Mister Rod," said Abacus, "It is not so much the tools that you have, but how you use them. We used to build intricate wands from rare and precious materials in Vivachanga, but we found the trees from which the wands were honed more magical than the wands themselves. Dragons or no dragons." When the evening simmered down, Abacus wove them all hammocks of ivy and to bed they went.

Later that night, rocking unnoticeably in his hammock, Rod was not well. How could such primitive cultures as Abacus' Tulikans be so much more advanced than industrial Gibbous Bizonia? As a disposable stirring stick manufacturer, MWI's highest directive was to sell as much product as possible, with style.

Rod began to tense up, listening to the sounds of the forest. Riding upon these sounds, crawling over Rod's nerves, was uncivilized fear.

In the city, fear was an overarching psychological blanket to be tapped into at random. One's mind was free to drift into nightmarish possibilities even when no danger was present. Out here, danger was very much present. Freakish sounds emanated from unseen sources in every direction. Strange, dark shapes lurked high and low.

The only thing that Rod could relate to, thanks to flaming Humbug Creek back home, was the sound of flowing water. The sounds from the creek were rich and varied. There were bubbling low notes, jingling high notes, and everything in-between. When he concentrated on the water's lullaby, Rod's caravan of fears marched off into the underbrush.

Then it happened.

A stifling *CRACK* in the wilderness.

Rod's mind flashed blood-red like the eyes of the dragon and he clenched his hammock. He fanned his ears open, for in the dark his ears could see more than his eyes. If it was out there—be it beast, dragon, baybeetle, *the* beast—his ears would know it first. Jake and Abacus did not appear to have noticed the threat.

Rod listened in a tense, motionless bundle, waiting for the next footstep to fall in his direction. None came. No beast would hesitate so long in suspended animation, so Rod's mind eased back into the array of water noises until…

*CRACK!*

Rod prayed to the Holy Beetle, reclenching after another crack in the woods. Awaiting death after a violent struggle, time passed. Again, the next fearsome footstep did not crush the ground and

# SAFFRON AND ANSWERS

Rod's mind again eased back into the water. Resigned to his demise in the jaws of the slowest moving carnivore on Nord, Rod closed his eyes and tried to relax into it.

Relaxation sharpened Rod's senses. He eventually heard another crack, and later, another. As his fears subsided to reality, the cracks increased in frequency and Rod was finally able to discern what the cracks really were.

Every time Rod heard a crack, it was followed by a fluttering, higher pitched note produced by the creek that before he could not hear. Every time he heard a crack, he could hear more of what was already there. These fearsome cracks were nothing more and nothing less than the experience of his own mind opening to fields of sound that had existed in this place for time immemorial. As the frightening cracks became a continuous, soothing element of Bankman's day off, Rod wondered what more there could be resting just outside of everything he thought he knew.

# CHAPTER FIFTEEN

# Razor Blades and Bear Claws

*It was dark. A grotesque, matted figure hung from the rafters. Despite its great size, the figure was held aloft in the delicate snare of a spider's web. It was a beast, though not a spider. Jake doubted that the creature would still be alive in its horrid condition. Upon closer examination, Jake saw that it was still barely breathing. What hung trapped and dying was not one, but two jaguars emaciated and damp from their own bodily fluids.*

*In the next room another jaguar, healthy and colored luminous purple and blue, attacked Jake head on, claws and teeth bared. Empty handed, Jake fended off the great, luminous cat.*

*As if to reward Jake for his bravery, there appeared a child waist-high to Jake with golden skin and almond eyes. The child was dressed in red and gold ceremonial regalia, the brim of his pancake hat as wide as the child was tall. To one side, the child held a circular gong. Deep tones resonated when he struck the black center of the gong with a padded mallet. The shadowy and frantic house of jaguars dissolved around Jake and the child. That which always has been and that which always shall be was revealed as the darkness fell away.*

*That which always has been and always shall be, that which surrounded all baybeetles but could not be seen through the cloaks of misery they pulled over their lives, were colorful paper lanterns. They dallied on threads strung in rows above the powdered brows of elegant baybeetles in a sun-gold mountain courtyard. The peace and harmony were forthright.*

As Jake awoke from this dream to a pale orange horizon and frozen ears, he said under his frosty breath, "I'm ready."

As for Rod, his expanded powers of perception culminated in a dream of his own head exploding. When the dream woke him up, Rod could still hear the report from the explosion of his head echoing through the landscape. Rod had fallen asleep with his glasses on and a thin layer of snow accumulated on the lenses as he slept. When Rod opened his eyes, he saw that everything in his world had been absorbed into a featureless white light. With the shock of this new reality, Rod failed to note the snow that was melting on his face and blanket. The only reasonable conclusion that Rod could reach was that his head had actually exploded and that he had passed the test and entered the great white light of Heaven.

Abacus had coffee.

"Here, Mister Rod," said Abacus, handing Rod a steaming gourd, "This is for you."

His jaw slack, Rod raised with two hands the sacred chalice. He reveled in pouring the elixir of eternal life all over his face and down the front of his shirt. Steam from the coffee turned the snow on his lenses to slush, and Rod was faced with the fact that Heaven was nothing more than a blurry version of Nord. He felt otherwise normal except for the burning on his face and neck.

Abacus joined Jake who was up and at it, inspecting a small pile of debris at the edge of camp. "This is most rare," said Abacus to Jake.

"My brother?"

Abacus laughed, "Nay, Jake. Rare is the snowfall and rare is this pile of debris."

Jake was bent over, fingering baggies, gum wrappers, ballpoint pens, cigarette butts, tiny plastic spoons, and dust mice. "Where do you think it came from, Abacus?"

"Most certainly the clouds, Jake. To be honest, it leaves me more than a little unnerved. Not in my lifetime has this slope been dusted with snow and we are ill prepared for inclement weather."

"I mean where did this pile of junk come from."

"I have not the foggiest notion, Jake. Nobody comes here. Not even Gino's…yet."

Rod had become a wreck of tears due to the shock of his own passing. What would he do without Mom and Dad? Without Jake and Slim? Rod found the blurry baybeetle figures who had also apparently passed the test and blubbered with his hands shaking, "When will I ever see Slim again? When will I *ever* see *Slim* again?"

Jake grabbed the cat and gave him over to Rod. Thinking Jake a heroic angel, Rod prostrated himself before Jake, rubbing Slim against his forehead, knocking off his glasses. Picking them up, Rod stuffed and buttoned his glasses into his shirt pocket. They were of no use here.

Abacus was apprehensive as he prepared breakfast atop a dainty campfire. They were near the end of their food supply. They had been relying on foraged meals, but with everything on the increasingly barren terrain covered in snow, even Abacus would be hard-pressed to scrounge up enough food to feed them all. Abacus and Jake ate in a hurry and began preparations for the final leg of their ascent to the cave. Meanwhile, Rod busied himself with elfin jigs and waving his hands in rippling motions in front of his face.

Witnessing his brother's mysterious liberation caused Jake some discomfort, but he was pleased all the same to see his stoic brother expressing a little vitality. Rod's suitcases were stashed in the crotch of a tree beneath a colony of hammocking chipmunks.

Abacus pulled out a rolled wad of banana leaves and wove them all banana belts that worked surprisingly well as barriers against the cold. Each were given tight food bundles that would have to suffice until their work at the cave was complete. As ready as they were going to get, the strange crew, growing stranger, put their heads down and began to climb.

Looking back over his shoulder in farewell, Jake saw the butterfly knolls below the snow line and below that, the sultry Sheel ruins of Lugan. Then, of course, there was Sister Ocean. Jake could see the jungles of Vivachanga fade into the high desert of Muzora. He wondered if Yuyu sat upon *Da Bufa* right now, looking his way, wearing a face filled with the confidence of love.

The once cane-wielding Abacus was nearly impossible to keep pace with as the terrain grew steeper, stonier and more arctic with every step. The still, humid air of the jungle below had turned to icy gusts. Winds lifted the snow and plastered it to one side of every stone, twig, leaf, and blade of grass. In areas sheltered from wind and snow, a crystalline fur of frozen vapor crept over every surface.

Higher up the mountain, snow and crystalline fur turned to solid ice. The trees sparkled under this thin layer of frozen rains—a breathtaking but dangerous beauty. As they ascended, the ice thickened to stoop entire trees with its weight. The wind cracked the sleeves of ice that coated the branches, each gust culminating in the din of calving glaciers. The landscape was antlered with fallen glass branches.

A thick tree limb was heard to snap.

# RAZOR BLADES AND BEAR CLAWS

The limb fell in an explosion of ice and splintering wood just one pace ahead of Abacus, directly in his path. Jake stumbled at the sight, slipping on the ice and landing on his knees. On all fours with pain ringing in his ears, Jake saw for the first time how close they were walking to a drop-off into nowhere on one side. This proximity to disaster had been hitherto obscured by trees, scrub, and the weather.

They hadn't spent the night deep in the forest, but behind the last row of trees that marked the edge of a sheer cliff. The dragon chased by Anisha hadn't sought refuge in the forest, but over the edge of the cliff, a mile in the air over Vivachanga. Taking up the rear, Jake kept closer vigilance over Rod who was steady and tranquil, feeling his way over the ice with slippery wingtips and a lack of decent vision.

"'Tis not a great distance from where we now travel!" shouted Abacus over his shoulder to the brothers. Anisha was tucked deep in Abacus' beard, saving her energy for the task that lay ahead. Slim scampered back and forth keeping watch over them all, his black and white tuxedo fur flattening in the howling winds.

Their path narrowed, pinched tighter and tighter between the drop-off and a raised cornice of snow that offered some protection against the winds. When the cornice of snow dwindled down to nothing, they were left to teeter, unprotected, atop a backbone ridgeline—the cliff on one side and a nearly vertical downslope of snow on the other. They could see where sections of the cornice had broken off to avalanche down through virgin powder for hundreds of feet into a distant valley. Every step had to be taken with the uttermost caution while leaning into the wind.

Rod was the first to lose his footing, but Slim was there to extend a claw and Jake dove to grab Slim's tail. Together, they hauled Rod back up to the ridgeline.

The ridgeline dead-ended into a gunmetal gray face of stone. Abacus disappeared, scuttling around one side of the stone face. Following Rod and Slim around the same turn, Jake was blasted from his feet by a gale wind, the most forceful yet. He got up clutching for Rod and Slim to combine their strength against the storm. Heads down, they ran straight into Abacus. Abacus did not acknowledge their presence. He was staring ahead, his face slack.

Before them grew a menace, the likes of which none had ever seen or even imagined. The hurricane winds were braided together, an octopus of cyclones entangled with malice. Each arm was heavy with smoke, spiked with the lexicon of baybeetle excrement—razor blades, glass shards, chewed gum, wire, wet string, buttons, batteries, electric can openers, and magic wands. Jake and Abacus knew that this was the funneled tip of the massive foxtailed spell.

Visible through breaks in the black magician's gnashing storm, a wall of ice adhered to the face of the mountain. Megalithic columns of fractured ice were pressed together, pinstriped with the narrowest of gaps between. Through the gaps, more jackknifing formations of ice were honed into bear claws and screens of barbed wire. Behind this, more fractured, lopsided tree trunks of ice. One could sense the darkness that lay behind the labyrinth. Massive sections of shattered ice pillars were strewn erratically about their iced-over shelf of mountain. The entire scene was peppered by flying sands of biting ice pellets.

"Here lies the cave of Tyrone Outlandish!" shouted Abacus. He was silenced by a deafening snap as one of the suspended columns of ice broke off from above and tore through the air. As the column struck the ground and was blasted into a million pieces, only the smallest shards struck their ankles, but that was pain enough to leave the adventurers trembling. They all thought to turn back.

"It used to be so quiet here," yelled Abacus, "that one could hear one's self from yesterday! The sun shone and the ground beneath us was warm with grass and buttercups!"

At Abacus' call, Anisha showed no hesitation in emerging from his tangled, ice-crimped beard. She hovered tight to Abacus' side, taking quiet assessment. Jake gritted his teeth, not knowing what lay ahead for them or for their smallish friend.

With a dime plume of her breath's mist, Anisha reared back, poised to take down the hungriest villain. Then she was gone, corkscrewing through the cyclones of howling detritus, into the unpredictable wall of falling ice, and into the darkness beyond.

"Vacation over!" growled a red-horned, gurgling demon. The soaring demon spread its black carbon wings and lashed with its claws at both Tyrone and the blue-tongued dragon. Ambushed while at play, Tyrone and the pearly green dragon found themselves flying side by side as fast as they could, breakneck down the vertical flanks of an impassable mountain escarpment, fleeing to live another day.

The green dragon banked to one side and Tyrone banked to the other as they both disappeared into the forest. Peeking over his shoulder for the demon, Tyrone smashed headlong into a brick wall. It was never there before. Tyrone fell to the ground with a thump but shook it off like he meant to crash into a wall at high speed. He flew to the top and tiptoed along the wall's crest of iron lance points. Through a haze of smoke, Tyrone saw a city inside the new wall that was filled with baybeetles.

Half of them were on fire.

The other half were lighting their fellow baybeetles on fire and didn't seem to give a care. One smoldering baybeetle was dropping flaming bundles into a blackened concrete cylinder. With a whoosh and a pop, out flew the flaming bundles beyond the city walls, igniting patches of forest. Lighting each other and the planet on fire was apparently just their way of doing business.

Tyrone swooped through the smoke into the city to save the baybeetles from their self-destruction and to awaken them as to who they really were. "Mreeow!" Tyrone cried, "Mreeow! Mreeow!"

Running through the legs of the baybeetles, jumping up on their cars, none took heed. Some mimicked Tyrone idiotically—"Well meow meow, little kitty"—but most did not seem to hear him at all as they stroked Tyrone's body and told him how pretty he was. They did not understand Tyrone, so Tyrone decided to try and understand *them*.

The baybeetles lived very close together, yet there were staggering disparities in workload. Half of them worked for money all of the time, around the clock, every day. The other half did not work at all. They could find no work so they lay heavy and still, sleeping in doorways, eating discarded food. Why didn't they divide the work up equally so that all may live? Two content baybeetles working twenty hours a week was better than one baybeetle working forty hours a week while the other starved.

Among those who could work, there were staggering disparities in abundance. There in the flaming city, some of the employed were heavy with riches, eating tantalizing cuisine, while the majority struggled, living hand to mouth under constant stress.

In the flaming city, some of the ill were treated, some were not.

Did these baybeetles not realize what they were missing? Did they not see Nord burning and crumbling all around them? Did they not know that they were the Mreeow, the Dreamers? Did they not know that they were in Heaven?

Tyrone found a ladybeetle slaving away inside of a glass high-rise. She was pretty and composed, though Tyrone could see that she suffered the heartbreak of her world. Tyrone thought that a walk in the woods would do this ladybeetle a world of good.

When the ladybeetle's office cleared out at dusk, Tyrone jumped into her convertible and hid in the back. Instead of leaving the cloistered city with its noise pollution and concrete floors, however, the ladybeetle drove directly to Gino's Emporium. Tyrone watched amazed as she gambled fifty-four million dollars on the purchase of a Gino's limited edition handbag. Her bet was that the better handbag would give her an edge in her heart and in her community.

She was happy with the handbag for seventeen days. It was the nicest handbag in the neighborhood. There was, however, a side effect. The handbag had increased the violence.

Attempts were made to steal the handbag. Muggings and deceptive business transactions ran rampant as many strived to acquire their own limited edition handbags.

On her eighteenth morning of happiness, the young ladybeetle awakened to find her fabulous handbag knifed. There it lay, limp as a wet tissue. Not knowing who to blame, her life turned dark as night from a ground that could have grown her back together. She lost her gamble and what was left of her money and her happiness. She was worse off than when she started. On top of that, someone had lit her on fire.

Homeless and in need of help, the ladybeetle walked off trailing a plume of smoke. Tyrone followed, assuming that she would soon find assistance in this city so filled with wealth. The ladybeetle's condition deteriorated as Tyrone kept watch for help and the city's leadership.

As the days passed, the closest Tyrone found to leadership was a collection of business managers and government administrators. They were not only in charge, but also getting rich off the system. The leadership was not overly concerned with the baybeetles who were getting burned because the leadership had the world at its fingertips. They were tapped into the big business that blanketed the city and extended universally, unconcerned with any particular town, baybeetle, or natural patch of Nord.

"The advantages," Tyrone sighed, "of governing a society of gamblers." There was no grounded, equitable economic system in place, so the populace was forced into gambling. Baybeetles in the city worked their lives away, gambling their pay on handbags and paper thin investments that were supposed to see them through hard times and old age. No wonder the city was nervous, always on edge. Fortunes could disappear in the blink of an eye.

Tyrone had no thumbs and was covered with fur.

Never would he possess the power of fire.

The baybeetles, on the other hand, had the power of fire. With their magic, the baybeetles could have it all—food, shelter, medicine, travel, fun, and relative security for all. Abundance for all. They had the gift of fire, but see how they used it.

# RAZOR BLADES AND BEAR CLAWS

The city's flames grew higher.

Violence continued to increase.

The baybeetles remained blind to the flames, in denial of the flames, or busy growing walls in order to hide from the flames—the flames that would eventually destroy the walls themselves. Their isolation from each other and from Mother Nature was what had caused their problems, and this same isolation was what they were turning to for answers. Their fear of the light of being one with the planet was greater than their desire for survival.

Tyrone's ladybeetle friend lay weeping and burning at his side.

She had quit.

Surrounded by burning buildings and burning baybeetles, Tyrone sat back on his haunches and closed his eyes.

In the void of his mind, Tyrone pictured the fires that surround him, the scorched and dulled hues, the threatening turbulence. Through the middle of the filthy rampage, Tyrone imagined a clear rivulet of water snaking along a street curb. Reflecting the water, he imagined a feather of blue sky breaking through the black clouds. Though still very new to the baybeetles and to the planet, the baybeetle way of doing business was already obsolete. Surely burning served a purpose for a certain era, but this burning economy no longer brought happiness to baybeetles nor did it preserve life on Nord.

Tyrone preferred a natural economic system. In a natural economy, when one is given twenty baybeetles standing in a pasture, the work that needs to be done—providing food, clothing, shelter, and a few other amenities—is more or less divided equally among the twenty baybeetles. There is no competition, no lighting each other on fire. The less work that needs to be done, the fewer hours each baybeetle works. There is no fixed number of hours to be worked day in and day out. When the work is done, it is done. The fruits of the group's labor are then distributed among its members. From the feather of blue sky in Tyrone's mind unfolded another bright blue feather as the swelling stream of clean water carried away a charred dollar bill.

Eyes closed, Tyrone saw a new level of guidance emerging from within the city flames—a new layer of leadership whose concerns were a content, healthy baybeetle population and a healthy, vibrant planet. These leaders were the sages, the teachers, the intellectuals, the philosophers, the scientists, the artists. The lovers. The elves. Unconcerned with unquenchable desires to line their pockets with riches, these were the ones who were born to guide the business managers and government administrators. They were not troubled by the riches accrued by those whom they were guiding, so although these new leaders were changing the world, the rich got to stay rich. The rich got to stay rich and be benevolent at the same time.

The sun glinted off the surface of the water now flowing broadly through the city in Tyrone's mind. The stream was extinguishing the flames and slowly but surely wearing down asphalt and concrete, slowly but surely nurturing grasses growing upon its banks. The baybeetles of the city began to inch their way back into the natural world as they addressed the quagmires they had made of their own nature.

They began by stopping.

By simply stopping what they were doing—namely destroying their planet by the way they lived and conducted business—the baybeetles improved Nord immeasurably. After ending the way that things were done, every baybeetle was able to work as many hours as it wanted on reviving the land. Due to the thorough devastation of the planet, there were infinite ways to go about restoring its beauty and functionality. The highest priority was given to moving the wealth of industry and the genius of technology towards the goal of natural restoration. More jobs were created in restoring the world than in destroying it and it didn't require years of training to teach a baybeetle how to handle a shovel.

A full, redirected workforce liberated from forty hours per week of nonsense began to literally move mountains—and rebuild them. Leveled forests were replanted, toxic rivers purified. Streams buried in pipes beneath cities were brought again to the surface. The air was made fresh again. The hollow ocean became thick with life again. Even the fisherbeetles who gave up the fishing pole and the rowboat to work in fish factories floated upon the waters again, waiting for the big one. With the restoration of the land came the restoration of the baybeetle spirit.

The baybeetles always said that money didn't grow on trees, somehow forgetting that food *did* grow on trees, for free. As the forested lungs of the planet beyond the city limits were restored, the cities themselves were slathered with fruit trees, berry bushes, and vegetable gardens. More jobs arose with the harvest of city crops and the mop-up of fallen apples left uneaten.

All of this investment in nature was an investment in who the baybeetles really were. A baybeetle could always lose its handbag, but it could never lose its nature. Turquoise whitewater gurgled against black obsidian boulders bejeweled by the sun. These water-worn boulders were all that remained of the flaming city's walls.

Tyrone opened his eyes. He blinked, finding the world outside his mind was no different than the one he had created in his imagination. It made no difference whether his eyes were open or closed, what Tyrone saw was the same. The fires were gone. Baybeetles were lounging, working, and content. The ladybeetle who had given up was now wearing a smile. Tyrone pawed and slapped the bubbles in the water.

His thoughts alone had changed the world.

A perishing prandali was the last remnant of the urban inferno.

As the prandali drifted past his whiskers, Tyrone heard its ashen song, its final words for this world. "I had to lose my hammer," it rang, "to believe in another day." After its cryptic farewell, the silenced prandali fell to Nord to become soil for the life of another generation of prandalia.

Licking his arm in the warmth of the day, Tyrone got vigorous and lost control, falling over backwards onto a bed of four leaf clovers. Tongue still in mid-air, Tyrone fell asleep on the clover and began to dream a dream within a dream.

In his dark cave, Tyrone dreamed of a demon, a dragon, and a city on fire. His precious scrolls circled above him, torn to shreds by the blistering winds that held him captive. His creed had been reduced to scraps of jigsaw puzzle passages.

Without the creed, how would the baybeetles survive? How would Tyrone survive? How would Tyrone stop the war? The fires? The destruction of Nord?

RAZOR BLADES AND BEAR CLAWS

Tyrone awoke to Anisha zipping back and forth between his ears, whirring to wake him without resorting to her talons. "Ahhhhrrrrrr..." purred Tyrone, the freezing wind blowing up his fur, "Welcome, little one."

In the scant light, the great cat appeared gaunt but unworried. Anisha dropped a small chunk of meat onto the ground next to Tyrone, his head propped against the cave wall. "Thank you so much, darling. Do we have company?"

Flitting and twitting, Anisha signaled in the affirmative.

"Then let us begin."

# CHAPTER SIXTEEN

# Boxcars

Tyrone explained to Anisha the nature of their mission. He then began to growl his concepts all over her. Conscious of his tendency to expound on minutia and derail his own train of thought, Tyrone tried to make his first words the most crucial were he or Anisha to fall during the course of their task.

To Tyrone's every rambling monologue, Anisha hurried her head in agreement. She wanted nothing more than to bring this ordeal to a successful close and return to a life of suckling warm, sweet nectar. When her memory reached its capacity, Anisha wound through the scraps of flying parchment, Tyrone's shattered creed, then disappeared into the ice maze of bear claws and razor blades.

In the raging storm outside, heavy flakes of snow had begun to fall and mix with the rest of the debris whizzing through the air. Jake sat cross-legged, swaddled in his sleeping bag. Abacus stood next to him, his black eyes riveted on the mouth of the cave, fedora crooked against the wind. Slim was busy corralling Rod who busied himself dodging this way and that, catching snowflakes on his tongue next to the edge of the cliff. When Rod was still, when he was in spellbound contemplation of the storm, Slim would wrap himself around Abacus' bare, freezing toes.

Anisha emerged in a tailspin, feathers bent, but otherwise in one piece. Slim lunged for her again and his banana belt fell to the ground. Anisha spoke to Abacus from within his beard. "Jake," said Abacus, "draw forth your purple journal and a writing quill."

Anisha piped her way through Tyrone's opening remarks. "Write this down, Jake, in contemporary Bizonian idiom."

Abacus reiterated line by line the words of Tyrone as related by Anisha, two written pages in all. When Jake had finished dictating, Abacus signaled for Anisha to continue. She peeped two more pages, emerged from the tangle of Abacus' beard, and turned to twist back through the snapping jowls of the tempest, into the darkness of the cave. Abacus repeated her last words to Jake and Jake's head grew light and dreamy as he logged them down.

"Abacus. What the *Dijouti* is happening here?" asked an adamant Jake.

"Young Jake. We are transcribing the creed as penned by Tyrone. Tyrone must now repeat the entire work from memory."

"I, uh…Tyrone is a cat right? Or did you mean a 'cat', like a baybeetle is a 'cat', a 'dude'?"

"Oh I do mean a four-legged, my friend."

"I don't think we're on the same page here, Abacus."

"But we are both on page four. Onto page five with any luck 'tall."

Many years ago, when Tyrone was little more than a cub, he sat before a flayed rat. One by one, he removed the rat's organs and aligned them on a flat stone. The cats have always been highly scientific, and rebellious young Tyrone was selected for a stint in the dissection laboratory. Most considered a position in the lab an honor, as it was an acknowledgement of one's high intellect. This is not to mention that nibbling on warm entrails was a daily opportunity.

# BOXCARS

Tyrone, however, was not cut out for a life of dissecting rodents with sanitized claws, sitting on his tail in the den all day, every day. After being caught chasing shrew for pleasure when scheduled for the lab on three consecutive Saturday nights, Tyrone was reassigned to a known baybeetle feeding ground for a daily head count of the herd. The reassignment was considered particularly brutal, for from where Tyrone stood on the cutting edge of science, baybeetles were, shall we say, idiots.

All of the *native* species of Nord practiced ancient and complex forms of language. They were possessed of the ability to understand the languages of other native species. The baybeetles were castaways from outer space who would never fully mature under Nord's gravitational pull. Their brains were simply too cumbersome—all that came out of their mouths was confused whining and barking.

At the completion of his sentence, Tyrone requested a stay in baybeetle head count. His superiors, though baffled, conceded to Tyrone's request.

Tyrone saw patterns.

Baybeetles nodded when barking "okay okay". "C'mon baby baby" was repeated over and over while in mating display. There would be back-and-forths over a freshly caught fish where one baybeetle would bark "nice one", a call answered by "oh yeah". Soon there were so many instances of situation specific whining and barking that Tyrone became convinced. Baybeetles could talk.

When Tyrone reported his findings to the Wildlife Council, the council's response was that these semblances of language were just that—semblances of language. Crude warning signals at best.

Tyrone persevered.

He picked up a few words.

The first time Tyrone approached young Abacus was a disaster. Though Tyrone did his best to growl the word for "hello", seeing the great cat rolling in the grass made Abacus run screaming for mamabeetle.

Days later in another part of the forest, Abacus heard the same voice. This time he swore he heard the cat say "hello Abacus" as best a cat could. Abacus did not retreat and the two became fast friends.

Using hand and paw signals, drawing pictures in the dirt, word by word, Abacus and Tyrone learned each other's languages. Abacus proved fleet of tongue, able to mimic a wide variety of cat noises. Tyrone, on the other hand, found these baybeetles devilishly difficult to immitate and contented himself with understanding the spoken word.

Once it was discovered that baybeetles were trainable, a myriad of species volunteered their time to teach the baybeetles their languages. Abacus' tribe from Tulika became specialized in the languages of cats and hummingbirds.

Living so close with the Tulikans, Tyrone soon gleaned the story of Woodrow Happyhouse, the great white baybeetle from a distant land. Abacus taught Tyrone the Olde Byzontian tongue and the Tulikans told Tyrone about the Happyhouse "relics", a collection of goods left in their care many moons ago by Happyhouse. As a caretaker of the wayward baybeetles, these relics were something that Tyrone simply had to see for himself.

Tyrone was taken high into the mountains.

On the edge of a buttercup spray near the summit of Mount Rancancan, there was a cave drenched in sunlight and songbirds. Tyrone and his party found the rears of the cave by torchlight. Wrenching aside an ornery slab of granite, the Tulikans revealed to Tyrone the nautical chest of Sir Woodrow Happyhouse.

∿

A calculating device with many rows of sliding wooden beads.

A brass navigational instrument set with lenses and mirrors.

Twenty scrolls of parchment.

One bound, leather pouch.

These were the Happyhouse relics.

All but two of the scrolls were still completely blank. One of the marked scrolls was Abacus' map. The other was Woodrow's warning, his letter foreshadowing Bizonian encroachment into Vivachanga.

Following the departure of Happyhouse, the meaning of Woodrow's warning had become lost on the Tulikans. Woodrow read the words on the scroll to them once and that was that. Tulikan life after Happyhouse carried on unchanged for generations.

Having no concept of written language, the Tulikans came to see Woodrow's written warning as purely abstract art. For this reason, when Gino's REZ workers were first spotted by the Tulikans, Gino's was not recognized as the vanguard of destruction. These exploratory incursions into Tulikan wilds by Gino's were regarded as curious anomalies.

After viewing the relics, most notably the map and the decorated scroll, the enigma of Happyhouse filled Tyrone's every dream. He must learn more about this Happyhouse and the world from which he came. Tyrone would travel in search of answers.

Tyrone, naked, embarked.

Although he could understand none of the conversation transpiring around him, the strange cities of Muzora were a fascination. Such substantial roads and dwellings Tyrone had never imagined. Marked parchments, not at all dissimilar to that found in the Happyhouse relics, were everywhere. Books of bound parchment would be held up and scrutinized by the Muzorans much more intently than one would ever scrutinize a work of visual art. They seemed to be interpreting the marks on the parchment much the way a Vivachangan would interpret the information contained in deer tracks or bear droppings.

Like Slim in days hence, Tyrone found his crossing of the Rutmus Strait most invigorating. Chased by sailors with sticks and nets, Tyrone leapt from his Muzoran cargo ship and skidded to a halt on the docks of Philistine Acres in the land of Gibbous Bizonia. He hid and feasted for days behind a bin overflowing with fish heads.

Tyrone first assumed that the Bizonian being spoken in Philistine Acres stemmed from a seafaring dialect, as all of the words slurred together and he could hardly follow a conversation. The word order was also somehow convoluted. Everywhere he went, however, the Bizonian tongue had the same flavor. Things had changed since the time of Woodrow Happyhouse.

The roads and dwellings in Gibbous Bizonia were even more substantial than those in Muzora. Tyrone discovered that every day, all of the young baybeetles in the neighborhood would come and occupy one of the most substantial of these dwellings. Creeping up to a window in the brick building, Tyrone began salivating when he realized what the children were doing in there.

With his white stick, the big baybeetle at the front of the room would draw a few lines on the wall then say a word. All of the little baybeetles would repeat the word. The longer the chain of white-sticked markings became, the more it resembled the marked-up parchments like the books and the Happyhouse scroll. These messy baybeetles, word for word, were able to capture their own speech and parlay it into inked markings upon the page.

It took some time for the domesticated housecats to overcome the shock of learning that their mentally sluggish feeders were capable of both written and spoken language, but once Tyrone convinced them that this was indeed the case, these locals were more than willing to lend a paw. The family cat, from this point forward, was always looking over Mom's shoulder during bedtime stories. Pages from children's favorite books would be chewed loose and drug away. Kittens brought for show and tell would refuse to leave grade school classrooms until the children's grammar lessons were complete. Homework would disappear from school bags to an endless parade of crying, innocent children being sent to their rooms. Tyrone and his minions would convene with their bounty of written material every Thursday for study, then relax over chew toys.

After two years of study, Tyrone was capable of reading and writing the Bizonian language. He could, of course, still only speak the words that one could imagine a cat able to pronounce, words like *mail, drawer, real,* and *maroon. Grow, muse, broom,* and *mucus.*

Upon his return to Vivachanga, Tyrone pounced on Woodrow's warning, his saliva threatening to bleed the ink. Tyrone became the only living being on Nord to have read Woodrow's words. Inclined to agree with the meat of Woodrow's warning, especially after gaining first-hand experience of the world at large, Tyrone knew that Vivachanga was in trouble. Gino's was the beginning of the end.

Tyrone told Abacus alone what he had read on the Happyhouse parchment—the longhand passage on the back remained a mystery. As if sensing the troubles to come, Tyrone sent Abacus off with not only Woodrow's warning, but the relic's bound leather pouch and the map of Nord for safe keeping.

Tyrone had seen the spell cast.

Perhaps only he knew the antidote.

The antivenin.

Tyrone had heard Bizonians say that their free market economy would be that antivenin. A free market economy would solve all of the world's problems. Under the free market system, anyone with money was free to spend or not spend their money at the market on anything they pleased. All of Nord would be put up for sale in the free market. None of Nord's natural resources—forests, oceans, baybeetles—would be free from the chopping block.

"Let the laws of supply and demand dictate the way we do business," Bizonians would say. By these dictates, if a fellow had enough money, he could demand that Vivachanga's krundle pine monarch sanctuaries be cut down and handed over. No questions asked.

Although the free market may eventually "fix" the world's problems, it was most definitely not the most efficient way to do so. The end results would be far from optimal. Tyrone knew that the power of the mind was the true antivenin.

Tyrone knew that he must write a creed, a creed to be delivered to Gibbous Bizonia and digested by Gibbous Bizonians. This was where the healing antivenin must be injected. The eighteen scrolls. The eighteen blank scrolls. In the cave of relics, on the Happyhouse parchments, Tyrone went about his work, keeping his project a secret, even from Abacus. Undue alarm was to be avoided.

Writing with a claw dipped in blackberry ink was slow and sloppy, but after twelve years of thankless labor, the creed was completed—the antivenin secured. Eighteen scrolls, eighteen chapters.

# BOXCARS

On what should have been a pleasant spring morning, the morning after Tyrone had put the finishing touches on his manuscript, he awoke to a nightmare. The sun had disappeared. The air in his cave, the cave of relics, had grown cold and damp. The mouth of the cave was no longer an exit, but a wall of ice behind which churned a cyclone of baybeetle disposables. His creed was in tatters, flying about the cave. Worst of all, a piece of old gum had lodged in his fur.

For hours Anisha's trial raged on.

Ever more plucked, Anisha's eyes grew wider and more anxious each time she emerged from the cave and the unholy tabernacle of biting refuse. With every return of Anisha, Jake's eyes grew wider and more anxious at the content of what he was dictating. These ideas and the way they were presented had no known precedent.

Come twilight, after more than thirty trips in and out of the cave's death trap, Anisha's work was only half done. She was glad to see the onset of night, as the darkness rendered her chore all but impossible.

With Anisha snoring in his beard, Abacus set himself to the task of constructing shelter from the storm. His final product of ice and evergreen spray was either an illusion or an actual physical impossibility. Regardless, the akimbo structure was enough for them all to sleep in and stay dry, if not warm.

In their hunger, someone made a stab for a scrap of someone else's food.

Beneath a cacophony of slot machines, Dijouti squatted at the craps table. She called "boxcars" and rolled the dice. The chattering dice rocked on edge and when they were still, the dice showed double sixes—boxcars. Gathering in her winnings Dijouti, called "boxcars" again, titillating onlookers. Rattling the dice on her wing, Dijouti let 'em fly.

Boxcars.

"Boxcars."

Boxcars.

"Boxcars."

Boxcars.

Dijouti couldn't lose.

The dice were fixed.

Won every time.

Dijouti called 'em "boxcars" one more time and this time she won big. Dijouti, The Ptarmigan of Peace, won the entire universe. Dijouti beamed as she flew the universe home to her nest. Once she and the universe were cozy, Dijouti stared into the universe with half-closed eyes, like one in love.

The deeper Dijouti looked into the snow globe of the universe, the more beautiful and miraculous it became. There were supernovas, dark matter horse heads, quasar discos, and loads of love burrows. Dijouti saw countless planets where loud and symmetrical life forms devoured one another, doing so in order to perpetuate life. When not killing for food, creatures on these planets lived off the dew from the leaves, singing songs and taking care not to destroy the land where they walked and slept.

Centuries passed.

# BOXCARS

Craving involvement, Dijouti dove headlong into the snow globe, the celestial menagerie. Inside the universe, there were stars everywhere, yet almost nowhere. Even riding the tail of a comet, Dijouti could not travel from one star to the next. She would have to fly, and fly she did, past worm holes, intergalactic space vehicles, and pods of fetal baybeetles.

Mature baybeetles were always there when she needed one. When Dijouti's curiosity would draw her towards rhinestone clouds of deathly gasses, a loving, weightless baybeetle would materialize to shoo her away.

A bright electric flash caught Dijouti's eye.

The flash had burped off of a miniscule, blue planet. The planet had only two significant land masses, separated by a narrow strait of water. In addition to an envelope of shifting clouds, Dijouti saw that this planet was obscured by a foxtail of dust and smoke. She became perplexed.

Planets were not supposed to have tails.

The tail was dynamic. Its contents flowed from one tapered end of the tail in the East, into a wide belly, and from there into another tapered point in the Far West. Following the flow of the dust and smoke, Dijouti saw through the western end of the tail a nation composed of great hives of concrete and steel. Instead of living off of the dew from the leaves, the hive creatures here engaged in a riot of consumption. Objects of every imaginable variety were drawn from the land then left to rot in piles or injected into the polluted seas. The creatures consumed for pleasure, but in so doing, they were forfeiting one of the greatest pleasures of all, their own gift of freedom.

One creature sacrificed its freedom by working to produce, say, toasters to be consumed by other creatures. In the process of creating toasters, more items such as staples, memo pads, work gloves, and machine oil were consumed at the toaster factory. Other creatures labored endlessly at other factories to create the staples, memo pads, work gloves, and machine oil. Electricity, cutting blades, sewing needles, and cleaning solvents were consumed while producing staples, memo pads, work gloves, and machine oil, so soon the entire hive did nothing but consume and work, consume and work, consume and work.

In consuming products that consumed the land, the creatures at this end of the tail were also forfeiting the pleasure of their own universally promised gift of natural beauty. The nation acted as a drain in a bathtub, sucking the pulverized planet into its spiraling depths, pulling on the planet at large.

Through the wide belly of the foxtail, across the narrow strait of water, Dijouti saw hives of wood and adobe. Here there was not nearly the level of consumption seen in the civilization of concrete and steel. Still, the creatures were forced into a life of work, work, and more work, feeding the foxtail with dust and smoke from their factories. They worked as virtual slaves and all of the items they made were shipped away to the hive of concrete and steel.

In this middle country, Dijouti saw another electric flash much like the first. Up close, she could now see that the flash was born of a violent blast that destroyed plants, animals, and the land. Dijouti had found the lonely anomaly called war. Nowhere else in the entire snow globe of the cosmos had she seen such slovenly nonsense.

Dust.

Smoke.

War.

# BOXCARS

The first nation, the nation of concrete and steel, produced all of the instruments of war, arming the entire planet. The production of weapons drove the nation's economy. The equipment produced in the name of war—tanks, bombs, jet fighters, sonar, radar, satellites, aircraft carriers—were this planet's most technologically complex items, demanding pound-for-pound more natural resources than any other product. In order to extract the resources it needed to build these complex war instruments and keep them running, the nation of concrete and steel went to war on the rest of the planet, warring against its own weaponry. The silliness of the cycle was twisted and disturbing.

War was not only destroying this planet due to the extraction of natural resources used to build war equipment, but war in and of itself was destroying the planet one bomb at a time. Pockmarks infected the land. Caves of stone were blown to shreds, never to grow back. War clogged the air, feeding the planet's tail with smoke from fires of every horrific variety—wood, oil, and flesh. When a city hive was destroyed by the fire of war, its remaining residents took to the countryside to extract more stone, wood, and oil to rebuild their hives and prepare for the next wave of war.

On this lonely planet at war, not only did they kill and let the bodies rot, but they felt no shame in obliterating the life support systems of their own planet. They were burning down their own home, their own hospital. Indiscriminate killing of all forms of life was not only commonplace, but celebrated.

Why was this planet at war with itself?

Why was it self-destructing?

What spell was it under?

The eastern tip of the foxtail was below her now. This end of the tail twisted into a vicious cyclone. Sailing through the frigid jet stream, Dijouti decided she had seen enough of this blood bath of a planet and turned her head towards better things in her new cosmos.

But Dijouti couldn't leave.

She had gotten too close to the tip of the planet's tail. The tail's pull was sucking the freezing upper atmosphere down into its vortex, along with Dijouti. Her wings could not tear her away.

Losing altitude, Dijouti saw a halo of virgin terrain surrounding the storm's vortex. The only hives down there were for honey bees. Sanity at last. She even caught glimpses of elusive, peaceful creatures with sensitive ears living off the dew.

Tumbling out of control towards the tiny planet, Dijouti was losing her breath and feathers. She entered the churning storm clenched with fear. Her world a whiteout, Dijouti could not tell up from down until the cyclone spat her out over a mountain peak in the thralls of a blizzard. Dijouti was content to have made it through alive.

From her pine branch perch, Dijouti saw a collection of creatures large and small huddled near the peak of the mountain. Three of them walked on two feet and one, a four-legged, was covered with fur. The smallest creature had a needle beak and was draped in iridescent plumage. Each held a rather small pile of provisions.

One of the creatures made a stab for a scrap of someone else's food.

A scuffle ensued and when the creatures retired for the night, each kept one eye open, on guard against the others. Once the food stabber was still, Dijouti looked into his heart and mind to see what made him lose his team spirit.

# BOXCARS

This two-legged had a good heart. His mind, however—a mind that used to work so well as an extension of his heart—had deviated from his heart. Looking deeper into his deviated mind, Dijouti saw that the deviation from the heart was not his fault. Dijouti could see that the deviation occurred thousands of years ago among this creature's ancient ancestors. The ancestors were the ones who had walked away from the abundance of food and warmth they found in their original jungles. When the ancestors of this freezing, hungry creature wandered into the planet's colder, less fertile lands, they lost their minds. They deviated from the heart.

So long ago was their deviation from an abundant, community-oriented frame of mind that the lot of them now believed in scarcity, stabbing, armored tanks, and war. Worse yet, they believed that stabbing was their nature and that they could not control it. They were not aware of their own deviation.

Dijouti wondered if this two-legged below would realize that to possess little, to demand little from his environment, was to have a lot. It was the origin and the future of his species. The less he demanded, the more abundance he would experience. There was enough for everyone on his planet and best of all, their hearts were still good. Their violence could continue if it must, but if even the victors of war were to survive, they would have to learn to fight with little more than their bare hands. Blowing up mountains to create devices for blowing up mountains was killing them all.

Dijouti the Snow Chicken and Ptarmigan of Peace awoke from her dream of winning the universe at craps.

She opened her eyes and let out a call into the dawn, rousting a motley crew in an impossible shelter below. Not to waylay their mission, Dijouti quivered the snow from her spring plumage and flew away.

At Dijouti's croaking call, Abacus and Rod awoke looking straight at each other, wondering if they had heard what they thought they had heard. Each was wondering if somebody wasn't trying to be clever.

Jake awoke unaware of the call of the Snow Chicken. Still half asleep he blurted, "Baybeetles migrated into coldness."

"Yes," added Rod, "In body and in soul."

"I do think that you boys are onto something," said Abacus, "Now let us finish our work."

Somehow Anisha made it through another five hours of circus survival then burrowed back into Abacus' beard. "Anisha says we are done," said Abacus, "Now tarry not. If Tyrone is to survive and live free, if there is hope to be had for life on Nord, we must deliver his manuscript into the proper hands."

As they crawled back down the way they had come, through rampart gusts of seething air, Jake looked back to the cave and swore that he caught—through the rarest trick of the light—the image of Tyrone, gesturing with raised paw from deep within the darkness. Through one luminous facet of a pillar of ice, Jake saw that Tyrone was small, white, and fuzzy, with a little gray nose and gray ears. Jake's head whipped back to the path with the thud of Rod being knocked to the ground. A forty pound rubber tire hoisted by the vortex winds had bruised him badly.

Rod rose to his knees covered in snow, both fists raging at God Almighty for the abusive blow. Rod howled from the hungry heart of his belly, "I HAVE BEEN A GOOD BAYBEETLE!" Rod's reverberating bellow jammed the mountainside and the ice-burdened ground fell out from beneath him. Rod fell at speed into a rushing white collapse. Anisha and Abacus, sliding to a halt hundreds of feet below, managed to swim and then surf the avalanche.

Rod, Jake, and Slim were nowhere to be found.

# CHAPTER SEVENTEEN

# Relinquished

Withered down to her last few feathers, Anisha covered ground. Heeding her call, Abacus plowed ahead, his legs falling through the snow up to the hip with each step. Anisha had found a boot resting on the crusty surface of broken snow. Abacus bent over and took a whiff to track its stench.

Jerking his head back with a screwed face, Abacus knew immediately where to find Jake and yanked on the boot with both hands. As Abacus sank up to his chin in the rough powder, Jake popped clean up from beneath the settling avalanche, backpack and all.

Drenched and shaking, Jake was looking around, insane. "Abacus! Where's Rod? Where's Rod!"

"Off we must to find him, Jake. There is no time."

They fell to shouting, risking yet another avalanche. There was no sign of either Slim or Rod. Remembering the chain in which they had been hiking down from the cave, Jake started digging in the snow and ice with his bare fingers where logic and fortune might converge. Having no more intricate scheme, Abacus began digging as well. Beneath the frantic sounds of shoveling snow and labored breathing, Anisha was peeping her heart out, unheard just twenty feet from the excavation.

Anisha rifled through the air, her surgically precise beak piercing Abacus' brow. Abacus looked to where Anisha was signaling and saw a seal pup struggling to push its way up through the snow. Abacus was arrived to find the poke of Slim's snout gasping for air.

Abacus cleared the melting ice from Slim's face and began to dig him out, careful not to aggravate injury. The moment a full mote had been scooped away from the animal, Slim exploded into Abacus' face and took off running.

"Slim!" yelled Jake, instinctively running off behind Rod's kitten.

"Jake! Please! We must find your brother!" yelled Abacus, for Jake was drowning in his own adrenaline and stayed after Slim. "Great Dijouti. I cannot lose them all," whispered Abacus, and he took off screaming after Jake and Slim.

Bumbling over a heavy berm of deep snow, Abacus caught sight of Slim and Jake in another frenzied excavation. Abacus joined the charade, but it was Slim who first latched onto a corner of Rod. Abacus and Jake burrowed around the visible patch of Rod and once Abacus had gripped a mound of flesh, he hoisted Rod up and out. Rod was pale and limp.

"Rod!" shouted Jake. Rod did not respond.

"Mister Rod!" shouted Abacus, slapping Rod across the face.

"Mmmrrowwrrrr!" roared Slim, sinking his claws into Rod's chest.

But nothing worked.

They laid Rod down on Jake's jacket and Jake put his cheek to Rod's mouth. What little breath he heard was raspy and torn. "Don't go, brother." Jake shook him. "Wake up, Rod!" But there was still no response. Rod's lips were turning blue.

"We must flock to a lower elevation," said Abacus, "Come now. I will carry him." Jake picked-up Slim and bled tears as the five of them headed downward through the snowfield.

Travel remained deep and slow.

The sky grew dim.

Rod remained despondent, sinking deeper into the light.

With each step shifting, falling, and disappearing beneath them, they struggled. The snow thinned no more than one wisp at a time. "I believe that in your country there is a saying," said Abacus, "'Tis always darkest before the spawn."

"The dawn," said Jake.

"Always darkest before the dawn, Jake."

Jake remained quiet and mournful.

"I had not thought of this story for a great length of time, Jake, but of it I was recently reminded. When I was but a weebeetle, an exceptional event came upon this Nord.

"As the sun burned towards day's end, I was sculpting a wee mud cake. You shall not believe it, but despite the clumsy work of cake before me, I was there blessed with a song that grew from the hush of nature. It was the song of one thousand angels. One thousand melodies, each unique, all one. This alone was extraordinary, but in a magical world, acceptable.

"Then something else happened.

"The area around me brightened ever so slightly. I thought nothing of it, giving credit to the sun, the parting of the clouds. The stirring in my head I credited to the hill of red ants I had eaten to spoil my supper. Still working the lump of mud cake, an active warmth spread from my heart, filling my entire body, head to toe."

Jake was reminded of his welling heart uncapped in Valgato.

"Quite pleased," Abacus carried on, "I continued my work until again the area around me grew brighter. My head bristled as if a bolt of lightning had struck the Nord nearby. More waves of light and warmth arose through and around me. The singing grew in beauty and complexity.

"The quality of the light was such that it could forever increase in intensity yet never become painful to the eyes. The warmth such that it could forever rise in temperature yet never become painful to the body."

Jake tried to envision such a situation.

"I thought the rising light and the increasing warmth *would* go on forever, Jake. The constant weight of my body all but lifted off of the ground. My heart flew clear away into the newborn sky. My vision rose to a higher place and I saw the world from just above the top of my head. The only word to describe what I felt there is 'peace'. An unstoppable peace, vibrating and rhythmic. Everything! The dirt on my hands, the sky, the trees. They were the ones singing this beautiful music! I could not move. Then, the honeymoon ended.

"Something unknown and horrific, albeit something limitless and euphoric, had just had its way with me. I fell into distress. Crying and running around, I was hoping, nay, *praying* that our camp might still be in tact after this Nord shattering moment.

"Lucky for me, I found everyone. They were all out in the clearing looking to the sky. My mother took me in her arms and bade me look as well.

"My eyes adjusted from the mud to the sky to see a cloud illuminated by the sun. Everyone giggled and took a deep breath when the cloud moved to squirm and twist. The cloud was in animal locomotion, beating a path towards the horizon. Stretching for one hundred miles, if not one thousand miles from end to end, was an enormous, heavenly caterpillar. The caterpillar traveled so very high in the heavens that it was impossible to assess its dimensions.

"It was not impossible, however, to realise that the caterpillar was the creator of its own light and the instigator of the magnificent songs and sensations I experienced on that day. The remaining sunbeams of twilight were mute in comparison to the luminous caterpillar."

"A caterpillar?" asked a distant, sad, and skeptical Jake.

"Surely 'twas not a caterpillar as we know the caterpillar in a common sense, Jake. A celestial caterpillar 'twas. Carefree and dignified."

Their path remained steep, challenged by snow and ice. As much as Jake, Abacus, Anisha, and Slim wished for Rod's immediate care, if he were still alive, there was simply nowhere to stop.

Abacus continued his telling in an attempt to keep Jake's mind occupied, "Soon after the crossing of the celestial caterpillar in my youth, strange objects carried upon the waves of Sister Ocean began to wash upon our shores. With their sharp edges and impeccable uniformity to one another, it was surmised that the objects had been crafted by magical forces heretofore unknown. This brought everyone general discomfort.

"Sadly, the beached objects were followed by a decline in migrating birds and butterflies. I wondered if the enormous caterpillar had not been feeding upon them. An elder descended from the hills and called a meeting to order.

"'Twas at this meeting that the elder told of another caterpillar crossing. It had been described to him by his great-grandfather who was told by his great-grandfather and so forth."

CHAPTER 17

"Abacus, will you please stop with these crazy stories," Jake implored.

"Ahem. Following the ancient caterpillar crossing described by the elder, it was not strangely uniform objects, but Sir Woodrow Happyhouse himself that washed upon our shores. From this point forward, the world was joined in a circle. A caterpillar crossing had marked a truly great change in the world.

"Great change, once again, had come.

"This was beyond coincidence.

"With Happyhouse came an ominous sense of foreboding, though no one could remember why. With the objects on the beach came the loss of our winged animal friends. Were the celestial caterpillars the couriers of planetary atrocity masked in a radiant glory? Our elders removed themselves from the proceedings and retreated to the secret place to scrutinize.

"We waited for seven days, an eternity for a weebeetle like myself.

"On the seventh day, the return of the elders was signaled with a sounding of the conch. Everyone abandoned the honey hunt and ran to the clearing.

"The elders, like everyone else, were disturbed by the caterpillars. It was declared, however, that caterpillars do turn into butterflies.

"I believe the elders spoke well, Jake.

"With the coming of the first caterpillar, Happyhouse showed us that Nord was small and round. Though foreshadowing severe trials for Vivachanga, Nord could not possibly evolve without a realization of this unity. The first butterfly was unity.

"With the coming of the second caterpillar, the caterpillar of my youth, the elders saw another chapter in the evolution of Nord unfolding. Another time of great learning.

# RELINQUISHED

"It so happens, Jake, that the second caterpillar passing coincided with what has been termed the 'industrial revolution' of Gibbous Bizonia. During this industrial revolution, it became commonplace to produce the same exact item over and over again. With this new ease of production came a new ease of consumption. The effects of this untidy revolution are still catching up with the planet and it is starting to get ugly."

"Why are you telling me this, Abacus?"

"To give you hope, my friend."

"To give me hope? How can the industrial revolution give me hope when it appears that this 'time of great learning' is going to kill us all, starting with the birds and butterflies?" Inside of Abacus' beard, Anisha quaked. Maybe the hummingbirds would be next in line for extinction.

"Perhaps, Jake, the industrial revolution was necessary in order for Nord to reach a certain level of technological complexity. This complexity, though dangerous and destructive, has allowed for global travel and global communication. Since the coming of the second caterpillar, Nord has deepened its unity. A great planetary peace has become possible. Perhaps this peace is the next butterfly.

"Remember the nature of the universe, Jake. Always darkest before the spawn. The caterpillar is indicative of the highest good, so keep your heart and mind open. There is inspiration at the bottom of your darkest hour.

"It was also shortly after the second caterpillar that Tyrone first spake upon mine ear…" As Abacus said these words, the chewing of the snow beneath their feet melted away. They trod on solid Nord once again.

241

Using Rod's dead weight as a shield, Abacus and Jake clubbed their way through a wall of cricket thorn and the mountain gave way to the first dry, level ground of the day. They spread their jackets at the foot of an aspen and propped Rod up against its trunk. He was still breathing, shallow and raspy. "Beetle blast it Rod!" Jake yelled as he shook Rod, but Rod seemed ever farther away.

"Please, Jake. Let us just try to keep him warm," said Abacus. Jake knew this was best and had to walk away.

Arriving at the edge of their narrow plateau, Jake faced their next obstacle—a deadfall of trees. An entire mangled forest. Jake beckoned Abacus and together they examined the trees that had been knocked down this way and that with their branches snapped off or sticking straight up into the air. Root systems clinging desperately to stones and beds of soil were torn from the ground.

"What did this?" asked Jake.

"'Tis a ghastly sight," answered Abacus, "I know not what wields this power."

There was no going around it.

No going through it.

No going over it, not even for wily Abacus, especially with a limp Rod tossed over the shoulder. The trees overlapped each other so densely that nowhere was the ground visible through the web of downed timbers.

As Jake wandered and wept, Abacus rustled over the terrain searching for materials to construct a litter, a stretcher to be carried between he and Jake. Rod would lie on the litter as they attempted the treacherous passage of the deadfall. Abacus lashed green pine boughs to the litter's frame, chanting Vivachangan healing songs in Rod's direction.

"Alright already! I've had it! You guys are stinkin' up the place!" Rod was suddenly awake and fuming mad. "I can't even understand the words to these songs! All I hear is, 'Beetle blast it Rod!' 'Rod this!' 'Rod that!' 'Wake up! Wake up!' *Rest In Peace* is a joke! Could anything be worse than you guys carrying me everywhere on your shoulders? Throwing me to the ground wherever and whenever you want? Yelling at me! Slapping me! Clawing me! Using me as a stinking battering ram! Where's the levity? Things aren't nearly as heavenly here in Heaven as I imagined. All I want is a little sleep. You know, *rest*. Hey—what's that?"

Rod eyeballed the very bed-like litter being constructed by Abacus. He gave up his rant and for the first time in Heaven, he floated weightless, landing upon the litter, snuggling and asking for his blanket.

Shocked, elated, and still mighty scared by Rod's sudden resurrection, Abacus shook him awake, "No! No, Rod! You cannot sleep right now. You may be hurt."

Hurt in the hereafter?

Absurd.

Pushed beyond frustration at not being able to "rest in peace" for even just a few hours, Rod laughed loud and hearty. What a joke. "Well. Alrighty then," he said puffing out his chest, "We'll have it *your* way then."

Taking a quick look around, Rod shook himself loose from Jake's brotherly embrace and dashed off at full speed—directly down into the treachery of the deadfall. He had shed his fearful mortal skin.

Rod's spectacles were back on, and this time Heaven was clear and in focus. Not only did he guide them at speed under, over, and through the impassable deadfall, but he did so with dashing strokes and daring strength moves in the disappearing daylight. Landing squarely upon a substantial game trail on the far side, Rod turned towards straggling Jake, Slim, Abacus, and Anisha and took a bow.

When Rod saw, for the first time in two days, the clear faces of Jake, Slim, and Abacus, his jaw fell in confused awe. They had all died. They had all died and were now joined together in the light. Rod was more happy than sad to have his brother and Abacus alongside himself and Slim. "Welcome," said Rod, and for the first time, he initiated a bear hug.

Regaining familiarity with his surroundings, Abacus took the lead. They were back in the dense foothill forest where the dark of night first takes hold of the land before reaching out to the rest of the world. Despite the velvet darkness unfurling around them, it was agreed that spending another night in the forest without food or safe camp was out of the question.

Jake imagined perhaps two hours of stumbling in the dark until they reached the safety and abundant food of the beach. They might be even closer, as they were travelling downhill. "Is there anything we need to know about walking through the jungle at night?" Jake asked Abacus.

"Leave me to think, Jake," Abacus replied, nearly invisible, "There is one nocturnal denizen of this jungle that spells death to any and all who cross its path. To sense its presence is to know death, for in every predatory skill and sensibility it is far superior to the baybeetle. It is always hungry for flesh. If you have sensed it, it has sensed you, and it will eat you in short measure. It can be anywhere at any moment, so we do not worry ourselves about it."

# RELINQUISHED

"Thanks, Abacus."

"You are welcome, Jake."

"Abacus?"

"Yes, Jake."

"Is that what I think it is?"

Creeping into silhouette before them, against stars peeping through twilight, was the Heart of the World. The ominous, top-heavy, and poorly aligned rock formation near the knoll of wintering monarchs.

"The Heart of the World, Jake."

Jake's calculations had not even come close. They were more than a half day's hike from the beach. Jake was already starved, scared, and physically exhausted.

"Shall we pick up the pace then, my friends?" proposed Abacus.

It would be trying, running across wild turf, their game trail lit only by stars, the moon, and fireflies. Better to risk physical injury though, than to be left in the woods as an easy meal. Rod started them off with a yelp, flying into the forest dark with Slim in pursuit. Rod was moving faster than Jake believed possible, but with three gazelle pounces Abacus shot past them all, disappearing into the velvet dark crawling with vermin. Crazy old hebeetle.

The Bizonians were now alone.

They jumped and scampered, attempted to keep up.

The trail forked.

Under the circumstances, so did their minds.

In his brilliant rage, Rod showed no hesitation in taking the path to the west.

"Can you see Abacus?" Jake yelled, breathless.

"Not at all, Jake!"

"Do you know where you're going?"

"Not at all, bro'!" answered Rod.

Jake managed to catch his brother by the shoulder and force him to reconsider. They shouted into the night for Abacus, but were answered only by their own distant echoes and one impotent howler monkey.

Surely Abacus would realize that he had left his friends behind at the fork. Or maybe Abacus hadn't sensed the fork at all and sat waiting in the dark for his friends to catch up. Or maybe he was still plowing ahead full throttle towards the coast. Maybe by the time Abacus decided that something was amiss, it would be too late.

Rod and Jake felt stares and heard stirrings in the pitch black around them. Back to back they strained to pierce the darkness with their eyes. "Jake," Rod said in a hushed voice.

"Yeah."

"Where's Slim?"

They both thought they heard a high-pitched giggle.

"Abacus?"

There was no answer.

"Where's Slim!" said Rod, again in a hushed voice. "Jake. Grab your flashlight."

"I don't have a flashlight. Wait..." Rod heard Jake rummaging through his pack. Jake struck a wooden match, then rummaged deeper. The match was extinguished and Rod heard the tearing and crumpling of paper. Jake held a second match to a torch of twisted notebook paper, hoping that Tyrone's manuscript and his sketches of Lugan were not going up in flames.

# RELINQUISHED

"Here kitty kitty kitty," called Rod, "Where's the kitty kitty? Here kitty kitty kitty." There were more eerie giggles in the darkness as the brothers turned in a circle searching for Slim. "Jake, I have to go back and look for Slim." Without argument from Jake, they began to backtrack. Rod and Jake hadn't gone fifteen feet when Jake dropped with burning fingers the last smoldering knob of their torch. As Jake was scrunching together another torch, the brothers were approached by a figure.

In striking another match, Jake lost his grip on the matchbox. The remaining matches were spilled from the box onto the floor of the jungle, wet with night. Jake held up their last match to see the figure moving towards them—a ghostly shape surrounded by a halo of fireflies. The full moon slipped out from behind a marauding night cloud. The match went dead.

A short, dark baybeetle draped in clean, white cloth emerged from within the gentle chaos of fireflies. His stare warmed and scared them. He lifted his cupped hands up in front of his long, peppered beard. Leaning towards them, the ghostly figure opened his hands to free a single blue flame. Over his tunic, the ghost wore a long necklace of thick flowers and on his shoulder was perched a cat named Slim. Slim batted at the ghost's beard as the blue flame lifted from the ghost's hands and moved off into the woods.

"Abacus?"

Before Rod and Jake received an answer, a bonfire erupted, ignited by the travelling flame. Two more bonfires were lit just beyond the first. Rod and Jake had no time to think as the gigglers in white tunics, all chocolate brown and too many to count, surrounded and hoisted them into the air. There were sounds of cheers, flutes, and rapid drumming.

Also atop the wave of joyous baybeetles were Slim and Abacus. Abacus shouted to his Bizonian friends, "Welcome to Tulika! Enjoy! For we are the guests of honour once again!"

Abacus had slipped into a tunic and a fog of monarchs were on the wing, loosened from their sleeping masses by the heat of the party. Bamboo torches lit those areas under the canopy not already aflame with bonfire and firefly. Prandalia were everywhere and the pleasant, penetrating vibration was a field of hummingbirds whisking through the air, cleaning what nectar they may out of everyone's flower necklaces.

Slim, for all his effort, still could not land a shifty hummingbird, so he gave up the hunt and began to hunt for a drink instead. Bouncing above the rejoicing mob, Slim had a hell of a time locating the liquor cabinet.

"Sextant!" yelled Abacus, hailing with raised arms another short, peppery hebeetle in a crinkled beard and ceremonial frock. The champions were thereafter lowered to the ground. "Come, my friends," said Abacus to the Bizonians, "There is someone I would like for you all to meet."

Abacus and Sextant engaged in an intimate, physical greeting the likes of which the Bizonians had never seen. "Sextant, my good friend, how be you?"

"Most excellent, my heroic friend. And how be you, Abacus?"

"Alive and well, friend."

"Of course. And who have we here?" asked Sextant as he gave Rod the same intimate greeting he had given Abacus. Abacus did what he could to intervene. Lucky for Rod and for Sextant of Tulika, their greeting was cut short by a lavish procession parading within the gaiety. Seventeen virgin Tulikans held aloft a royal litter

# RELINQUISHED

bedecked with candles and flowering vines. Every shebeetle virgin was paired with a shaved and prancing eunuch sporting a red hip scarf and strumming his dill harp.

Double-chinned and sloshing about atop the royal litter was an engorged and languid Anisha. She was anointed in fragrant oils and awash in ploon blossoms pulsing with sweetness. Rumpled sparkles from a crude bottle rocket shot through the air. All the old-timers laughed at the show.

They were in the heart of a nomadic Tulikan village—their homes were invisible and there were no roads. "I do believe," said Sextant to Abacus, "that I am in posession of what it is that you might now treasure." Snapping his fingers, Sextant signaled for one of his sons to present Abacus with the bent cone of a hollowed rhinoceros horn.

"Ahh. Ye olde horne," Abacus sighed with a smile.

As Abacus tucked his head in through the horn's shoulder strap, Rod, Jake, and Slim were given each their own freshly gutted horns. The point of Slim's horn was shoved into the ground and each horn was then filled to the brim with the most vile beverage—not exactly the gin and tonic that Slim was after, but it would have to do.

Vile as the beverage was, it did help Rod understand the dance of the Tulikans. One step to the left and one to the right, a step to the left and one to the right. Sextant showed Rod the shift of weight from one foot to the other, back and forth. After the nightclubs of Bottom Junction, Rod never knew it could be so easy.

"Sextant. Where has my little Lyric run off to?" asked Abacus.

"She *is* trouble, you know," Sextant replied, furrowing his brow.

"Oh yes. Thank goodness," said Abacus as he left arm in arm with Sextant. They were off to find Lyric, Abacus' granddaughter.

Abacus wanted his new friends from afar to explore the celebration on their own terms.

"Long time no see, bro'," said Sextant, dropping his formal Olde Byzontian in favor of the relaxed Tulikan vernacular, "How's Tyrone doin'?"

It felt like a lifetime since Abacus had conversed in his native Tulikan. "Tyrone's hangin' in there," he answered, "but the scene at the cave is a freaking disaster. Speaking of caves…"

"Nine years, bro'. I'll tell ya one thing. You are a brilliant being of beautiful light."

After spending nine years in the absolute darkness of a lowland cave, Sextant had emerged just a week ago to be dazed by life in the outside world. Dazed—as he felt he should be, as he felt they all should be, all of the time. The beauty. The mystery. He was also up for some partying and spending time with his buddies.

Whenever the planets were aligned just so, a chosen one was sent to the lowland cave where he or she would endure nine years with no source of light. As the Tulikan cave sitter looked into the darkness, crisp diagrams of the past, present, and future would form hour by hour, week by week, month by month. Food would be brought in silence to the cave sitter and the cave sitter's feces would be silently hauled away. In this manner, the Tulikans gained precious perspective on life.

As if nine years in a cave weren't enough, after his reintroduction to the world of light, Sextant was chosen by his tribe to serve a term as governor. Sextant spent all of his worth trying to prevent his successful confirmation, as did all proposed governors. Governing was far too costly on the mind and body, requiring far too much work. The Tulikans, as with all Vivachangans, were content baybeetles who found no pleasure in working more than they had to. The typical Vivachangan labored no more than twenty hours per week to provide for an excellent life.

When Sextant asked Abacus to tell him more about his curious Bizonian companions, Abacus replied, "You wouldn't believe these guys. They're cool, but weird as shit. Leave any one of 'em out in the woods for more than a couple days and I swear to Dijouti they'd just *die*. And they're like, 'This is *my* land.' 'This is *my* tree.' '*My* this.' '*My* that.' 'Blah blah blah.' 'Blah blah blah.'" Sextant and Abacus both laughed until they cried.

When bearded buddies Sextant and Abacus found Lyric, she was setting the crowd on fire with Abacus' favorite antelope joke. "And then this antelope says, 'These aren't my *horns*, they're—"

"Lyric!" smiled Abacus, "Come 'ere dang it! Give grampy a hug! And there's sombody I want you to meet."

It was uncanny.

Despite her chocolate butter skin and tightly wound black hair, Jake found in Lyric nearly another Yuyu—light as a feather, cheekbones regal, eyes dark and feisty. Rod had emptied his horn several times and was fairly inebriated as he watched Jake and Lyric dance on the other side of the bonfire. Rod shoved his hands into his pockets and grinned as if looking upon a completed masterpiece. Heaven at last. He just wished and had always thought that Heaven would be a little more sanitary.

Feeling around in his pocket, Rod found a list scratched out on a piece of paper. The list—a list it appeared he had written himself— was titled "Jake's List". With one glance at his little brother, the list of Jake's shortcomings and suggestions was tossed into the bonfire.

A prandali in the coals of the bonfire delighted in the unexpected fuel. The prandali tossed herself into the flames bursting off the list and as she ascended, she told Rod to go find a place where he may sing his heart song—the song that has never been sung.

Rod walked away from the party into the woods.

He pondered the words of the prandali until he was greeted by a creek to sing to. Unsure of how to proceed, Rod started humming a couple of notes with pursed lips. His lips parted and his tongue started to toy with the roof of his mouth. Once he set the song into motion, it wasn't long before Rod was belting it out, spontaneous and deep, from the soles of his feet up to the stars. Nothing had ever felt so good aside from lunch with Dorothy Tarnuckle. Loud and strong, Rod started down the creek's edge taking small, loose steps, singing no one else's song. He was unabashed, alone in the wilderness, or so he thought.

Right in the middle of an extended gut note, Rod spotted a Tulikan shebeetle seated next to the creek, cleaning the fringes of her tunic. As he hadn't seen her until he was nearly on top of her, Rod stopped his song abruptly. "Sorry," he said, embarrassed beyond the bone.

"Not at all," she replied, "And please, do not stop. Not ever."

CHAPTER EIGHTEEN

# The Creed

In the green morning sunlight, Rod and Jake sat petting the fur on golden horseflies. Scattered about in the woods were the bodies of nearly one hundred Tulikans. Judging by those who had stripped off their tunics in favor of the daily loin cloth, there was not an extra ounce of fat on any one of them. A few were awake, drinking again.

Some were still drinking from the night before, filling their horns from a shriveling bladder hung from the branch of a tree. As more of the Tulikans awoke, they stretched out and began eating each other's mangos. The hot fluid in the Bizonian brothers' horns was rich and it renewed their vigor. They knew better than to ask its ingredients.

The hot horns were given to them by Lyric, marking the first time since leaving home that their morning elixer had not been provided by Abacus. Rod spoke to Lyric, "Your grandfather is sleeping in then?"

"Not," replied Lyric, "Were he to be sleeping, 'twould be not in, but out o' door, Mister Rod."

"Yes, of course."

"Alas, he is somewhere gone," she said, kneading a pumpkin leaf.

"Come he not presently hither?" asked Rod, trying on the olde tongue.

"Not."

"Not?"

253

"Not. And henceforth 'twill be upon us to sail the wat'ry seas of life, mine grandfather only in our dreams."

"I understand thee not," said Rod.

"My grandfather is yon, not set to return. Chosen hath he to cross." Jake, who had tuned out the meaningless interaction, was now intrigued. Lyric continued, "Our Abacus now belongs to that which lies beyond."

"I don't understand either, Lyric," said Jake, "Has Abacus left? Is he okay?"

"He is okay. However, most simply put, Jake, my grandfather hath chosen to cross over. To pass on. To die."

"Can't happen," chuckled Rod, "Not here."

"Yes, Mister Rod, Mister Jake. Upon the break of day, Mister Abacus departed in only his hat to seek that which his eyes may last see."

"But why, Lyric?" asked Jake, his jaw quaking, "What's going on?"

Lyric looked at Jake with a sharp gleam, "Our Abacus, whom gav'st life to my father and me, was a seasoned elderbeetle. Thou hast seen with thine own eyes that his purpose here has been served. My grandfather's is a timely and well-deserv'd passing, friends. In Tulika we live life like prandalia."

A tear fell from Jake's shaking chin into his horn.

Jake remembered last seeing Abacus late in the night, during the peak of the festivities. He was dancing and grinning as the smoke of the bonfire wrapped around his hands and face. When they were both cross-eyed from the local juice, Abacus pulled Jake aside and whispered in his ear, "The future is always longer than the past," and then jerking on Jake's arm, "Vivachanga is magic! Vivachanga is *everywhere*!"

# THE CREED

"My grandfather wished that I remind you, as your adventure is only just beginning, that we are always safe. We are the children of eternity and the infinite universe. You cannot destroy us." Lyric paused. "Abacus also wanted for you to take these."

Lyric produced from below the berry scrum in her pumpkin leaf a scroll bound with a braided satin ribbon. It was the map of Nord penned by Happyhouse so that the wayward travelers might find their way home. Lyric handed the map to Jake. She then produced a top-notch cigar of hand-rolled catnip and passed it through Slim's whiskers, handing the cigar also to Jake for safe keeping. For Rod, Lyric produced a small, sturdy, perfect cube woven from tree bark.

The cube had an unfamiliar nut anchored to one corner with a ram gut tether. Holding it out in the palm of her hand, Lyric said, "Abacus performed a spontaneous contraption for you, Mister Rod," and Rod felt the sting of being cheated.

"Lastly, this is for all of you to share. It shall perhaps serve as trade for food and transport to the land of Gibbous Bizonia." Lyric laid before them a bound leather pouch. "It is from the relics."

Rod lifted the pouch, assessing its surprising heft. Untying the pouch, he poured its contents out onto the grass. The pouch was filled with solid gold doubloons.

"We can't take these," said Jake, scanning the priceless artifacts, "Those have got to be worth a fortune."

"Oh, Jake, what does it matter?" asked Rod in earnest. Heaven was again looking pretty good.

"Yes, Jake," reiterated Lyric, "What does it matter?"

That settled, they had celebrated heartily and slept late, so Lyric brought it to their attention that the day was well on. "It is my charge to see that you embark very close to now," she said, "Please do gather your belongings and make haste. There is much that rests upon your shoulders."

After an emotionally charged and culturally awkward send-off from Lyric and Sextant, Rod, Jake, and Slim got themselves lost in the wilderness of the *nooshtah*. It was not for the Happyhouse map nor for a lacking sense of direction. Gino's had been through. The brothers were forced into a landscape of clearcuts, landslides, blast zones, and flooded river gorges. They couldn't even locate the elephant lake. Nature fifteen billion years in the making had been reduced to sludge and rubble in a matter of seconds at the hands of baybeetles.

Under the stars, muddied and torn from traversing a slice of Nord turned nightmare, Rod, Jake, and Slim gave way to a dark silence. Behind them lay the loss of Abacus, before them a lost trail home. Jake sat and tried to hide his exhaustion from the world by wedging himself into a rock fall. Rod just wandered off.

Before dropping down next to a pile of plastic forks and flattened plastic mustard packets, Rod dug in his pants for his spontaneous contraption. He pulled it out then dropped and wedged in.

Rod couldn't believe how strange life, and death, had become. He remembered spending his days in the flat comfort of MWI. Then just as life was becoming an adventure, he goes and dies in the mountains of Vivachanga, only to find that death was even more interesting than life.

Now this.

# THE CREED

This nothing.

This emptiness.

In an attempt to maintain his sanity, Rod began to fiddle with the inane contraption—sliding his fingers along the edges, turning it about on a corner in the palm of his hand, flinging the nut. When Rod touched the dangling nut to its opposite corner on the cube, the cube shocked his fingers.

Rod lost his grip and the spontaneous contraption rolled off his stomach onto the Gino's Yellow Mustard packets left behind by REZ workers. Rod scrambled to his feet to give the contraption a wide berth as it shot wiry sparks into the night air. With the recoil of each spark, the gadget tumbled backwards. Two sparks were emitted at once and the gadget leapt as high as Rod's knee.

"Jake! Come quickly!" Rod yelped.

By the time Jake arrived, still lugging his backpack, the contraption was dancing wildly within a mad wig of shooting sparks, lighting the faces of the brothers as if night were day. Wise Slim kept his distance.

A low trumpeting vibrated the ground beneath their paws and feet. The note grew louder and was joined by a harmonious trombone, higher in pitch. A beam of pale green light shot straight up from within the cube into the sky above. The rest of the brass section kicked in. The combined peal of so many horns was deafening.

A red beam of light shot out to one horizon followed by another red beam to the opposite horizon. Blue beams and yellow beams followed, finding every direction until there was a rainbow sent to every tree in the forest and to every star in the heavens. Then the sky itself pulsed from the north in a sheet of white light. Then came a pulse from the south, then the east and the west. A final shrieking of trumpets made Rod cover his ears.

The next moment, the world returned, black and silent.

"Spectacular but useless," said Rod tipping the contraption over with his toe, resting one limp hand on his binoculars. "I would have preferred a cooked ham. A potato."

Jake's arms hung lifelessly at his sides.

The wind scraped a gust over the forest canopy.

Behind them the wind grew louder, more fierce. It blew down from the treetops, penetrating to the forest floor.

In a rare moment of defeat, Jake dropped his head, "It's going to be a very long night. A very very long ni—" At that instant, Jake and Rod were hit from behind at the knees, snapping both of them flat onto their backs. Their feet lifted off the ground.

With the wind and an ugly odor rushing up into his nostrils, Rod was flipped from his back up and over, facedown onto a warm, furry log. He was climbing higher through the forest, head into the wind, holding onto the fur for dear life. Rod turned his head to the side and saw the great pearly green wing that had picked him up then folded him over. Rod yelled for Jake.

"I'm okay!" came Jake's voice from somewhere near his feet.

"Where's Slim?!" yelled Rod.

Jake did not respond.

"WHERE'S SLIM!"

The dragon's blue tongue flailed in the wind, its flaming eyelashes peeled backwards, illuminating the dragon's enormous, windswept ears. Just as Rod was preparing to eject from the dragon's back, Slim's little head, unscathed, poked out of the dragon's mane, right between the ears. Slim was at the helm, piloting their psychedelic apparition.

# THE CREED

Looking back to Rod and Jake, Slim's cat face was not one of panic, resignation, or defeat, but one of quiet perseverance. "Slim's okay!" yelled Rod back to Jake. Unable to see Slim for himself, Jake crossed his fingers in the dragon fur.

They raged through the sky, rising high above the fractured terrain. Where were they going? Would the dragon take them out to sea? Back to the top of Mount Rancancan? Would it simply reach the end of Abacus' *oolazoo batoom* spell and disintegrate from beneath them, leaving them to tumble through space to their death? Yet another death? All they could do was hold on and hope that Slim knew what he was doing.

For hours they sailed through the night.

Rod and Jakes' backs froze from the altitude as their chests burned from the heat of the dragon. They could see nothing but themselves and the stars. Everything else was black. Even the moon had gone missing.

In the void below, Rod came to imagine purple shapes arising in sublime, geometric patterns. The kaleidoscopic movements of his mind's creation left Rod in trance and he forgot his freezing, burning body. When red, molten veins appeared, seeping up through the blackness of Nord below, Rod believed it another element of his kaleidoscopic illusion. The molten veins knifed through the land in shattered glass splinters.

At once with the appearance of these scarlet veins, the dragon began to lose altitude. The enflamed gashes marring the surface of Nord grew nearer. A stinging scent, worse even than that of the dragon, raked across the Bizonians. The unrelenting stench snapped Rod out of his kaleidoscope and he could now see that the crimson glowing trails were indeed ablaze. A web of fire was dredging the land. Without warning, they dove into the heat.

The heat increased as they fell, becoming less and less bearable. Above the rush of wind in their ears, there was heard a scream. Both Rod and Jake presumed it was the other finally losing his cool. The scream loudened, crystallizing into shrieking missiles, concussive blasts, and the ungodly cries of baybeetles being torn apart.

The war.

They could now taste death in their mouths, feel it on their skin. Jake's fists dug, clenching harder into the pelt of the dragon. As they flew lower and lower, Rod identified the players in this war in Heaven. Half were baybeetle—dirty, poorly armed mavericks attempting to hold their own. The other half, the invaders, were unrecognizable as baybeetle. They were engorged monsters, drones that spewed fire from their fingertips, mechanical beasts that cut baybeetles in half.

Everything was tinted red with blood.

"Out of sight. Out of mind," whispered Rod, "like the disappearing monarch forest." Bizonians would not support their nation's wars were they to see such carnage up close, on their own soil, in their own neighborhoods.

As if to stop the massacre, Jake closed his eyes and forced into his head a blossoming of daffodils, heavy with dew. He imagined the blossoms falling by the millions from the sky, raining to fascinate the soldiers below as the daffodils turned into butterflies. This madness of war had to stop. Nord was a lonely gem in the universe, a gem that cradled the beauty of life—a gem that was on the verge of being lost to baybeetles forever.

"Why am *I* still alive?" Jake asked of the wind.

A heinous cry from the dragon was his only answer.

A missile.

# THE CREED

They had been hit.

Jake felt the dragon flesh beneath his hands give way, liquefied. They lost a wing. The dragon struggled in noble, silent pain, unable to prevent them from spiraling into Nord. Flames reached up to char the fur of their dragon as the dragon disintegrated beneath them, becoming ever more ghostly, turning from liquid to vapor.

What was left of the dragon went into an unchecked tailspin.

Not even Slim could save them now.

All Jake could see was a smear of stars followed by a flash of burning Nord, over and over as they spun. For a fleeting moment, in a flash of Nord, Jake saw a two-headed beast walking through a wall of fire, lost and chewing on a family of Muzorans. Then there was a flash of white stone and a smear of stars, a flash of white stone and a smear of stars—repeating as they spun ever faster towards the ground, the dragon's spell broken.

Their heads were clouded and dizzy where they lay on cobblestone. The shifting outline of a mythic warrior loomed large overhead.

The knight was clad in the throne's armor, his helmet crested with the crimson plumage of the Harlequin Dickcissel. "What eez you doing here?" the warrior demanded, swinging his spiked mace.

"Where are we?" asked a still blurry Jake.

"What are you meaning?" asked the warrior. The warrior bent over and grabbed Jake and Rod by their arms, pulling them up to stand. Fear snapped Jake's head into clarity. Before them stood Romiel Sando. They were surrounded by the white stone edifices of central Valgato.

Romiel wore nothing more than patterned boxer shorts and a burlap sack for body armor. Strapped to his head as a war helmet was a teakettle, its bottom removed by a can opener. Jake recognized the bottomless teakettle as the very same one that had served he and Yuyu rose petal tea. It was the same teakettle that had served the Sando family for generations, pouring love potion after love potion. Stuffed into the spout off the back of the helmet was one of Romiel's bright red nose hankies. In lieu of a spiked mace, Romiel brandished one palm frond beaver tail that had, until now, served only to spank the cobblestones during festivals. Even as such, Romiel appeared a formidable combatant.

There was a fresh cut under Romiel's left eye the crimson of the hanky.

"Romiel?" said Jake, mixed in emotion and still unwilling to believe his eyes.

"Yes Jake, my friend. I am the Romiel." Romiel gathered Jake in his arms.

"What is going on, Romiel? Is this party a masquerade?"

"I am sorry, no. The war eez come to Valgato on tomorrow."

"We saw it, Romiel. We saw it! Where's Yuyu? Is she okay?"

"Yes. The Yuyu she eez okay the last time I see her."

"Where is she? Is your house safe?"

"Yes, I am think the house she eez safe. Until tomorrow. But the Yuyu—you will not find the Yuyu in the house."

"Where is she, Romiel? Where can I find her?"

"Jake. We have sent all of the shebeetle and all of the babies off to the secret place. Anyone who does not know the secret place already, we are held by the oath not to tell. I am sorry, Jake, but thees eez how it must be."

# THE CREED

"But Romiel—"

"I am sorry, my friend."

They had been dumped in the central gardens, *Gronau Esquito*, but there were no striking shebeetles to be found, no lean charioteers. Though deserted, in its white stone and chipped paint charm the town was even more beautiful than before. The Valgatans had been very busy.

Flowers covered everything. The sidewalks were scrubbed and polished with lambswool. Banners of welcome hung over the streets, lilting with bushels of inflated balloons. Every tavern and public house glowed with doors open wide. The amber street lanterns were lit, every one.

"It eez our wish," continued Romiel, "to welcome the soldiers of Bizonia and have a very next party. Maybe drink together as fellow manbeetles. We can have a talk and a smoke with them. You can remember thees good talking, yes? But they do not return our invitation. I do not think the Bizonian eez very interested in enjoying the life. But you my friends, you have already been to the Vivachanga? Where eez the Abacus?"

"Yes, we made it to Vivachanga," said Jake, "but Abacus is not with us. There is a lot to explain."

"I am sure yes, but the most very important thing right now eez for getting you and you and the Slim to my house where you are to be more safe than right here. If the Bizonians accept the party invitation, I will send for you very first thing. Do you remember how to get to the Romiel house?"

"Of course," answered Jake.

"Then you are taking thees key and locking the door. Very good?"

Jake hesitated, considering the fight that lay ahead for Valgato, possibly for the life of Yuyu. Should he forego the relative safety of Romiel's home and stay in the garden to do battle? Tyrone's manuscript, the cure for this madness, was in his hands. Jake was the keeper and messenger of the creed. "Very good, Romiel."

"Remember, Jake," said Romiel handing the giant key to Jake, "the greatest fight...eez not to fight."

Rod, Jake, and Slim suffered the walk to Romiel's under the chilling silence of the once bustling township of Valgato. After turning the key, they trudged up the stairway through Romiel's empty, echoing household. Rod took one bedroom while Jake moved on to the next, on to Yuyu's room.

The door to Yuyu's room was as heavy and cold as the door to her crypt. He went inside, accompanied by Slim, and closed the door to a crack behind him. Yuyu's cello was resting in the corner with her horsehair bow.

Jake heaved his backpack onto Yuyu's bed then turned to collapse and sit. Everything in the room was so pretty, so full of life. A tiara of dried flowers. A pink candle stuck into an empty bottle of bubbly. Lace curtains, a collection of seashells, and a calendar with pictures of kittens tangled in yarn. Parties Yuyu hoped to attend were marked on the calendar in bright colors.

At least they had the manuscript, Tyrone's creed.

The solution.

Jake twisted around and unbuckled his pack. Reaching inside, he pulled out his purple notebook—a singular hope in this time of despair. He laid the manuscript atop Yuyu's quilted bedspread next to Slim.

# THE CREED

Listening to Rod in the bedroom next door whistling and rearranging the furniture, Jake dropped his forehead into his hands and began to weep. Staring at the two puddles of tears, one pool from each eye, growing on the dry floor, Jake heard Yuyu's bedroom door creak.

As Rod was still in his room blundering with what sounded like a chest of drawers, Jake imagined Yuyu, bows in her hair, flowing into the room and into his arms. Jake was greeted instead by a rush of putrid air and the sight of a lone magic wand, gyrating to a stop on the concrete floor in a mist of settling dust. Jake raced to the door to see who it could be and found not a soul in any direction.

Grabbing the errant wand, Jake saw next to it one monarch butterfly wing, torn in half. What life remained in Jake's body fell through the floor and his heart cured to stone. He became weak.

Then he remembered the creed.

Salvation lay on Yuyu's bed in this very room.

Jake looked to the bed, to his backpack, and to mighty Slim. Tyrone's manuscript, their purpose, was gone, turned to a pale streak of ashes. Jake snapped the errant wand in two and dropped to his knees next to Yuyu's bed, trembling. Slim raised to his haunches, staring directly at silent, raging Jake.

Jake lifted his eyes to Slim who yawned and twitched a whisker. As Jake succumbed to his deepest darkness, as the future of his kind burned before his eyes, the room around Jake brightened ever so slightly. A strange, familiar warmth emerged from Jake's chest like a fire started from yesterday's coals. His body grew lighter as if wanting to lift off the ground. More waves of light and warmth arose through and around him.

The quality of the light was such that it could forever increase in intensity yet never become painful to the eyes. The warmth such that it could forever rise in temperature yet never become painful to the body.

"*Vivachanga is everywhere.*"

Jake heard a whisper and a whir and snapped back towards the door. It was Anisha.

Fed, feathered, and rested.

Ready for things to come.

Made in the USA
Columbia, SC
23 August 2022

65283091R00171